PRAISE FOR

Sadie on a Plate

. . . .

"*Sadie on a Plate* is a joyful, satisfying romp. I loved it—and I'm still hungry!"

—KJ Dell'Antonia, *New York Times* bestselling
author of *The Chicken Sisters*

"*Sadie on a Plate* reads like the ultimate cooking-show comfort watch—with the added spice of a forbidden romance. A delicious love story and heartfelt ode to Jewish cuisine."

—Rachel Lynn Solomon, national bestselling
author of *The Ex Talk*

"Amanda Elliot's debut, *Sadie on a Plate*, is a foodie delight. Fans of *Top Chef* will cheer on Sadie Rosen as she blazes through the *Chef Supreme* competition. The Jewish meals Sadie cooks are from the heart as is her steamy romance with Chef Luke Weston. This sweet sufganiyot of a novel is deliciously delectable."

—Roselle Lim, author of *Vanessa Yu's
Magical Paris Tea Shop*

"My goodness—Amanda Elliot knows how to write swoon-worthy food! Amidst all the inventive dishes and luscious food descriptions, *Sadie on a Plate* mixes the drama of a culinary competition, a slow-burn forbidden romance, and a salty-sweet cast of characters into the perfect bookish bite."

—Amy E. Reichert, author of *The Kindred Spirits Supper Club*

"*Sadie on a Plate* is a delectable mix of humor, reality show drama, foodie vibes, and heart-fluttering love story. Amanda Elliot has crafted an endearingly imperfect heroine whose hot mess–ness and tenacity will resonate with readers. You'll swoon, laugh, and cheer as you watch Sadie earn the happily ever after she so deserves."

—Sarah Echavarre Smith, author of *On Location*

"This novel is perfect for any fans of cooking shows who also love to curl up with a beach read. It's fun [and] breezy, and [it's] clear that Elliot did her research into the behind-the-scenes world of *Top Chef*."   —*USA Today*

"*Sadie on a Plate* reveals the arduous, exacting tasks of making really good food. Light as a soufflé, it's delicious."

—*The American Jewish World*

"A love letter to Ashkenazi cooking, and food in general, as a means of connecting with one's identity."

—*The Canadian Jewish News*

"Foodies with a hunger for juicy cooking-show competitions will eagerly lap up every last drop of *Sadie on a Plate*, Amanda Elliot's delicious rom-com. . . . Detailed food descriptions, recipes, and kitchen culture—along with a diverse cast—spice up a well-plotted story warmed with romance, humor, and heart."   —Shelf Awareness

"Luke and Sadie are likable characters with magnetic, slow-building chemistry and sympathetic, realistic backstories. The fast-paced, delicious plot is as much about food as romance. . . . Readers, especially those who enjoy shows like *Top Chef*, won't be able to put down this fast-paced romantic comedy."   —*Library Journal* (starred review)

"Elliot's first adult novel . . . has the perfect amount of reality show high jinks and food innuendos that help dial up the heat. . . . A satisfying debut for foodies and romance lovers alike."   —*Kirkus Reviews* (starred review)

Best Served Hot

....

AMANDA ELLIOT

Berkley Romance
New York

Berkley Romance
Published by Berkley
An imprint of Penguin Random House LLC
penguinrandomhouse.com

Library of Congress Cataloging-in-Publication Data

Names: Elliot, Amanda, author.
Title: Best served hot / Amanda Elliot.
Description: First Edition. | New York : Berkley Romance, 2023.
Identifiers: LCCN 2022022238 (print) | LCCN 2022022239 (ebook) |
ISBN 9780593335734 (trade paperback) | ISBN 9780593335741 (ebook)
Subjects: LCGFT: Novels.
Classification: LCC PS3605.L4423 B47 2023 (print) | LCC PS3605.L4423
(ebook) | DDC 813/.6—dc23
LC record available at https://lccn.loc.gov/2022022238
LC ebook record available at https://lccn.loc.gov/2022022239

First Edition: February 2023

Printed in the United States of America
1st Printing

Book design by Ashley Tucker

If you've ever worked in a restaurant, especially during the pandemic, then this book is for you.

1

RUNNING DOWN A MIDTOWN MANHATTAN SIDE-walk during rush hour might as well be running an ob-stacle course. Leap the pile of garbage spilling out from glossy black bags. Dodge the woman weaving from side to side, eyes fixed on her phone. Zero in on the tiny opening between a row of businessmen spread out about as wide as they can go, blocking almost the whole pathway. Try not to sweat through your silk work blouse.

I jerked to a stop, panting, in front of the address. I didn't even need to confirm the restaurant name etched on the great glass window because Alice Wong was standing in front of it. Frowning at me. "You're late."

"I've had a *day*." I drew in a great deep breath. "I woke up to a text from my bank saying that my account had been overdrafted, and then there was a troll in my DMs and comments who wasn't even creative with his dick metaphors—come on, sausages have been overdone—and then Mr. Decker was grouchy all day because it's tax season, and with New York raising its tax brackets on the ultrarich, he keeps saying he might have to sell one of his yachts—"

"My God." Alice pressed the back of her hand against the blunt black bangs cutting across her forehead. "The poor man." She turned to go inside the restaurant, but I stopped her with a touch to the shoulder.

"One second. Let me make sure BiggerBoi69 hasn't popped back up under another name." I grabbed my phone and flicked open the app. My profile, JulieZeeEatsNYC, scrolled across the screen, little shots of restaurant meals I'd reviewed and video stills of me biting into things, which, no matter how I timed them, always looked awkward. My last few comment sections were clear. Well, mostly. A small-time troll was arguing with my commenters about the optimal doneness of steak, but I could deal with that later.

I sighed. Such were the trials and tribulations of some-one who ran their own restaurant reviews on social media instead of doing it for real in a newspaper or other well-known blog. They had a support staff for this kind of thing so that their reviewers could focus on the food.

Though I knew better than to complain aloud. I knew exactly what Alice would say. Not because I was psychic or anything, but because she'd said it all before. *You* are *a real reviewer, babe. You review restaurants, and you have a pretty big following, too. That makes you no less real than the others and their fancy papers.*

Alice cleared her throat. I looked up to find her staring at me, her slash of red lipstick pressed tight in a way that meant *I'm starving.*

"Alice," I told her. "You're a genius."

The frown smoothed out. "I know. But how so?"

My phone dinged with an email notification, and my heart skipped a beat as my head ducked back down. I couldn't help holding my breath as I opened it up. I'd been doing that for days now, hoping for one specific email asking me in for an interview. Dreading the email that would start with *We regret to inform you that . . .* or *Thank you very much for your application, but . . .*

It was my bank offering me more overdraft protection. I sighed again. It was a little too late for that. "I'm ready. Let's go in."

The restaurant was dark, narrow, and cluttered, the tables set so close together I'd have no problem leaning over and taking a bite off my neighbor's plate. The walls were hung with kitschy representations of boats and lobsters, the ceiling strung with garlands of twinkling white lights. The tacky decor was, fortunately, not a reflection of the food. I'd learned that on my two previous visits.

I didn't answer Alice's question until we were seated, glasses of tepid water before us. I preferred it tepid. Too cold and it was a shock to the system, numbing the taste buds. "You were giving me a pep talk in my head. That's why you're a genius."

"Unfortunately, I haven't mastered telepathy yet, so that pep talk was all you talking to you," said Alice. "Let me guess: 'I' was telling you that you're real and valid in what you do?"

I didn't have to nod. She knew what it meant when my eyes ducked down and stared intently at the starched white tablecloth.

"I was indeed right," Alice said. "I love saying that. It doesn't matter if you don't have a byline or a salary. You're out there doing the work, and you have a devoted following for it."

I'd heard this before, from her and from my parents and even from one of my three older brothers, which was a surprise coming from someone whose preferred mode of communication with his younger sister had always been belching the ABC's in her face.

So what if I couldn't quite bring myself to believe it? I snuck another glance at my phone. If the *thing* I couldn't even think about or risk jinxing came true, I wouldn't have to worry about it anymore anyway. I'd have the respect I craved. Even someone like my boss, Mr. Decker, would listen to me then.

This wasn't the time to argue with Alice, though. "How's the coding going?"

Alice's face brightened. "Fabulously. For real. My team just hired another girl! Now there are two of us."

"Compared to how many dudes?"

"Seven."

"Progress." I lifted my water glass in a toast. "To very, very slowly getting to equality!" By the time we clinked, drank, and set our glasses back down, the waiter had arrived with our menus. I didn't even have to page through mine. "I'm ready to order, please."

As I listed off everything I wanted to feature in my post, I did my best not to cringe at the prices. If I reviewed restaurants for a real outlet, whether it was a prestigious paper like the *New York Times* or the *New York Scroll* or a blog like *Eater*, I'd have an expense account to cover these checks. But alas, all I had was a small advertising revenue. I mostly broke even, or sometimes just went broke. Hence the overdraft fee.

"So hey," Alice said as the waiter walked away, scribbling on his pad. "How's Greg?"

I tried not to grimace. I'd gone on three dates with Greg, a thirtysomething marketing guy and surprise taxidermy enthusiast. Despite the weirdness of being watched as I slept by eight pairs of beady black fake squirrel eyes, I'd still texted him the next day. And had not heard back in the two days since. "Pretty sure he's ghosting me."

Alice swiped the back of her hand dramatically over her brow as if wicking away a nervous sweat. "Oh, thank God. I was kind of afraid you'd end up with your head mounted on his wall."

"Whatever." I shrugged like I didn't care. To be honest, I didn't care *that* much. It was the rejection that stung more than anything. If I'd been the one to ignore *him*, I probably wouldn't even be thinking about it. "There are plenty of fish in the sea."

"I've never understood that metaphor," said Alice. "Are we fish, too, in this scenario? Or are we fishing for the guys, as it implies, and then killing and eating them?"

I was saved from having to answer by the arrival of the food. If I was indeed seeking a mate by fishing for him and then eating him, I hoped he'd be the lobster in the fried lobster and waffles. Anything fried well always looked delicious—light brown, glistening slightly with oil—and these chunks of lobster in their coating of crispy batter couldn't have looked more appealing atop the delicate squares of golden waffle smeared with a sunset of sweet potato butter. "Let's take our pictures and then set up the phone to film me for a quick teaser as I eat."

Every time I had to stand up on my chair in order to snap a good angle of a plate, I said a silent prayer in thanks to my fellow millennials, who were also out there taking pictures of their food. Nobody so much as spared me a funny glance. Not that I would notice; I was too busy focusing on keeping my balance on the slick wooden chair while making the food look beautiful on my phone.

My mouth watered. The lobster and waffles was extremely delicious, but I also loved the fancy toast topped with snow crab and avocado (rich, sweet, and texturally balanced, given nice contrast by a zing of black pepper on top). And the soft-shell crab BLT, where the sweet, earthy tomato met the crisp, watery crunch of the iceberg lettuce and thick, chewy smoke of bacon, and then the sweet, crispy crackles of the soft-shell crab. And Chef Stephanie's version of New England clam chowder, which was rich with cream, but not heavy, and delicately spiced; the clams were big and briny, and the bits of bacon throughout somehow still crispy. It would have qualified as an excellent but not all that memorable clam chowder if not for the salsify root, which had the texture of a parsnip but the taste, almost, of an oyster or a clam. It made for a marvelously interesting bite. Unfortunately, it looked like a bowl of white sludge, which meant I couldn't feature—

My phone buzzed with a push notification. My eyes flicked to it quickly in case BiggerBoi69 was back, and I caught, *New York Scroll* names new rest–

I slipped. "Eeeek!"

One of the reasons Alice is my best friend: she always catches me when I'm down, both figuratively and literally. She slipped out of her seat and caught me neatly before any soft-shell crab or salsify root could go flying onto the table next to us. "Maybe let's get our photos from a less vertical angle going forward," she told me once I was safely back on solid ground.

But my heart was thudding, and not just because I'd almost broken destiny's choice of bones. The thing I'd been dreading was staring at me from my notification list, and it had the nerve to not even be in personal email form. A breaking news story. *New York Scroll* names new restaurant critic, Bennett Richard Macalester Wright.

Suddenly, none of the food looked all that appetizing anymore.

"What is it?" asked Alice.

I sat back down with a thump. "I didn't get it," I said

dully. And it wasn't like I'd expected them to read my passionate cover letter and résumé and social media stats and immediately roll out the heirloom tomato–red carpet. But they hadn't even bothered sending me a rejection email. Or any kind of acknowledgment at all. Maybe my application had been one of a million, even though the job hadn't been listed online for the general peasantry to apply for. (I'd been tipped off about the opening through an email my boss had gotten and I'd read.)

Or maybe they hadn't taken my résumé seriously. Laughed about it in the office. *Who does this girl think she is? She thinks some followers and some videos make her suited for us?* The *New York Scroll* had never hired a critic who wasn't a white dude over fifty. They had social media, of course, but they still published trend pieces where they gaped at it and how it worked like it was a zoo exhibit. *And over here we have people—wait for it—actually getting their news on their phones. Thank goodness the protective bars are here, or they might attack us.*

Not unlike my boss, come to think of it. I was pretty sure he didn't know about my second "job," but I'd heard the way he snorted as he watched his daughters take selfies or the older one herd her kids into the perfect light for a family snap.

Alice made a sympathetic *mmm* in response. "Who'd they name? Is it at least someone good?"

The name sounded vaguely familiar, but I was already frantically googling to learn more, leaving the food to cool before us. "He went to Dartmouth," I reported. Which, if I judged by the alumni I knew—my boss and his daughters—was stereotypically rich and fratty. "And he played on the squash team." Which was basically code for "has an enormous trust fund." I scowled down at my screen. "Hobbies include boating and collecting ancient coins."

Bennett Richard Macalester Wright had almost certainly never misbudgeted and run out of food money his freshman year of college and had to subsist on ramen and scrounged-up free pizza from various club meetings to get by.

"And then it looks like he was a food reporter at the *Times* for the last five years," I said. I scrolled through a few of his past headlines. A profile on a chef semi-famous for his cooking and very famous for his string of ever-younger actress wives. A report on why high-end restaurants were trending toward smaller but more expensive wine lists. A few reviews of pricey restaurants—it looked like he'd filled in for their regular critic while she was out on maternity leave.

"At least he seems like he's qualified," Alice said.

I scowled at her. I didn't want to hear that he was qualified. I wanted to hear that he sucked and that they should've hired me. But I didn't say that. I continued my googling but turned up nothing except dead ends. Like most major food reviewers, he'd clearly done his best to take down as much as he possibly could about himself, especially photographs. No serious food reviewer wanted to tip off a restaurant that they were there since that might lead the owner or the kitchen to offer them special treatment that would bias their review. It was why I never made a reservation under my own name, though I couldn't do much about my face. Sometimes, if I got recognized on one visit, I'd go back with a wig or glasses the next time.

"Excuse me, ladies?" Our waiter smiled down on us. "How are we doing?"

"Not great, but the food is delicious," I told him.

His smile wavered, not quite sure what to do with that. "Would you like anything more to drink? We have some lovely wines on offer tonight."

"No thanks," Alice said. "She doesn't like wine."

"Alice!" I hissed. Which was always fun. Alice had a particularly hissable name.

The waiter nodded and went off to bring our check. Alice turned to me, blinking. "What?"

"We've had this discussion before," I said. "Don't tell anyone I don't like wine."

"But you *don't* like wine," Alice said.

It was true. Wine tasted like literal sour grapes to me, whether it was the cheap boxed stuff our roommates used to bring home in college or the ultra-fancy kind my boss gave me last year for the holidays. It made my lips pucker and my cheeks suck in. I'd never been able to understand why people actually enjoyed drinking it.

But my followers wouldn't agree. Again, they were mostly young women around my age or a bit older. There was a whole meme industry around wine. The wine moms. Giant wineglasses. Social media love turned on a dime. Not like I was hiding it hard-core. It was just that I'd rather the truth not be known, because I didn't want to do anything that might alienate me from my followers. Sometimes being loved on social media meant being loved as someone who wasn't really you.

"You know who I bet loooves wine?" I said, rather than continuing my lecture. "Bennett . . ." I couldn't remember his two middle names, so I made some up. "Bennett Rigatoni Mushroom Wright." Alice giggled, which made me go on. "The *Scroll* always includes a wine list in their reviews, and the wines they choose always cost a fortune."

Alice blinked for a moment, processing, then leaned in. "Bennett Ratatouille Meatloaf Wright is probably one of those guys who swishes the wine around in their mouth and then says they taste oak or cherry or chocolate underneath."

I held up my water glass and swished it around. Lowered my voice so that it honked out my nose. "Hmm, this wine is quite delicious. I believe I'm getting notes of pine and banana and . . . hmm, is that a Krispy Kreme doughnut under there?"

Alice giggled. My lips perked up in a tiny—genuine—smile. I continued, "Taking bets on if he includes that in his first review tomorrow."

"Either that or something equally pretentious," she said. "Unlike you and your delightful videos."

I sighed. "That reminds me that I never actually *got* my video."

"It's not too late."

And it wasn't. Even if I was in no mood to perform right now. After all, as I'd just told myself, sometimes I had to be someone else online. So I forced myself to smile— my day job was great practice for that!—and seem enthused about the lobster and waffles, which were now cold and un-appealing, the grease congealing on my tongue, the coat-ing soggy. "It's sooo good," I said, rolling my eyes back in my mock-orgasm face. This short video wouldn't be part of my official post, but I'd post it to my profile in advance of the actual review as a teaser. "I'm so happy to be eating this right now!"

I finished in one take, and just in time. The waiter set the check gently on our table; I grabbed it before Alice could. Though, to be fair, she no longer bothered trying. Sometimes I wondered if she actually just came out with me for the free meals and not the company, but Alice wasn't that good of a liar.

"We still on for the food festival this weekend?" I asked, trying to push all thoughts of Bennett Wright aside.

The Central Park Food Festival was the most exciting day of my shooting calendar, the way I truly knew spring was here. Tens of booths and stands sent by not only some of the city's most exciting new restaurants but people try-ing to raise money to open their own restaurant or food truck. The application process was fierce because the heat of the attention from all the food bloggers and reviewers circulating throughout could make that investor dough rise. "Don't worry. I'm planning on doing all the research this week so we have our route plotted out exactly."

"Um, obviously," said Alice. "I can't wait."

In between all my research (and probably some expense report filing and conference room shining for my actual boss), I'd post a couple days of teasers, then livestream a bit on the day of, and prep some epic videos and reviews for the week after. I already knew some of the booths I'd definitely have to check out. All I had to do was figure out how to zigzag between them to get the most food in me.

"I can't wait, either," I said. "I wonder if the *Scroll* will go." They didn't usually. It was like they were saying, *We don't need to do the discovering; we'll wait for you to do the discovering, and we'll do the judging.* Like they'd swish all those new exciting chefs between their teeth, straining them out, looking for undertones that I'd swallow without even noticing.

Now they had a new guy to do that for them. *I hope you choke, Bennett Ranch Dressing Milkshake Wright,* I thought fiercely and then felt bad. *Not, like, choke to death. Just choke enough to be embarrassed, like maybe cough up a bite of fancy food onto your boss or something.*

That mental image almost made me feel better.

2

TWO DAYS LATER, I WAS AT WORK PUTTING THE finishing touches on my post. *Ahoy, maties! I've always thought of the Midtown restaurant scene as expensive, mediocre food aimed at stuffy businessmen trying to outspend each other, theatergoers impatient to bolt down their food before* Hamilton *starts, and tourists, but Chef Stephanie Lynch is changing that up with her seafood-themed Daily Catch. Are you drooling over that lobster and waffles? Just wait until you smell it . . .*

I finished reading over my caption for the millionth time, then fiddled with my photo of the caviar dip that went with the potato chips, trying to make it look less like . . . well, less like fish eggs. *Not happening.* I scheduled it to post later in the day during peak hours but posted my video to my story. Got to get people excited.

Done. Okay. Now I could focus on the work I was actually getting a salary and benefits for. Or, realistically, I could do a few half-assed tasks for the work I was actually getting a salary and benefits for, then work on my research for the Central Park Food Festival. I answered a few phone calls and emails, then turned to the assortment of newspapers tossed in our office hallway each morning. Mr. Decker wouldn't be in today—he was up at his Connecticut estate watching a grandchild's play or baseball game or something—which left all the papers to me.

I chewed the inside of my cheek and surveyed the office. One of my favorite things about working here was the privilege of hanging out in this space all by myself (at least when Mr. Decker wasn't here). And that wasn't sarcasm. Even though he was officially retired, Mr. Decker's previous tenure as CEO of the major TV network LBC granted him a legacy office space in Rockefeller Center until he retired from life itself. He spent most of his days doing charity work, including heading his ovarian cancer charity, Ellen's Promise, named after his sister, and sitting on boards, where he got paid absurd amounts of money to give other rich people advice a few days a month, if that. I existed to answer his phone and collect his business mail and coordinate between his house managers and make sure he got where he needed to go when he needed to get there.

It was a plum gig. And it was a plum space, twice as big as the two-bedroom apartment I shared with a roommate, with a massive office space for Mr. Decker, the central room where I spent my time, a conference room, a kitchen, and a storage/copy room, with no other occupants to bother me or judge me when I wasn't doing my work. Massive windows lining the walls showcased Fifth Avenue and Saks; posters of movies and TV shows Mr. Decker had greenlit while at LBC plastered the walls with slick, colorful designs. A gleaming glass cabinet in the corner showed off his four Emmys. Had I taken them out of the cabinet and snapped selfies with them that I would never share to social media, hugging them close and pretending that I'd finally won Outstanding Lead Actress after four totally unfair snubs? I'd never tell. (But yes.)

"Throw the *Scroll* in the recycling bin the way you promised Alice you would," I murmured to myself. I pulled the *Scroll* out of the stack and splayed it out on my desk, covering up the expense reports I was supposed to be reviewing and filing. "Do not open it up to the food section and obsess over Bennett Radicchio Mustard Wright's first review." I opened it up to the food section. "Oops," I said. "That was an accident."

I was not convincing.

Anyway, Bennett Wright's first review took up the whole front page. I frowned at the centerpiece photo of a luscious-looking duck confit placed on top of haricots verts and potatoes. Which, okay, looked delicious, but didn't look especially *interesting*. Another fancy, ultraexpensive French place? Boh-ring. "Let me guess," I murmured to Bennett Wright as I skimmed his review. Imaginary Bennett turned his nose up at me in response, fish belly–white jowls jiggling from his old-man chin. "Next you're going to take us to a fancy, ultraexpensive New American place and then a fancy, ultraexpensive modern European place. All will be cheffed by pretentious white men and—"

My phone vibrated on the desk. I turned it over to see a text from Alice. **You're reading it, aren't you?**

I shook my head. *My ass, she's not psychic.*

"Anyway," I told Mr. Decker's copy of the *Scroll*, "all the places he covers will be cheffed by pretentious white men and will be some variant of American or European food, or maybe present some kind of 'ethnic' food, but only a token amount and only if it's got some kind of 'modern' twist. And . . ." I trailed off as I hit a line three-quarters of the way through. "Really, Bennett? 'I don't personally care for octopus; I find it unpleasantly squeaky against the teeth when cooked well, and even more unpleasantly rubbery when not.' That's super pretentious, isn't it?"

"What's pretentious?" somebody asked.

My head whipped up. How had I missed someone coming into the office? Had I really been that wrapped up in this stupid review? *Bennett Ricotta Macaroni Wright, this is without a doubt your fault.* Beneath my desk, I slipped my feet back into my work shoes, trading plush carpet massaging my toes for fake leather pinching them. "Emerson Leigh! Hello!" I said, rising to my feet to greet Mr. Decker's younger daughter. "How are you doing? Are you looking for your dad? He's up in Connecticut today."

Emerson Leigh glanced down, a few strands of blond hair slipping free of her messy bun, and it was then I realized that she was holding a stack of flyers. "I finally got these just the way I wanted them. I thought I'd surprise him with one . . ."

Curiosity got the best of me. "What are they?"

She perked up so fast it was almost as if she'd been electrocuted. Circles of pink rose on her otherwise very tan cheeks. "My first advertisement for my business!"

"I didn't know you had a business," I said. As if in reply, Emerson Leigh shoved a flyer in my face. I took it. "Wow, Emerson Leigh." I blinked as I read it. "This is quite . . . something."

The flyer was advertising Emerson Leigh's new pet yoga business. *Is your dog, cat, rabbit, or fish stressed-out or anxious? Call me, a soon-to-be-certified yoga instructor, and I'll help them stretch that stress away! (No snakes.)* An email address was listed below, but instead of a contact name, it just had a big photo of Emerson Leigh's beaming face. Her face was bigger than any of the text, actually.

"I decided I didn't want it to have a real brand name," said Emerson Leigh. "I thought it was better if the brand was just my face. It's, like, a metaphor for the human condition. And how my business is a part of me."

Last year, on December 8, Emerson Leigh had come into the office and wished me a happy birthday with an actual gift. I was surprised because I had never told her my birthday: she'd gone into my employee file and found it herself, telling me that everybody should feel special on their birthday. When I unwrapped the gift, touched almost to the point of tears, I found a framed picture she'd painted of herself. In the nude, sprawled out on a tiger fur rug (fake, she assured me, as if that changed anything).

That story tells you pretty much all you need to know about Emerson Leigh.

"So, Emerson Leigh," I said. "What made you decide to start a pet yoga business? Are there really that many stressed-out pets in New York?"

She drew herself up. "Well, I did a cat yoga class with my cat, except it was really just a bunch of moves I did with my cat there next to me, so it might have de-stressed me, but it didn't do anything for her. And I just thought, why not? She might not be able to talk, but her life really isn't that different from mine. So if I'm stressed and lost and worried about . . ." She trailed off and cleared her throat as she shuffled her flyers. "Anyway, I researched online how to become a pet yoga instructor and discovered there was a real hole in the market!"

"I see," I replied dubiously. "So how does a fish do yoga?"

"Oh, it's not that complicated. You just—" She looked down at my desk. Her eyes widened, sunny circles of green on white. "Oh! Wow! Look at that!"

I looked down, too. Now we were both looking at that large photo of duck confit, Bennett Relish Marmalade Wright's name stamped in official black and white beneath it.

Most of my followers didn't even know my real name. When anyone recognized me in public, they always called out my handle. *Hey, it's JulieZeeEatsNYC!*

"It's duck confit," I said, but she didn't seem to hear me.

"It's Bennett's first review in the *Scroll*!" she cried instead. "How exciting! I'll have to save this! Maybe even frame it for him!" She snatched the paper from my desk and held it up in the air before her. It made a noise like thunder. "Wow, that duck confit looks luscious, doesn't it? So good. I have to go there and try it out sometime. Don't you think it looks good, Julie?"

"It's a really nice picture," I said. "Do you . . . know . . ." It took me a minute to remember his actual names. "Bennett Richard Macalester Wright?"

Her airy laugh pealed in the air. "He sounds so stuffy when you say his full name like that! Yes, I've known Ben for years. He went to Dartmouth with Maisie." Her older sister. "They actually dated for a little bit. He used to come to our cottage in Martha's Vineyard for half the summer. They broke up, but we're all still friends."

I'd been right. Totally right. Maybe not about Bennett's oldness—the picture in my head de-aged from a fifty-something to a thirtysomething—but of course Bennett Wright ran in the same circles as the Deckers. His parents were probably childhood friends with the paper's CEO. Both the *Scroll*'s and the *Times*'s.

It was really competitive, getting a first job as a food reporter at a place like the *Times*, and I realized now that Bennett would've been young when he got it. The opening had probably come up and his dad had leaned on the CEO, said conspiratorially into his ear how nice it would be for his kid to get a byline in before he grew up and moved on to the business world like all the proper kids in that circle, and the CEO had said go ahead. And then the same for this restaurant critic job. If there was anything I'd learned from working for Mr. Decker, that was how the world worked.

Emerson Leigh was still talking. ". . . but Maisie was cheating on everybody then, so it wasn't personal." She set her stack of flyers down on the ledge above my desk. "I was probably angrier at her than Bennett was, since that meant he wouldn't be coming around to Martha's Vineyard anymore, and he always knew the hot places to eat before they had lines." She laughed again. "But we kept in touch, and I was so excited when he moved back to the city! Look, this is us last week."

She thrust her phone in my face. I hated to admit it, but if Bennett and I weren't already mortal enemies (whether he knew it or not), I probably would have found him attractive. From the way he had to stoop to pose with Emerson Leigh, who was five-eight, I assumed he had to be pretty tall. Wire frame glasses shone against the flash, nearly hiding the blue-gray eyes beneath. Pale skin on a narrow, angular face, a high forehead beneath a swoosh of brown-blond hair. Nerd cute, very different from Emerson Leigh's usual type. "Looks fun, Emerson Leigh," I said. "Is he going to take you restaurant-reviewing with him?"

Her shoulders sagged as she pulled her phone back. "It's hard because I'm doing this cleanse right now where I can't eat anything that has color, and he said you really have to be able to eat everything."

"Except octopus," I said.

"Yeah, Bennett really doesn't like octopus," Emerson Leigh said. "Octopi are really smart, though, aren't they? I feel like I shouldn't be eating anything that smart. Why do we eat them?"

"I don't know," I said. My computer pinged with notifications. More emails I had to answer before getting back to my research. "So, do you want to leave the flyers here for your dad? I can make sure he sees them first thing when he comes in."

Emerson Leigh dumped the *Scroll* back on my desk and picked her papers back up. "It's okay. I want to start hanging them up in the lobby downstairs and give some out to my friends to put them up in their buildings," she said cheerily. "But you can keep the one I handed you in case Dad meets with anyone who mentions their anxious pet!"

I eyed it skeptically. "Great. Thanks."

"Yeah, and if you ever want to mention my business online on your page, that's cool, too!" she said. "I'm of course putting it on mine, but I'm really trying to get it out to as many people as possible."

Eek. The last thing I needed was my boss's daughter pressuring me to advertise her ridiculous business on my professional page. *Change the subject, quick.* "You know what I bet would be really fun and that would get the word out?" I chirped. "A business launch party. Rent a space, invite all your friends and your friends' friends. I bet there are a lot of people in your circle who need yoga for their pets."

She gasped so loudly that for a moment, I thought she

was choking. "Yes! You're brilliant, Julie!" She flashed me a dimpled smile. "I'm always down for a party, but even better if it's celebrating me, right?" She didn't wait for an answer. "You'll come, right? You have to. It was your idea."

If nothing else, it would be entertaining. "Wouldn't miss it for the world!"

"Fantastic," Emerson Leigh said over her shoulder as she swished away. The door closed with a click behind her, and I slumped down in my chair, the smile sliding off my face as my gaze settled back onto Bennett Richard Macalester Wright's review.

I want what you have.

I jumped in my chair. Had I really just thought that? *You have plenty*, I told myself. *Be happy with your followers and your status. You're going to achieve everything he has, only you'll be proud because you actually worked for it.*

You'd be happier if you got paid a salary and benefits and had an expense account to do what you love, if you got to take risks and be yourself, instead of having to spend most of your time fetching and smiling for the top one percent, I said back. *It's not fair.*

Always a good sign when the voices in your head were arguing with each other.

To be clear: I knew I had privilege. I had a good job that paid me almost enough to live on and a safe place to live and a family who loved me. If I suddenly lost my job and my apartment burned down, I could move back in with my parents until I got back on my feet. A lot of people didn't have that. I was lucky I did.

Still, spending my time with people like the Deckers, it

could be hard to remember that. It could be hard to not feel like I was the dirt beneath Emerson Leigh's high-heeled shoes.

"I don't need your prestige," I mumbled at the page. Then sighed and swiveled away from it to my computer. Mr. Decker's Florida house manager had emailed me to complain that their cable bill hadn't gotten paid last month. Unless I woke up tomorrow morning to the news of a trust fund established in my name by a previously unknown, mysteriously rich, and very dead great-aunt, who was some-how prominent enough in food media to give my résumé to someone important at a place like the *Scroll*, this was my life.

And there was no point obsessing over it.

3

IF I COULD LIVE IN ANY APARTMENT IN THE CITY, I'd choose one with a view of Central Park, the most expansive green space in Manhattan, full of trees and grass and water and one very fancy duck. I didn't even care which part of the park I lived by. The zoo with its sea lion fountain. The knotty, wild Ramble. The Reservoir surrounded by its running track, or the elegant Conservatory Garden. Not just because it would make me happy to sit out on my balcony and sip tea while gazing serenely over the coveted green space, or because it would be really nice to step outside and unwind with some plants instead of the gray concrete sidewalk and one sad tree planted outside my current building in Brooklyn.

No, because it would mean I'd have had a quick, easy, relaxing commute to the Central Park Food Festival today instead of having to take a circuitous, construction-fueled route that took me over an hour to get to where I stood now, outside the Museum of Natural History.

I took a deep breath. The topiary dinosaurs gazed down at me with their blank black eyes. My underarms were slick with sweat, even with the application of deodorant this morning that should've made me smell like baby powder, and wisps of hair were fraying free from the high bun I'd piled it into this morning to keep it out of my face while eating. I cursed under my breath, digging into my satchel for my tiny emergency bottle of gel. "There you are," I said under my breath, pulling it out . . . and immediately dropping it. I reached for it, but like I'd accidentally fallen into a comedy of errors, a group of masked tourists tromped by, chattering in French as their feet ground the bottle into the dirt.

I cursed again, not under my breath.

"Someone's not having a great morning," Alice said from behind me. I jumped. One more point in the "Alice is Magic" column. I turned to find her looking way more put together than me, her red sweater sweat stain–free, her round, serious face neatly framed by her frizzless black bob.

"It's better now that you're here," I said. "Do you have any gel, by chance? Or hair spray?"

She shook her head. "Sadly, no. I don't like anything that makes my hair feel stiff or crunchy." She paused and considered. "If it's any consolation, I like the frizzy bits. I think they make you look relatable."

I sighed. "We'll go with that." It wasn't like I had any other options. "What's going on with you?"

She linked her elbow with mine, and we moved forward into the park. The path was crowded; streams of people were making their way toward the assemblage of tents and booths in the distance. "Nothing, really. Except I've been getting to know the other girl on my team." Her face lit up. "It's been *so* nice having another girl around. Her name is Kelsey and she's so smart. I've been walking her through our database and our libraries, and I'm making sure she's up to code on our framework—"

"Ha, up to code!" I said. "I get it."

She looked back at me blankly. "Get what?"

"Your pun. It was an excellent pun," I said, but when she continued to just look at me blankly, I sighed. "Never mind. Go on."

Her face lit back up again as she continued to talk about coding minutiae I knew nothing about, but I nodded along, genuinely smiling, enjoying the excitement in her voice and the passion behind it. When she'd first started taking computer science, she hadn't been in love with it; she'd grown up poor, and her goal wasn't to follow her passion but to make a sizable salary in a career field where she'd always be in demand, one that—unlike lawyering or doctoring or finance—didn't typically have ridiculous hours, leaving her time to follow her passions on the side.

But she'd found once she started that she really enjoyed coding: the way it presents you with a problem that has a hundred routes to fix it; the beautiful symmetry of the screen, with its rainbow of colors; the power to bend computers and robots to your will (she usually cackled when she said this, but her eyes were dead serious). She'd even found herself taking freelance projects in her spare time because she enjoyed it, though I didn't think it was her passion in the sense that she'd keep doing it if she wasn't being paid for it, which was the way I felt about food writing.

She finished up with a story about how she and Kelsey had fixed a bug that had caused their team's code to duplicate everything that came out. I had no idea what was going on, but she was laughing, so I laughed, too.

By the time she was done talking, we'd reached the gates of the festival, where throngs of people were waiting for the bag check. Excitement bubbled inside me. The tents were colorful, the voices joyful, the smells incredible. Seriously, my mouth was already watering as we strode onto the expansive green lawn that would soon be tromped muddy and brown. I barely noticed the city skyline painting the horizon as I pulled out my phone and scrolled to my list.

"Let's film a quick introduction," Alice said, because she was the absolute best. She was also the absolute rightest: I had to get the intro out of the way. I couldn't get distracted by all the delicious smells. I tried to push the thought of my messy hair out of my mind as I plastered my usual smile on my face.

"Hey, everyone! I'm here at the Central Park Food Festival and I'm so, so sorry"—dramatic pause—"that nobody's invented smell-vision yet, so you can't smell what I'm smelling right now. How many times can I smell the word *smell* in one sentence?" Let my smile relax wryly, poking fun at myself. The viewers loved that. "We'll see.

Anyway, come along with me while I taste the very best the food festival has to offer!"

A quick pan around, and we were done for now. "I'm thinking we'll do a short video at each stand, and make sure to photograph everything well so that I can do recap posts later," I said.

"Affirmative."

"I think we should go to the shaobing stand first. The *Times* just ran this whole feature on the cook yesterday after his Beard Award nomination, so I think the lines will be longest there."

Alice nodded, and we set off. I goggled at everything we passed, wanting to stop and try it all. It seemed like most vendors had stuck to a street food theme this year, which made sense. We passed booths handing out empanadas bursting with traditional fillings like shredded beef or cheese and less traditional fillings like five-spice pork and tofu or buffalo chicken. Hot dogs charred crispy on the grill and piled high with pineapple relish and chicharrones and cheese sauce. Cool cups of ceviche, the translucent chunks of fish and shellfish just barely cooked in a bath of citrus juice and onion.

I wanted it *all*.

But it would have to wait, because the lines were indeed longest at the shaobing stand, stretching all the way past the next nine booths. I took a quick video of the line to share, then stood at the end.

Alice nudged me with her elbow. I winced. She had very sharp elbows. "Is that Jada Knox over there?"

My heart leaped. *Be cool, Julie. Be cool.* I swiveled my head as slowly and coolly as possible, glancing coolly off into the distance as if thinking hard, picking coolly at my cuticles—there! Jada Knox was standing right there, grinning into her phone and waving an empanada around in the other hand as she talked rapid-fire to her followers.

"You know, I always assume that all influencers are using filters and things to make themselves look better online," Alice said thoughtfully. "But she's just as pretty in person."

Jada Knox was the queen of New York City restaurant-reviewing streamers—a small niche, sure, but one she'd dominated. I might have over fifty thousand followers, but I was fingerling potatoes compared to Jada Knox's four hundred thousand. If we were comparing our follower counts to potatoes, then she was one of those five-pound bags of Idaho potatoes I eyed at the grocery store but couldn't bring myself to lug all the way back over the sidewalk to my apartment.

"She seems to really like that empanada, from the way she's smiling," I said. Though it was hard to pay attention to her mouth when she had literal art painting her eyes: her eye makeup was beyond on point, an ombré of glittery pinks fading to purples that looked like a sunrise on her deep brown skin. Her dress matched it perfectly, a puffy pink skirt with flouncy sleeves that looked like something Glinda the Good Witch might have worn for an afternoon picnic but was somehow absolutely perfect both on her and for this occasion, and her box braids were tied up in an elegant bun. I was suddenly warm with how bad my hair looked, how sweaty I was in the armpits. Jada Knox didn't look like she'd ever sweated in her life. "We should definitely get one later."

Alice was already staring at her phone. "I'm going to see if she tells us what flavor she got."

"She might not actually be posting right now, just recording," I said, turning back to the line and stepping forward as it jumped ahead. "Though I guess she could be live . . ."

I trailed off as I focused on the person in front of us, another familiar face. Only this one I wasn't used to seeing in my feed, literally sparkling as they talked up the city's best food. No, this was one I wasn't supposed to know at all. I'd last seen it pressed up against Emerson Leigh's cheek, smiling for a photo.

Bennett Richard Macalester Wright, literally so close to me that I could smell him, the clean scent of soap and spice cutting through the grease of the doughnut stand beside us.

I hated that he smelled good.

I hated that he looked good, too. Those wire frame glasses flashed in the sunlight high above me; I wasn't close enough to measure for sure, but I probably came up only to his angular chin. He must share the same superpower as Jada Knox, aka knowing exactly what to put on his body to make him look his best for any particular occasion, because the way his blue plaid button-down and pressed khakis hung on his skinny-but-not-spindly frame was Just Right. He stood with two other guys, both white, both dressed like him; the other two guys were laughing with each other, but Bennett stood on the outskirts, a faint smile on his face. What the heck was he even doing here? A street food festival wasn't exactly the *Scroll*'s scene.

I nudged Alice maybe a little harder than I had to, just to make up for the fact that my elbows were decidedly rounder than hers. Then leaned in to whisper in her ear. "That's Bennett Wright right there."

She pulled away, wincing. "You spit in my ear."

"Sorry." It was a consequence of having to whisper loudly enough to be heard over the hubbub around us. We inched past the doughnut stand and were blasted full in the face by taco steam. Not that I was complaining. If all exfoliation steam smelled like tacos, sign me up for a spa day right now. "Did you hear me, though? That's Bennett Wright in front of us." She blinked at me, uncomprehending. I sighed. "Bennett Wright, the new reviewer for the *Scroll*!"

"Oh!" She blinked again, her eyes widening. "What do you want to do? Should we post a video and out him? Wait, how do you even know what he looks like? Didn't he hide all his photos online and things, which you'd think would be impossible, considering we live in the Internet age?"

I quickly explained yesterday to her. Her mouth dropped open as I spoke. "Please tell me you brought me one of Emerson's flyers. Do you think she'd take me seriously if I asked her about yoga for the mice in my kitchen?"

"I have one, but I left it at work," I said. "Yes, she probably would, and she'd choreograph an entire routine for them. And it's Emerson Leigh. She goes by two names, like Katy Perry." Which was something that had always rankled me a tiny bit. Didn't Emerson Leigh take up enough space in this world without that extra little bit of time it took to say an extra name? "Did you know Perry isn't Katy Perry's last name?"

"Now I do," said Alice. "Kelsey has a first name for a last name. Courtney. That's her full name, Kelsey Courtney."

"Who's—" Right, Kelsey was Alice's new coworker. "That's a pretty name." But we were getting way off topic here. "I don't think we should make his image public. That's going too far." No matter how much I loathed him, there was a code of conduct among food writers. I could still be professional. And the *Scroll* probably wouldn't be happy with me if they heard I'd outed their main reviewer; I could wave goodbye to ever writing for them.

But it wasn't like there were only two options here. The corner of my lip twisted mischievously.

I had to tamp it down a minute later when I stepped up to their group. The two guys Bennett was with stopped talking mid-sentence and swiveled to look down on me like I was an empanada filled with crushed cockroaches. If I hadn't been on a mission, I might have shriveled in my fashionable sneakers. I tossed my head to the side, trying to feel more confident, and fulfilled the exact opposite of my goal when tendrils of flyaway hair stuck to the sweat on my forehead. "Heyyyy," I said, trying to sound as much like Emerson Leigh as possible. Confident. Friendly. Oblivious. "Do you guys know who John Waterford is? The name sounds sooooo familiar."

They exchanged glances, eyebrows raised like, *How stupid is this chick?* Or at least the two random guys did. Bennett was squinting at me, like he knew me from somewhere. *That's not possible*, I told myself. *There's no way a reviewer from the* Scroll *follows you.* Though he didn't have to recognize me from JulieZeeEatsNYC, did he? Maybe he'd seen me the same way I'd seen him, from a photo of me with Emerson Leigh. *Curse all those selfies she made me take.*

Stop overthinking, I ordered myself. *Stick the landing.*

"Yeah, I know who John Waterford is." It was the guy in front who'd spoken: blond, pink-cheeked, and wearing a pastel yellow polo with the logo of a rhino on the chest, which probably meant it was from some fancy brand I didn't know. "He's one of the most famous chefs in the world. He's even a judge on *Chef Supreme.*"

Yes. Obviously, I knew all that. But I fixed my face into a look of wide-eyed, O-mouthed surprise, the same one Emerson Leigh gave me when I told her I'd "summered" as a child in the same house I "wintered." "Oh! Wow! Because I just heard that he's at the crepe booth down there"—I leaned out of line and pointed back toward where we came, at the opposite end of the festival—"doing an impromptu cooking demonstration!"

I'd figured that would be a draw for any fancy food writer, and, sure enough, Bennett almost jumped out of his textured gray sneakers. Were those made of wool? I wasn't all that up on the latest fashion trends, but Alice told me all the tech people were wearing those now. "At the crepe booth, you said?"

"Yup," I said, trying to beam disarmingly the way Emerson Leigh did. From the way Rhino grimaced, I assumed I looked like an orangutan ready to fight. "But from what my friend texted me, it doesn't sound like he's going to be there very long."

Bennett nodded, a jerky, abrupt motion. "Thanks for the tip." Ignoring the non-Rhino friend, who was groaning about how they'd been waiting in line soooo long already, he stalked off into the crowd, pulling them along behind him. We moved forward, filling their open positions.

"That was masterful." I turned to find Alice goggling at me. "When did you become such a good liar?"

I widened my eyes innocently. "Me, lie? Never."

Alice giggled. Actually giggled. I wasn't sure if I'd ever seen Alice giggle. Laugh, sure. Giggle, no. "That reminds me of this thing that Kelsey does when the guys ask her to take notes in meetings, because she's new and she's the girl. She makes her voice all high and . . ."

I spent the rest of our time in line listening to how great Kelsey Courtney was, drooling over the smells of the food we passed, and laughing over how confused Bennett was going to be when he got to the crepe stand and found no famous chef cracking eggs. Hopefully, it threw him off. Ruined his day. Even if he wasn't here in an official capacity.

Finally, we got close enough where we could see the menu. There were some tempting-looking little salads and teas, but it appeared that the main centerpiece of the booth was the shaobing. My previous day's research had told me that shaobing was a type of layered flatbread popular in Northern China, super flaky and often flavored with sesame, which could be filled with anything sweet or savory. It looked like the chef had chosen some of the traditional fillings as options, including red bean paste or mung beans with egg and tofu, along with some less traditional options, like Cubano pork, and s'mores.

"We should try some traditional and some less traditional," I said.

"Definitely the red bean paste," said Alice.

So we decided on that, plus the s'mores and whatever the chef recommended, because they just sounded so good. Any more than that and we might not have room for more food, and we still had to try a lot more booths.

I was going to have so many leftovers to bring home. Which made me very happy.

The shaobing smelled so good I wanted to tear into them right away, but of course we had to step to the side and get some good photos first. Fortunately, the lighting in this area was great. Once the photos were done, I had Alice film me taking my first bite of the shaobing recommended by the person at the window—the one with the Cubano filling. I closed my eyes as I chewed. And swallowed fully before I spoke.

"If you don't try the shaobing with Cubano pork today, you're missing out," I said. "It's just an explosion of flavor. The pork is tender and practically falls apart at my teeth, and the pickles add a nice vinegary crunch against the meatiness of the pork and ham and the richness of the cheese. And that structure! I'll never be able to eat a Cubano sandwich on ordinary bread again, not after the flaky crunch of the shaobing. I hope you caught the steam that billowed out when I took that bite. I'd *bathe* in it." Was that too weird? Too late. I couldn't wait another second before digging in. The s'mores and red bean ones were already getting cool from the way we'd pulled the outsides apart to get good photos of the filling.

An hour later, I was just about full-term with a bouncing, beautiful food baby. Alice and I had photographed and eaten jerk chicken over plantains, spicy and sweet; cups of icy, sweet, rich halo-halo piled with red beans and fruit cocktail; lobster roll sliders stuffed full of delicate shellfish on buttery brioche; pani puri, the fried Indian hollow rounds of dough loaded up with mashed potato and chickpeas and sweet, tangy tamarind chutney. My camera was happy. I was happy.

Alice was stuffed. "I don't think I can eat another bite," she moaned, swaying as she walked. "I couldn't even drink anything. Not even wine. And I love wine."

I was swaying as I walked, too, but I had my own superpower. I never really got full. My food baby just turned into twins. Or triplets. "Okay, that means more for me. Or more leftovers," I told her, eyes swooping from side to side. I still wanted to try the empanadas Jada Knox had been eating . . . or would it be a waste of time for me to eat the same thing as her, since she'd broadcast it to her hundreds of thousands of followers before me and my own would just swipe through? Should I focus on some of the more obscure booths? "And you know I think wine is nasty, so I definitely can't drink any right now, either. I still really want to try Chef Dominic Nguyen's bánh xèo with prawns and mint. Here, take my phone, film me talking, and I'll do a viewer poll."

I handed it over and she held it up; I talked a bit about the bánh xèo again and then went on. "There's Chef Liz Branch's fancy pizza that I've been eyeing all day—I hear the crust is crispier than most, even with all her toppings piled on—and there's that Belgian waffle stand that's a wild card but could be amazing . . ." I trailed off as I noticed Alice staring over my shoulder, eyes wide like she'd seen a guy flicking peeled-off toe skin into the fryer. "What is it? Is there something in my hair?"

"I think you meant, '*Who* is it?'" someone said from behind me, and I could hear the sneer in his voice even before I turned around. It was the guy in the rhino polo, blond hair plastered tight to his head with sweat, Bennett and his other friend standing to his side. "John Waterford was never here at all. Was it really worth it to steal our place in line?" He scrunched up his broad face. "They were out of the s'mores shaobing by the time we finally made it up there."

"It had nothing to do with stealing your place in line,"

I told him hotly, then remembered that I was supposed to be acting like Emerson Leigh around them. I pushed my shoulders back, lifted my chin, tried to relax my brows so I wasn't frowning. "Hey, I'm sorry! Someone told me that thing about John Waterford and I passed it on. I had no idea it wasn't true."

Rhino snorted—ironically, exactly like a rhino—and turned to go. I relaxed my shoulders, hunching a little, figuring that would be the end of it.

And then Bennett said, suddenly, "No, I know you."

"Me?"

"Yes, you." He had a plummy way of speaking that I absolutely should have expected, like he was enunciating every word, making sure the ends didn't trail off and the beginnings didn't mumble. "You're Emerson Leigh's friend. Julie Zee Eats NYC."

I kind of liked how he separated out my username, making it four separate words rather than the one run-on word it tended to slur into in my head. The sentiment was another thing. "I don't know if I'd say *friend*," I told him. "More like father's employee."

He waved a hand in the air, his blue-gray eyes pinning me in place. "That's irrelevant." I felt a little bit like a butterfly on a corkboard. "She told me she'd shown you a picture of me. She called me right after she did it since she felt bad. I'd asked her not to share any photos of me with anyone, because of the *Scroll*. I had to look you up to make sure you hadn't posted it."

I bristled at the way he said *had to*. Like clicking on my name and looking at my face was *such* an imposition.

"So you knew who I was, and you know food, and I estimate there's at least a ninety-five percent chance you know who John Waterford is, which means you were probably lying." He cocked his head. "Why?"

All their eyes on me made my skin hot. My eyes darted frantically to the side. I could run. And probably disappear in the crowd. I'd escape.

But for what? Everybody knew who I was and where to find me. I'd be considered a coward. And I wasn't a coward. I raised my chin defiantly, though my cheeks still burned. "It was just a joke. A prank from a fellow restaurant reviewer, if you will." A dumb explanation, and knowing that made my cheeks burn harder, but it was better than the truth. "I didn't know you were reviewing any of this today."

He raised his eyebrows with amusement. Or bemusement. I could never get those two down. "Reviewing? No, I'm not reviewing the festival. Not officially. I would never *review* a place like this in print."

A place like this. He was still talking, but I couldn't hear him over the roar building in my ears. Could barely see his mouth moving through the film of red forming over my vision. *A place like this.* Bennett Wright was exactly who I'd thought he would be: a spoiled brat who looked down on every restaurant that didn't charge at least fifty dollars a plate. Sure, he might deign to pick up food at a fun festival and throw a few dollars at the vendors, but feature them in the hallowed, unsullied pages of the *New York Scroll*? No. Oh no, that wouldn't do.

A place like this. He was talking about *me*. About what *I* did. Putting *me* down. I barked a not-at-all-humorous laugh, one that stopped him mid-whatever he was saying. Maybe because it sounded like I was about to vomit all over his fancy wool sneakers, which probably cost a full week of my salary.

Suddenly, I wished I *could* vomit on command, something I'd never wanted before. "That's right, you're so much better than me," I spat. He blinked, eyebrows raising this time with surprise behind those wire rims. "What restaurant did you pick for your first review? I can't remember the name, since it read exactly the same as every other review I've read from the *Scroll*. Pretentious, expensive, and boring."

It was like a door closed over his face. "Wow."

"Yeah, wow," I said, and it was like pushing someone off a cliff: there was nowhere to go but down, down, down. I was hitting all the trees and rocks on the way, and the injustice of this whole thing was burning in me, a sharp pain like a broken bone, the fact that this guy had gotten the job I'd so badly wanted.

I would have done such a good job. I would not have chosen to go after the same restaurants they'd always done, the same restaurants that resonated mainly with middle-aged office workers in their white collars and expensive suits. "But it's not so surprising," I said. "You're basically the same as their last critic. And the critic before him. A rich white guy. You're all that's wrong with food media today. Is your dad all BFF with the *Scroll*'s CEO or with the food editor, or are they only business buddies?"

Beside Bennett, Rhino let out a long, low whistle. "So, just because someone's rich and white, they can't be a food critic? Wow, talk about reverse racism."

"That's not what *reverse racism* means," I said, my eyes still on Bennett. Like I needed both hands to concentrate, I dropped my bag of leftovers onto the ground beside me. "That's not even a real term. And I'd say it's probably more classism and sexism in this case. Though in food, most of the actual cooks aren't rich and white, but the people featured disproportionately in your pages and in food media are. Why is that? How is that fair?"

Meanwhile, Bennett dropped his gaze, and without those eyes stabbing me, for a moment I felt bad. A little bad, like a hitch in my breath, a missed step at the bottom of a staircase. I took the moment to look around us. I guess I'd assumed that people would be clustering nearby, murmuring excitedly and filming, but no. Everybody was mostly ignoring us.

"For your information," Rhino said, his voice trumpeting like an actual rhino's, "Bennett's mom might have grown up with the paper's CEO, but that doesn't mean he didn't get the job on his own—"

"Stop it, Ryan," Bennett said, his voice low, but the burning inside me was already crawling up my throat, bursting out in a hot, scornful laugh. I didn't even have to know whether Rhino was talking about the *Times* or the *Scroll.*

"You are everything that's wrong with food writing and restaurant reviewing today. You could *never* do what I do."

Those eyes came back up, and I had to swallow hard at the intensity aimed at me, the scorching anger magnified by the lenses of his glasses. "Is that right? What is it again that you do, exactly?" He held his palm up to his face, mimicking a phone as he talked into it. "Hey guys, check out this really pretty food! What does it taste like? What's the historical context behind it, and who's the chef that cooked it? It doesn't matter! It looks cool!"

The fire spread to my cheeks, then to my eyes. If looks could kill, he'd have two neat holes drilled into that pale forehead by now. "That's not what I do," I bit out, but I couldn't deny that the words hit home. I spent so much time thinking about lighting and placement and which dish looked best on camera, and also how nice it might be to capture each dish in writing, where it didn't matter how pretty it looked. So much time focusing on how I looked before the camera. "How many subscribers do you have left, anyway? Isn't print dying? How long until it's actually dead and you're out of a job?"

I knew I'd hit home when he winced, like I'd actually hit him. For a moment I felt that bad missed-stair feeling again, and then I remembered what he'd said to me. So no more of that. I lifted my chin challengingly as he replied.

"The food page is one of the only sections that's expanding. Doing well and drawing people in. That and real estate, surprisingly enough."

I supposed the scions and CEOs flipping through the paper each morning preferred to browse their third homes or vacation yachts or design schemes off real paper. I'd found my apartment on Craigslist, but I'd had to scroll through scams and sketchy listings of older men looking for younger women to live with for reduced rent in exchange for "chores."

"There's only so long those numbers can carry you," I said wisely, like I had any idea what I was talking about. "I wouldn't do what you do in a million years." Bennett's eyes flashed, and for a moment, panic squirmed in me that he'd seen my résumé lying on someone's desk, would respond with a clear-cut, *If you wouldn't take my job, why did you apply?*

Thankfully, his mom's friendship with the paper's CEO didn't extend that far. "Whatever you say. How much do you make doing this again?"

Ryan the Rhino guffawed behind him, as if that had been some great crack. I pressed my lips together. Why couldn't Bennett just take his salary and benefits and expense account and go? Preferably somewhere far away. Like the middle of the Atlantic Ocean. He could review seaweed salad and gull meat and clams, all deliciously brined. And maybe also dehydrate himself and die. *Julie, you may be going a little too far.* But it didn't feel like it. He wasn't just attacking me, he was attacking all the dreams I'd ever had.

"It doesn't matter how much I make doing this," I bit out. "Some things aren't about the money, though you and your friends probably don't understand that." I waved my arm around wildly in the air, as if that proved something. Or anything aside from that fact that I had at least one working shoulder socket. "I *love* what I do. I get to eat the best food in the city and tell people about it, and have *way* more of an effect on my followers than your official byline does."

He raised one elegant eyebrow behind his wire rims. It really was elegant. I couldn't help but wonder if he manscaped. "Are you joking?"

"I don't joke," I said, which was a lie. "My viewers like me and trust *me*. I thought Emerson Leigh told you about my account. You didn't look me up?"

His lip curled. "Just to make sure you didn't post anything of me. I don't use social media. At least, not in my personal life."

Of course he didn't. My blood heated even more. Sometimes people weren't into social media, and that was fine. Just like some people were vegans, and that was fine, too, because people should be able to make whatever choices for their personal lives they wanted as long as they didn't hurt anyone else. But from the way his lip was curling, I knew he wasn't one of those people. He was one of those people who thought social media rotted your brain and made you stupid. He probably sat down every day with his print newspaper and smiled smugly at it, thinking of all the poor, stupid souls scrolling through Twitter headlines instead.

I curled my lip back at him. "On social media, power comes from the people. Not an institution. Your readers don't care about you; you're just the byline in the *Scroll*. You might get more readers, but mine are way more passionate."

"Is that so?" He looked as if he'd bitten into a fine torte and discovered it was filled with ground liver instead of chocolate. "All right, then. Prove it."

I tossed my hair, or tried to toss my hair before I remembered it was all up in an actually messy, not just artfully messy bun, and of course, this was the moment my actually messy, not just artfully messy bun chose to entirely explode. My hair tie pinged off and vanished forever into the trampled grass. Hair everywhere, no survivors.

I have a lot of hair. That's not specific enough, so let me try it again: I have hair like the mane of an especially aggravated male lion, like the "before" photo of a nineties teen movie makeover, like a storm cloud crackling with electricity. So it wasn't a surprise when their eyes widened and they took a step back as my hair sprang free. I lifted my chin, feeling a little bit like an avenging goddess. "I prove it in the comments of my followers and the thank-yous from businesses when they report a spike in reservations after my reviews go live." Was it my imagination, or was my voice deeper, an echo behind it?

It was definitely my imagination. I was losing it a little. "I don't need your byline and your health benefits. I am the future, and you are the past."

Bennett, Ryan the Rhino, and their third friend seemed to shrink a little bit beneath the force of my voice. Ryan actually took a step back. But Bennett swallowed hard and forced out, "That's a shame. Remember when I said the food pages of the *Scroll* were expanding? If you really could prove it, I bet that and a good word from me could get you in. At least an interview. Maybe even a column."

For a moment, all I could see were those blue-gray eyes behind his glasses, and the frames seemed almost like windows to another world. One where we were working side by side for the *New York Scroll*. Those eyes squinted in laughter as I cracked a joke across our shared desk. (Why was I sharing a desk in my own fantasy?) They widened in impressed enjoyment as they read my first column, one that persuaded stodgy old print readers to get out of their comfort zone and try new things.

But I couldn't back down now. So my hair and I glared him down, and I thought so hard about how I didn't want that, that I almost believed it. He glared back, and the air practically sizzled between us. I wouldn't have been surprised if the grass actually burst into flame.

He was the first to look away, and I found myself a little disappointed when he did, as if the sizzle had been the thing keeping me standing. I stumbled back a step, then two. "Well, I'm not going to waste any more of my time," Bennett announced. "I'm going to go eat more delicious food." He took a step back. "You might want to find a hair tie."

"*You* might want to find a hair tie!" I called after his retreating back, which, I admit, was not one of my finest comebacks. I turned to Alice, feeling a little sheepish, at least until I noticed she was still holding my phone up in front of her. "Wait, have you been filming this whole time?"

She lowered it, goggling at me. "You didn't tell me to stop."

My first instinct was to sigh and grab my phone and delete it all, but I paused after the second step, phone in hand. My interaction with Bennett played silently out on the screen, and yes, I did look extremely fierce.

Maybe I could use this, I thought, and didn't realize I'd murmured it aloud until Alice said, "What?"

4

FOR MUCH OF THE COUNTRY, SUNDAY WAS A DAY
of rest. The Sabbath. Not for me, and not just because I
wasn't Christian. The afternoon after the food festival
found me at my laptop in my little bedroom, occasionally
glancing wistfully out the window between editing work
at the quiet Brooklyn street of brick row homes and my
one sad tree.

I was lucky enough that my work at Mr. Decker's allowed me to do a lot of other work on company time, but
I didn't have my photo or video editing software at the
office. Which meant that weekends were my time for editing. I'd already touched up my photos from the food festival that I'd be including in my post—no major filters or
anything; I just wanted to quiet any distracting background noise, make the colors of the food really pop, and
edit out some of my extra frizz. Now I was left staring at

the video of me and Bennett yelling at each other, our voices loud and clear over the buzz of people in the background.

Watching it made me want to yell in chorus with my past self.

Though now I could catch the part of his speech I'd missed the first time, after he'd told me he'd never review "a place like this" in hallowed print, when I'd gotten so pissed off that my thinking had drowned him out. He'd gone on to say that he was here to capture some highlights from the day on social media, because part of the deal of him getting this restaurant critic job was that he'd share a lot of his behind-the-scenes life online, which was new for the paper (they had robust food social media pages with cooking and recipes, but not so much restaurant or fine-dining stuff). That was actually who the guy who wasn't Ryan the Rhino was: a social media intern from the *Scroll*.

Guilt flickered inside me at the thought of my behavior in front of him, but it quickly roared into a blaze of anger. How dare he swagger in to do exactly what I did and then proceed to make fun of me for doing *exactly what he was trying to do*. What a jerk. The *Scroll* deserved to go out of print if that's how their employees were going to talk about other people.

My phone buzzed. A text from Alice. **Did you decide what you're going to do with the video yet?** Before I could respond, another buzz. **You should just delete it and forget it. Focus on your own code.**

I assumed those were words of wisdom from her

workplace, but they applied to me, too. I couldn't control what Bennett did, or what the *Scroll* did. All I could control was my own screen. And sometimes—I thought ruefully, glancing at the video—not even that.

And yet, the anger was still boiling away in my chest. Shouldn't the people know what the *Scroll* thought of them? Shouldn't the people who would follow them online and see what they had to say be aware of what their food critic thought of them and of people like me?

It doesn't hurt to edit the video into something usable, I told myself. *You don't have to post it right away. You can think about it first.*

So that's how I spent the next hour or so. Fixing the sound so that Bennett's and my voices came through clearly and didn't get drowned out by background noise. Editing out pauses and awkward coughs. Not changing anything either Bennett or I said, or cutting anything out to make it sound like either of us said something that we didn't—that would be wrong. Just cleaning it up. Blurring out Bennett's and the other guys' faces, because yeah, I was mad, but I wasn't going to tank Bennett's whole career because of it. Editing in pauses so that I could write in some reactions in text and emojis.

When my phone buzzed again, I jumped. I'd never gotten back to Alice, so I assumed it was her, but the name that flashed on the screen was my roommate's. **You still alive in there?**

A smile twitched at my lips. Most of the roommates I'd lived with in New York (aside from Alice in college) wouldn't have cared if I'd died in my room. To be perfectly honest, I wouldn't have much cared if they'd died in their rooms, either. Sometimes I thought I'd rather have a ghost as a roommate than the girl who never washed her dishes until roaches were eating her crusted-on food or the guy who brought random club hookups in every weekend until one stole his laptop.

But Marcus was different. Yeah, he was a Craigslist roommate like most of the others, and it wasn't like we were best friends hanging out every night, but we sometimes watched *Chef Supreme* together in the living room and shared our kitchen staples. And he cared about whether I'd died, which was really nice considering I'd only been in here for—

My eyes bugged out as I saw the time. "It's been *seven hours*?" How could it be nine o'clock already? I never lost myself inside my work, no matter how much I loved it. I might be able to hold my bladder for ages, but I never forgot to eat. As if it was furious with me, my stomach let out the loudest growl I'd ever heard. I gave it a pat. "I'm so sorry!" When I stood, my knees cracked, and my back groaned. I winced. My looming thirtieth birthday had never looked less appealing. "Let's feed you."

I hustled out of my room to find Marcus sprawled out on the scuffed white couch left here by a past roommate, something with a laugh track blaring on the TV. The framed poster of the New York City subway map—also left behind by a previous roommate—hung slightly crooked above him. He clapped his hands when he saw me. "She lives!"

"She's starving," I said grimly, but I smiled. Marcus was wearing worn-in blue basketball shorts and no shirt, the scars from his top surgery a dark brown against his light brown skin. He'd been self-conscious about them after the surgery and had only recently begun going shirtless around the apartment. I typically didn't enjoy seeing my roommates in various stages of undress, but my feelings made an exception for him. "Is Edna's still open?"

My hopes for shrimp roti and curried potatoes deflated fast as Marcus shook his head. Most of the restaurants in the area were small mom-and-pop Caribbean joints that served cheap, delicious food cafeteria-style to the immigrant population and closed relatively early; I could order delivery from farther away, but it would take ages to get here. My stomach growled at me again at the very thought.

Marcus let out an overly dramatic gasp. "Does this mean you're going to . . . cook?"

"Don't sound so surprised," I said. "I *can* cook, you know."

"When's the last time you've cooked?"

When *was* the last time I'd cooked? I actually had to think about it. I used to love cooking in college, but since I'd moved to New York and started JulieZeeEatsNYC, I'd been eating out so much keeping my page current that cooking had kind of taken a back seat. When was the last time I'd even gone grocery shopping?

I ran out of time for an answer. Marcus scoffed, turning back to his show. "I made extra pasta salad if you want some. It's in the fridge."

Well, now I *had* to cook. "I don't need your pity pasta salad," I said, sticking my nose in the air. Then lowering it back down. "Though I'm sure it's delicious."

"It *is* delicious."

Unlike most New York City kitchens, which were long and narrow and dark, ours was big enough to fit a kitchen cart and even a tiny table for two under the big window; Marcus's herb garden was green and cheery on the sill, and he'd covered the old but serviceable (and only slightly leaky) fridge with magnetic poetry. *Light the world on fire*, it told me now. I hoped it didn't mean literally.

"Let me know if you need any help," Marcus called from the other room.

"I'm good," I called back as I opened the fridge. And grimaced. Marcus's side overflowed with a bounty of fresh greens and violently purple eggplants, little jars of sauces and plastic Tupperware filled with an expectedly tasty-looking pesto pasta salad, with . . . were those roasted carrots and asparagus? Yum.

My side was barren in comparison. I had a bottle of ketchup, a half stick of butter, a slimy bag of what had once been spinach, and a few eggs that had expired only a week ago and so were probably still good. My cabinet situation wasn't much better. I had some flour and stale popcorn, which weren't all that appealing or helpful. A dusty bag of rice, which smelled fine.

Okay. That was it, then. I'd make eggs and rice and mix it up with some ketchup and Marcus's soy sauce. Ketchup fried rice had been a college staple, even if back then I'd included some more vegetables. But ketchup was kind of a vegetable, which made this a nutritious and filling meal. Sort of. The annoyance was simmering inside me again just looking at it all, not as hot as the anger but from the same source. *I'd be eating delicious roti and potatoes from Edna's if* Bennett Wright *hadn't distracted me with his extremely punchable face on video.*

I took a deep breath and assembled my mise en place. I might not cook often, but some things were muscle memory. My half stick of butter, the rice, the eggs, the soy sauce, and the ketchup. Oh, and salt. Everything needed salt. And maybe pepper, except that my pepper grinder had run out. How sad was that?

I could practically see Bennett sneering at me with disdain.

"Shut up," I hissed, even though he hadn't said anything and he wasn't here, anyway, but even so, after I turned the heat on under the skillet on the stove and dumped in a pat of butter, I cracked the eggs maybe a little bit too hard. Okay, definitely a lot too hard. And maybe I shouldn't have done it on the edge of the skillet, because the whites oozed over the side, little flakes of shell falling into the pan with them. I cursed under my breath and stuck my fingertip in the pan, trying to scoop the bits out, only to stick my skin right up against the searing metal. I cursed again, not under my breath.

"You sure you don't need help?" Marcus called.

"I'm good," I called back again. I was not good. Why had I started off by cooking the eggs? They were already done, but the rice would take at least—I peeked at the back of the bag—twenty minutes. I was so out of practice. The only thing that kept me from cursing again was that I didn't want more of Marcus's pity.

Okay. The rice went into the pot, followed by twice that amount of water and a good pinch of salt. I put it on the stove and turned the burner way up so it would boil quickly, then turned the burner under the eggs off. I sighed, flopping onto one of our little barstools and resting my cheek against the table.

Somehow, over the furious battle cries of my stomach, my thoughts drifted back to the video. To post or not to post: that was the question. It really depended on how I framed it. If I posted it and used the caption to tattle on Bennett for being a classist jerk, I'd look spiteful and petty, and people would sympathize with him. If I just posted it alone, that was the Wild West. People would be able to interpret it however they wanted. They wouldn't like that. Followers didn't go on my social media to think hard and analyze; they went on because it was easy and fun. And there was nothing wrong with that—they probably thought hard and analyzed all day at work, listening to music or podcasts, reading books and articles. It was okay that they came to me to unwind, but that meant they'd want some kind of frame or fence herding them to a conclusion.

I could post it if I knew the frame would make my followers and anyone else who saw it sympathize with me. Even better if I could make *them* feel under attack. I could frame it as a public service announcement. *Hey, people on social media, do you put a lot of stock in the* Scroll's *reviews? Here's a PSA on what the reviewer thinks of you.* The thought of people's reaction was enough to make my nose wrinkle, like I smelled something burning.

No, not *like*. I *did* smell something burning.

I jumped up from the barstool. Marcus called out to me again from the other room, though our smoke alarm wasn't going off. *We should probably get that checked out.* I grabbed the pot lid, then shouted because it burned my hand.

"Out of the way!" Marcus to the rescue. He pushed me to the side—in a gentle way—and, somehow with a pot holder already on his hand, lifted the lid off my pot. Smoke escaped, and I wrinkled my nose harder but didn't turn away. I felt like the guy in *Game of Thrones* who gravely told his son they had to see firsthand the dirty consequences of what they had to do, and even though they'd been talking about beheading lawbreakers, the sentiment felt similar. Kind of.

"You know, you're supposed to pay attention when you've got something on the stove," Marcus said once the smoke had cleared and we could both stare into the pot. The rice had scorched black and stuck to the pot and burned while I was sitting there thinking about the video. He gazed into the pot, reaching in and poking some of the grains gingerly with one finger. "It's somehow over- *and* undercooked at the same time. Truly impressive."

I knew my cheeks were flushing from embarrassment

from how hot they were getting, but still, I stepped back. Took a bow.

Marcus laughed. "Maybe don't feature this one under your handle," he said, pulling the pot off the stove and dumping it into the sink, then filling it with water. "We'll let this soak for a while. In the meantime, you have some . . . overcooked, rubbery eggs with shell in them?"

I gritted my teeth. "My favorite."

Marcus sighed. "Do you ever think about how ironic it is that you literally review restaurants for a living, but you can't even boil water?"

I didn't quite review restaurants for my living, but yes, I had thought about this before. Maybe I should dedicate one night a week to cooking again just so I wouldn't be so embarrassing in the kitchen. I ground my teeth harder. "I can so boil water," I said. "The problem was that I boiled it too hard."

He patted my shoulder. "Keep telling yourself that."

As it turned out, the pasta salad *was* delicious.

5

I WOKE UP THE NEXT MORNING DETERMINED AND decided on the course of the edited video. No, that wasn't exactly true. As usual, I woke up determined and decided on nothing but stumbling into the bathroom and brushing my teeth and pouring some coffee into my face. So the truth was that I strode into Mr. Decker's office and plunked in my chair and kicked off my shoes and then, just then, I was determined and decided.

I pulled up my account. It was early, but this wasn't a review where I was worried about staying on theme and maximizing engagement. Besides, I didn't want this video to interfere with any of my scheduled posts on the food festival, which were coming later today and tomorrow. I let my thumb hover over the touch screen for just a moment before bringing it solidly down.

Post.

And then, before I could chicken out, I tagged the *Scroll*'s food page, because I wasn't hiding.

I exhaled slowly as I set my phone down on my desk. Then picked it back up again to put it on do-not-disturb mode. Back down. Somehow I was still exhaling, all the air leaking out of me like a deflating balloon. Something with tentacles was swimming in my stomach, which was murky with acid. I was afraid it might swim up my throat.

Deep breath in. Had I just done an incredibly stupid thing? It had only been a couple of minutes, but I picked my phone back up again, flicked my social media open.

To, already, a storm of comments. I thought I might pass out as I opened them up. Squeezed my eyes shut for a moment, trying to gird up my nerves, and popped them open before I could lose my resolve.

WOW what a dick that guy is

Hey @newyorkscrollfood are you really ok with your reviewer talking about us that way??

Ahhhh Julie you're a queen!!! Tell him!!!

My shoulders relaxed as I continued reading, lowering from their tense perch around my ears. Most of the comments followed in that vein—true, the people seeing it this early on were likely my fans who spent a lot of time on social media and were on right as I posted, but I wasn't alone. I wasn't overreacting. People were on my side.

That knowledge made it easier to put my phone back facedown and leave it there while I dealt with what quali-

fied as a crisis in the Decker office (one of the TVs on his
Florida yacht was down—gasp). You'd be amazed how an
entire morning can fly by while you're focused on something that, in the grand scheme of things, matters not at
all. There were three other TVs on the yacht. Mr. Decker
wouldn't even be down there to watch any of them until
late fall. By the time I picked up my phone again, it was
almost noon. I ran downstairs for a salad—shoes on—
and then back up—shoes off—settling into my chair to
see what had gone on over the last few hours.

My jaw dropped. A few pieces of farro dropped with it,
falling onto my lap. I blinked at my screen once, twice,
three times, not thinking until then that I should probably
clean the farro off so that the oil of the dressing wouldn't
stain my pencil skirt.

Six thousand followers: that was how many I'd gained
since I checked last. My heart pattered against my rib cage
as I scanned the comments. They were still mostly supportive of me, but—whoa! I'd been reblogged by *Eater*
and *Grub Street* and Jada Knox. Jada Knox! She'd even
done a little reaction to the video, all, *this is why the old guard
is dying, bring on the new guard.*

We were the new guard. I thought so, anyway.

My breathing grew shallow as a new notification popped
up on my screen. From the *Scroll*'s account. Before I even
read it, I wondered if it was from the social media intern
who'd accompanied Bennett to the food festival. Hey,
everybody! Our food critic Bennett was glad to meet up with Julie
Zee at the food festival and discuss their careers. Please know he

greatly respects her and all of you. He looks forward to continuing these conversations with Julie Zee about how the old guard and the new guard can coexist and respect each other in the restaurant-reviewing space!

We'd be "continuing these conversations"? That was news to me.

Just as I was thinking that, my screen pinged. I instinctually reached for my phone, but of course it wasn't my phone; I always had sound notifications turned off at work. It was my work computer. I spun in my chair, exhilarated, ready to run down to Florida and beat that nonworking TV into submission . . . only the email wasn't from the Palm Beach house manager. Or a member of the charity board. Or Mr. Decker himself. Or . . . well, anyone else in Mr. Decker's prodigious address book.

It was from Bennett Wright.

I inhaled so loud I started to cough. And amid that coughing, before I could even check the email, the office door flew open and in breezed Emerson Leigh, a big paper shopping bag crinkling over her shoulder. "Julie!" she trilled in greeting. I had no idea how she managed to trill a word with no Rs in it; maybe that was something you learned at prep school. "I saw your post! It's going viral!"

She set the bag down on the reception table, skewing the pile of glossy magazines from the past several years, all of which featured Mr. Decker somewhere in their pages (he was most proud of his write-up in *Golf Fancy*). The bag slumped, and some garment wrought of plush emerald silk peeked out the top. "That was quite a bold thing to post, wasn't it?" she asked, smiling. She sure smiled with a lot of teeth. "Calling Bennett out like that? Making it seem like he's some kind of jerk?"

"I don't know," I said mildly to Emerson Leigh, because she was my boss's daughter, and I couldn't say that her friend *was* actually a massive jerk. "I mean, I didn't edit the meaning out of it. Everything on that video was something we actually said."

She put her hand on her hip and cocked it. Though the physical gesture wasn't similar, it reminded me of cocking a gun. "You guys really seemed to be hitting it off."

That was so different than what I'd expected her to say that I blinked in surprise, stunned into silence. She only blinked back at me, her high blond ponytail shivering, her mouth set seriously.

When I finally managed to speak, it came out almost as a cough. "Are you sure you watched the right video?"

That was the wrong thing to say, evidently, because the corners of her mouth turned down. "I watched the video you posted. There was a crackle between the two of you. Of chemistry."

"The only crackle between me and Bennett was anger," I said, barely holding the laugh back. "Besides, his face was blurred out. How could you even tell?"

"Right. That's true. Maybe I was just seeing things." And then she turned her brilliant smile on me. "The food looked soooo good, by the way. And your follower count is climbing really fast!"

"Thanks, Emerson Leigh," I said, and yawned, maybe

tired from the whiplash. My eyes strayed back to the screen, where Bennett Wright's email lurked beneath my screen saver of obscure words. *Nikhedonia* was currently bouncing around the screen with its definition: the feeling of excitement or elation that comes from anticipating success. I took it as a good sign. "Your dad's not here—he's still in Connecticut. Do you want me to get him on the phone for you?"

She wrinkled her nose. "No, I just came in to . . . say hi to you." I expected her to wave goodbye, but she plopped down on the couch instead, crossing her leather-booted ankles. "What's new?"

By the time she'd finished prattling on about all the deals she'd found on today's shopping trip, my stomach was growling again. It really had not been happy with me lately. "Well, I'm going to finish my salad," I said. "It was good to see you, Emerson Leigh." And I picked up my bowl, taking another big bite.

"Ooh, that looks good. Is it from downstairs? Maybe I'll get one," she said, making no move to get up. "By the way, I started planning my party! Or really, my business launch. I'm going to send invites to everyone in the local animal rescue community. I bet their animals are particularly stressed and could use some yoga."

"I bet," I said.

"Maybe I'll donate some hours pro bono to local shelters." She pulled out her phone. "That's what I was doing before shopping: making a list of everything I still need to get done." She blinked at me prettily. "Do you think my dad would get mad if I swiped his address book and sent invitations to, like, his famous friends and colleagues? If a big actress or singer or someone showed up at my launch and posted about how they couldn't wait to get their pet a yoga lesson, I'd be swamped with business!"

I did my best not to shudder in horror at what Mr. Decker's expression might be if he learned I'd given out the top secret email addresses of the actors and actresses and assorted other big names he'd worked with at LBC. Even if it was to his own daughter. Even if I'd secretly noted down Tina Fey's and Amy Poehler's email addresses just in case I had a brilliant idea for a comedy one day and was willing to get fired.

But again, I couldn't come out and say no. Because again, boss's daughter. "It seems like you're doing a great job with the planning!" I non-answered instead, hoping that I hadn't sounded patronizing.

She looked at me the way I'd looked at her the time she'd told me all *her* friends who were trying to be influencers were doing it full-time, because having jobs took up too much of their focus, and I should try out the same thing if I wanted to succeed. "Of course I know what I'm doing," she told me. "I was the head of my sorority's event planning committee." She perked up. "You can help me, if you want! I'd be happy to teach you some of my tricks!"

"That's so nice of you, Emerson Leigh," I said. "I wish I could, but my schedule is packed right now."

She nodded gravely. "I know you've been busy. Dad told me about the broken TV on his Florida yacht that you've been trying to get fixed. Things are rough."

"Okay," I said.

She popped up. "Well, I guess I'll head out," she said. "There's a big sample sale downtown I'm dying to go to. Don't forget to save the date for my party! You got the email with the details, right?"

It was somewhere in my inbox. "Yup," I said. "Have fun at the sample sale!"

Once the door had closed behind her, I swiveled back to my computer. Heart thumping, I waved the mouse to clear the screen saver and entered in my password. Finally, my email was back up. I ignored the one from the TV repairman and clicked on Bennett's and read, holding my breath. Then stopped holding my breath, because it was kind of a long email.

Julie,

I attempted to "DM" you as you requested, but unfortunately you've blocked DMs from people who aren't following you, and I can't follow you, as I don't have a personal account. So I asked Emerson Leigh for your email, which she so kindly sent me.

I'm going to trust that you won't post this email online, though I'm not sure why I'm trusting in you, considering you posted our conversation online. Honestly, I'm annoyed by that. And I'm not writing to apologize, unless you want to apologize first. You were, after all, the one who fired the first shot, if you will.

What I am writing to you to do is to propose a partnership. I'm sure you've seen your numbers jump from your association with me and the *Scroll*. What you may not have seen was that our social media following jumped as well, and, as you so kindly shouted at me at the food festival, print subscriptions are falling and online engagement is rising, so my editor and the other higher-ups here are very happy about that.

I don't particularly want to spend more time shouting at each other, but perhaps a partnership could be mutually beneficial. My editor suggested that you and I go to the same restaurant, and we both talk about our differing takes. He hopes it will lead to more engagement for the both of us. Let me know your thoughts.

Best regards,
Bennett Wright

I rolled my eyes at the ending salutation. "Best regards"? Really? Somehow I doubted he was actually offering me his "best regards."

My first instinct was to roll my eyes at the actual proposal, too. Continue our conversation? No, thank you. I didn't want to give myself a heart attack by thirty.

But then again . . . it was hard to deny the increase our interaction had had on my numbers. I clicked back to my profile. I'd gained another couple thousand followers since I'd last checked. Each thousand followers meant an increase in ad revenue. If I could get enough legitimate followers and publicity, I might actually be able to quit my job and do this full-time like Jada Knox. That wasn't even speaking of the actual paying publications like the *Scroll* that might come knocking if I became a *name*. Like, Jada Knox did her social media thing full-time, but she supplemented it with articles in various food magazines and online publications (though not the *Scroll*, of course), which got her name out there more and shined her with prestige.

I hesitated with my fingers over the keyboard. It was tempting to wait and think on it and reply later, but, having been involved in social media for so many years, I knew the public's attention was short and fickle. By tomorrow, they may very well have moved on to some newer, more interesting scandal, and the *Scroll* might feel safe rescinding their offer once they were out of the spotlight. No, thank you. So my fingers danced over the keys, then jabbed the enter button to send.

Bennett,

For someone who's not interested in social media, you sure seem to mention a lot how you aren't on it. Are you sure you're not compensating for something?

I don't particularly want to spend more time with you, either, but I have to admit our interaction was beneficial to me and my following. How exactly are you proposing we do this?

We don't have to go to the restaurant together, do we? I'd prefer it if we could do this without having to see each other.

By the way—you said I may have seen my numbers jump due to our interaction and the association with the *Scroll*. I submit that you saw your numbers jump due to your interaction with me. Just saying.

Julie

I probably should have gone right back to my email to talk to the TV guy—you would be surprised how difficult it could be to get a yacht repairman in Florida off season—but I couldn't stop my eyes flicking to the number in parentheses beside my inbox. Every time it jumped, indicating a new email, I clicked over to my inbox so fast my mouse juddered under its force.

Julie,

We don't have to go to the restaurant and sit together, but I do think we need to be there on the same day. Otherwise, what if the menu changes or a different chef is in the kitchen, meaning the food could theoretically differ? But yes, absolutely, let's sit at different tables. And ideally face opposite directions so that we literally do not have to lay eyes upon each other. If this is acceptable to you, what restaurant would you like to try? Ladies first, after all.

I will not dignify the rest of your email with a response. I take
my job seriously and I recommend you do, too.

Bennett

No more best regards. I folded my hands in my lap,
taking a deep breath at his last sentence, trying not to let it
pressurize into steam and shoot out my ears. He was a jerk.
I already knew that. I wouldn't be doing this to help him;
it would be to help *me*. It was worth putting up with a jerk's
presence for a little while if it meant a better future for
myself. I mean, I did it every day.

What could be fun, though, was saying I wanted to
review a dollar pizza joint next. Or a grungy diner. Just to
see him squirm.

No, I told myself. *You need to do this right. Like how you
blurred out his face. Don't stoop to his level.*

So I clicked over to the list of restaurants I wanted to
get to in the next few months. My eyes snagged longingly
on Wander, a diasporic Jewish restaurant that had just
opened in the West Village, headed by my favorite *Chef
Supreme* contestant, Chef Sadie. I'd been dying to try it. Except I hadn't managed to get a reservation.

Down the list, then. I sent him a few choices, and we
hammered it out. I actually signed off my last email: Warmly,
Julie.

He didn't have to know I was declaring only the first
three letters.

6

THE NEXT WEEK FOUND ME AT CALABAZA, A NEW tapas place all the way downtown. Calabaza was one of those places where you didn't need to wear a jacket to get in the door, but you probably wouldn't feel comfortable wandering in off the streets in your cutoffs and T-shirt. Hopefully, a good middle ground between my followers and Bennett's readers.

I came straight from work, a little overheated with my blue paisley sundress and white cardigan on top. At least I'd switched out my pinchy work flats for my sneakers, which made me feel like walking on clouds. Well, maybe not clouds. Not unless clouds were littered with literal piles of garbage, like the streets of New York. Sometimes I really loved this city, and sometimes I didn't, and those times were usually when I was walking past a particularly pungent garbage pile. Or a man pooping on the subway floor.

The inside of the restaurant was a portrait in warm elegance, with rustic wooden furniture and wall art in various shades of sun, but I had eyes only for Bennett. Not in a romantic way, in a know-your-enemy way. I swept the room, glancing into each little nook as the host led me to my table, but he didn't seem to have arrived yet.

"Hey," Alice said as I approached, already seated facing the door. "I see you got the outfit memo." She was also wearing blue paisley, though in a flowy blouse over slacks.

"You didn't notice the camera I installed over your closet last time I was over? I wanted to make sure we matched all the time," I said. She rolled her eyes, smirking. "Hey, do you mind switching seats? I want to be able to keep an eye on Bennett." I'd told him I didn't want to have to look at him, but when I really thought about it, it seemed worse to have my back to him than my front. Better to be prepared.

She stood, obliging without a word, and let me take her spot. Which was perfect. From here, I had a clear view of the door and the rest of the space. And the tiny golden pumpkin sitting in the middle of our table, a candlewick serving as the stem. Alice said, "We really need a good code word for him. Something that truly expresses what a dick he is. I'm thinking 'Dick.'"

"The main thing I love about you is how subtle you are," I said, and she snorted. "Hey, thanks for coming again, by the way. I know you've been seeing a lot of me lately. Some might even say too much."

"Who would ever say that?" Alice said sarcastically, and now it was my turn to roll my eyes. "To tell you the truth, I wasn't that upset about missing tonight's work happy hour. The guys on my team have really been grating on my nerves lately." She pursed her lips in a frown. "It's like now that there are two of us—two women—on the team, they're feeling threatened and they're acting out."

The waiter came by to deliver our menus and give us a spiel about the restaurant. I barely heard him, tensed as I was. When he finally left, I leaned in and said, in a low murmur, "What have they been doing to you?"

Alice held her hands up, palms out. "Nothing!" she said. "They've just been kind of annoying lately. And it's nice, at least, that I have an ally now to face them with." But her shifty eyes meant that she might not be telling me the whole story. "Maybe you can come with me to work trivia night or something and hang out on my turf."

I'd definitely do that. "Just tell me when and where."

"Will do."

The door opened, and I sat up extra straight as two people entered, the same way I sat when my doctor asked me if I'd been slouching lately. It was Bennett, his narrow face gold in the reflected light, his brown-blond hair styled into a high swoosh over his forehead. And with him? A woman around our age, short and a little chubby, with a pixie cut so glaringly pink it almost distracted from the bright orange lace of her dress. His girlfriend, maybe?

What do you care? I asked myself fiercely.

I don't *care*, I answered back, just as fiercely.

He craned his neck to look throughout the restaurant; when those blue-gray eyes settled on me, they narrowed just the tiniest bit. He didn't smile. He didn't nod. But then again, I didn't smile or nod at him, either. We just regarded each other in a chilly fashion, like we were opposing generals preparing to order our troops to war. When he sat, he first pulled out the chair for his companion, who fluffed up her skirts as she sat, then he took the seat facing me, placing his back to the door. *Unwise move*, I tried to communicate through my eye-beams. *If an axe murderer runs through the door, you won't see him, and your head is going to get chopped off.*

He looked away toward his companion, lips breaking in a smile, and he said something I couldn't hear. The pink-haired girl's shoulders shook in what I assume was a laugh, and suddenly I felt like a creep for still staring their way. I tore my eyes off them, fixating on the menu before me. I cleared my throat. "Anything on the menu especially calling out to you?"

"I want everything patatas," Alice said. "Especially when the patatas have been fried or smothered in cheese."

The Spanish did love their potatoes. But who didn't love potatoes, whether their country's or not? I loved all my potatoes equally, whether they were the french fries on my plate or the Tater Tots on Alice's. Alice could attest. I'd nearly lost a finger to her butter knife more than once. "Got it."

The excellent thing about tapas was that you could order a million different things to add up to a full dinner, and yes, it was expensive, but you also got to try a lot more than you did in a standard restaurant. So we ordered a ton of food, at least one thing from every section, and when I closed the menu, it was with such a sense of anticipation and excitement that I nearly forgot about my adversary across the room. Which, of course, made me focus on him. He was still laughing with his companion. What could possibly be so funny that they would *still* be laughing?

I hesitated with my fingertips on the menu, then flipped it back open. "Can I send a dish as a gift to another table?" I asked.

Maybe because it was only one dish versus many, it came out before either of our real orders. The waiter set the plate down on Bennett's table and said something I couldn't hear; Bennett glanced over at me. Our eyes met again; only this time, his were crinkled at the corners, unable to meet the force of my serious ones. His dropped away first, his laughter dying, which gave me a sense of victory.

Though it might have been less due to the force of my gaze than the pulpo I'd had sent to his table. I hadn't forgotten what he'd written in his review. *I don't personally care for octopus; I find it unpleasantly squeaky against the teeth when cooked well, and even more unpleasantly rubbery when not.*

He looked back up at me. I smiled wide, then mouthed, *A gift for you.*

He scowled. In return, I smiled wider. His companion exclaimed, her shoulders jumping, and pulled the octopus to herself. His face relaxed as he watched her enjoy the dish, which, in turn, made me scowl.

"So how is Emerson's business coming along?" Alice asked. "Is she taking investors? Because I'm considering investing in some—"

"Not Emerson—Emerson Leigh," I said reluctantly. "And no, I will not allow you to even joke about that. But she is planning on throwing herself a big party to celebrate her launch." I perked up a bit. "I bet she'd let me invite you if you want to come."

Alice perked up, too. "A room full of absurdly rich people being ridiculous? Yes, please."

Anything else she was going to say was interrupted by the arrival of the waiter, a tray on his shoulder. "Wow, that was fast," I said, impressed, ready to take a note on my phone as soon as he walked away, except when he lowered the tray, none of the food I'd ordered was on there. Just two goblets of bloodred wine. Which we hadn't ordered. "What's this?"

The waiter set them on the table, then nodded toward the entrance. "They're a gift from the gentleman over there. The one you sent the pulpo to."

I took a deep breath. I was not going to rope the waiter into this battle. Bennett must have overheard me right before he confronted me, when I was talking about my distaste for wine. And what lurked beneath: the uncertainty around it. Because it wasn't just that I didn't like it; it was that I couldn't tell the difference between wines. And that made me feel like a little kid who didn't know anything. Especially given the company I kept. I stared at the goblets, my forehead growing painfully hot. He was doing this to get back at me for the octopus, to embarrass me. To rub it in that I would have no idea whether these glasses he sent were the good stuff or the cheapest stuff on the menu. Whereas he'd probably grown up with his own personal sommelier.

To make things worse, Alice was nose deep in her goblet. "Mmm, smells fancy," she said. "Very rich and full-bodied. The kind I . . ."

She probably kept talking, but I didn't hear her, because I'd finally looked up. Bennett was looking at me with a cheesy grin. His companion had turned around, too, and was grinning in our direction as well. Great. They were both mocking us. Should I make a big show out of drinking it? Or of ignoring it, pushing it all the way to the side of the table like I didn't even care?

I didn't really want to drink it. It wasn't like he'd eaten the octopus. But I didn't want to leave it on the table, either. Every time I looked at it, it would be like it was mocking me.

I pulled the goblet away from Alice before she could take a sip, so violently a few drops sloshed over the edge of the glass. I stood, one goblet in each hand. It looked as if I'd cut myself and bled on the table. "I'll be right back."

I just want you to be aware that stomping across an entire New York City restaurant is not an easy thing to do.

They're always packed with people, the tables and chairs shoved as close to one another as possible in order to fit even more profit margins into the day, and of course they're also filled with the obstacles of restaurants everywhere: waiters carrying precarious trays of food and drink; bussers clearing off tables full of breakable porcelain and glass and sharp silver tines.

But I did it. I stomped across the whole room, not breaking my heavy stride as I twisted and squirmed between tables. Waiters and bussers jumped out of my way.

And all without spilling another drop.

"I think you left these at my table," I told them from a few feet away. *That definitely sounded like more of a burn in my head.* "We don't—"

Something slammed into the back of my legs. A chair? My knees buckled. I shrieked.

And the goblets of wine went flying. My mouth dropped open in horror, and it all played out in what seemed like slow motion. The pink-haired girl clapping her hand to her mouth, her fingernails a vibrant shade of neon green. The waiter's howl of *NOOOOOOoooooOOOOOOoooo.* Bennett's eyebrows shooting up to his hairline as he dived to the side.

All in vain. Because the wine found its mark: all over them. Splotching the pink-haired girl's orange dress into a sunset. Drenching Bennett's sharply creased khakis so that he looked kind of like he'd peed himself. If he had a severe kidney infection and he was peeing blood.

Oh my God. What had I done? I opened my mouth,

ready to vomit apologies all over them, horrified by their wide-eyed looks of panic and . . . was that fear?

Maybe . . . I could use this.

I stood up straight, clearing my throat. "That's what I think of your wine," I said, and then I turned tail and ran away. Yes, ran away. I couldn't handle their eyes on me anymore, or having them believe I'd thrown those glasses of wine on them. In theory, yes. In practice, no, because they made me feel kind of like I was going to throw up.

But the look I got from Alice when I got back to our table wasn't any less horrified. "Why did you do that?"

"It was an accident," I said, stumbling over my words even though it was the truth. "Somebody hit me with their chair, and I just rolled with it."

Her shoulders relaxed slightly. "I knew you weren't the type," she said. "I just didn't have a good view from over here."

"If you knew I wasn't the type, why'd you ask?" I said, and probably she would have answered if her mouth hadn't fallen open like she was trying to fit a double club sandwich in there. I turned to see what she was looking at, and my mouth dropped open, too. I could've stuffed a double-double club in there when I noticed the pink-haired girl had climbed on top of her chair and was now addressing the entire restaurant, her voice a megaphone.

"I would like everyone in this restaurant to be aware that it was Julie Zee Eats NYC who dumped goblets of wine on us!" And like the hand of God descending from the heavens, she pointed at me. Everybody turned at once.

I felt a little bit like a pointed-at lobster in a supermarket tank, paralyzed, waiting for the hand of the seafood counter guy to pluck me up and stuff me in a bag for boiling.

But the stares only lasted for a few seconds before the first murmurs broke the silence. "Who?" "Are we supposed to know who that is?" "Is she on TV?"

"The food blogger!" added the pink-haired girl hastily, but she'd already lost the room's attention. This was Manhattan. Once, I'd ridden the subway and not even noticed the guy next to me was Tim Gunn until somebody else asked for a selfie. "Almost sixty thousand followers, and none of you are here? Seriously?"

I blinked, and the waiter was next to our table again, regarding me solemnly. "Ma'am, I'm afraid I'm going to have to ask you and your friends to leave."

I wasn't sure what I was most offended by in that sentence. The "ma'am," implying I was old? Being disgracefully kicked out of the restaurant? Having it implied that Bennett and the pink-haired girl were my friends?

"You saw it was an accident, right?" I asked the waiter. "Somebody hit me with their chair."

He regarded me impassively. You knew you were toast when a waiter got unfriendly, because it meant they were no longer worried about a tip. "You've all disturbed the experience for our other guests, and I'm afraid you'll *all* need to leave."

I snuck a glance over at Bennett and his friend. He was still dabbing grimly at the wine stains on his khakis, but the girl's feet were planted firmly on the ground, and she was tossing a scarf around her neck. Getting ready to go.

Well, if they were going to go, I wouldn't stop them. Or stay myself. "This was a disaster," I whispered to Alice as we swept past Bennett and the pink-haired girl's table. I was careful not to turn toward them at all, but I imagined venomous looks drilling into the back of my head as we exited. We'd been in there long enough that it was starting to get dark. The night crowd was coming out, beautiful people dressed in expensive clothes, groups of friends laughing in the windows of bars.

Alice sighed, glancing wistfully at the menu. "I really wanted my patatas."

Great. I swallowed a lump of guilt in my throat. "Never fear. I'll get you your patatas."

They might not have been Spanish, but potatoes were just as good frenched.

MR. DECKER WASN'T in the next day, meaning I was all alone in the office. Also meaning I had all morning—after pointlessly laying out his papers and going through his overnight emails, which were all spam—to obsess over what to say to Bennett. Because as indignant as I was, once I'd gone home and lain down to go to sleep and instead lain awake for hours thinking about everything I'd ever done wrong in my life, it had come to my attention that the night's wrongs rested mainly on my shoulders. I'd started out with the pettiness by sending him that octopus, and his wine had been a retaliation. His companion's outing of me was pretty uncool, but if she'd thought I spilled the wine on her purposely, could I really blame her?

So finally I dug my toes into the carpet for strength, brought up a fresh new email, and gave it the subject line Sorry. Then typed, The wine was an accident. I really didn't mean to ...

Ground my teeth. Backspaced. Started again. I meant to give you the wine back, not spill it all over you. Blame the guy in the chair behind me. Sorry. Let me know if I can pay any dry-cleaning bills for you or your friend.

Backspaced again. Just because I was curious. . . . if I can pay any dry-cleaning bills for you or your girlfriend. Or should I put wife? No. I would've noticed a ring. And Emerson Leigh hadn't mentioned him being married. Not that she would have. I was totally overthinking this, so I hit send before I could overthink anything more.

His response came back almost immediately, which felt kind of insulting, considering how much time I'd spent obsessing over my email. Or was it actually a compliment, considering he might have been sitting on the edge of his seat, clicking refresh over and over just in case the notification took an extra second, waiting desperately to hear from me. Yeah. I'd go with that. He wrote, I'll get dry-cleaning money from the guy behind you in the devil chair. And she's not my girlfriend; she's my twin sister.

No word about the restaurant. No word about what we should do next, if we should go back to Calabaza or never darken their doorway again. No word on if this—

collaboration? Or whatever we were doing?—was continuing on. So I replied, Twin, huh? I always wanted a twin. I thought it would be fun to have twin telepathy or to be able to switch places at will. Also, thoughts about netx steps? I considered going back and changing the typo, but I really wanted to project a laissez-faire attitude. Send.

This time, it took a bit before he got back to me. Yes, the whole idea of the pink hair was to stop people from confusing us, because otherwise Penny and I look so much alike. I snorted a laugh. Re: next steps, I've already told my bosses I planned on reviewing Calabaza. I'd rather not go back on that so early into this gig. And we can still help each other.

I also really wanted to do Calabaza. Last night I'd dreamed of patatas and paella, pulpo and granita (those last two had been served together, and in the dream, I'd thought the sweet octopus ice was delicious). So I responded, We might have been kicked out, but it's not like they'll remember us. They see so many people each night, that place was packed. If we go back on our own, or with different people, maybe with a wig on me and no glasses for you, I bet we'll be fine. Two nights from now? Thursday? And truce while we're there?

Him: Sounds good. It was unclear which question he was responding to, but I'd just assume he was assenting to both.

So. The option was to bring somebody other than Alice or to go alone. There were a few college friends I could ask, and I figured I could decide later based on who was free. But it was all moot after I finally called for a reservation an hour after setting up a conference call for

Mr. Decker. The restaurant was full, though they were able to reserve me a single seat at the bar. I gave them a fake name, Harper, scribbling it down along with the place and time and Bennett's name on a Post-it so that I wouldn't forget, then stuck the Post-it to my monitor so that it would be staring at me until the actual event.

I had more invoices to go through, but I spent most of the day dreaming about octopus desserts, about my date two nights from now. *Not a date*, I told myself sternly. *Not anything even close to a date.* I would spend the night sitting alone at the bar, my back to the room and anyone who happened to be dining there, and I would eat delicious food. Alone.

7

THE TWO DAYS PASSED. SLOWLY. FITFULLY. EMER-
son Leigh stopped by at four fifty-five on Wednesday afternoon and chattered about how she'd sent her business pitch
to her dad's friend who was a producer for *Good Morning
America*, and maybe they'd feature her on the show. I nodded along for fifteen excruciating minutes until I lied that I
had a hair appointment and beat it out of there. Thursday I
spent most of the day wrinkling my nose, because Emerson
Leigh had sprayed something foul that lingered in the air; I
finally tracked down the spray bottle in her dad's office and
found that it was a bottle of Maisie's handmade artisanal
perfume (the scent: "Horse Sweat").

And then it was time. Nerves tingled in my stomach
as I exchanged my pinchy flats for cute sneakers and
shrugged on my light spring poncho, then the blond wig
I'd found at a thrift shop and kept around for emergencies.

The blunt bangs tickled my forehead, and the ends of the bob brushed my shoulders as I breezed out the door, keeping what I hoped was a pleasant expression on my face for the whole ride down (which was quite a feat on the subway). Bennett could pop up any moment, the way killer clowns did in nightmares, and I didn't want to look frazzled or nervous or weak in any way.

At least until I spoke to the hostess. "I'm afraid I don't have any record of your reservation," she said, squinting at her screen. Fortunately, she hadn't been there three nights ago. Even so, I doubted she'd recognize me in the dark, crowded entryway. "What was the name again?"

I thought back to the Post-it note. "Harper? For one at the bar, seven o'clock?"

She squinted even harder, like it might make my fake name pop into existence. "I'm sorry, I'm not seeing it here." She glanced to the side, her eyes flitting past me, alighting on the groups that had lined up in the entryway. I was holding her up. "And I'm afraid we're full tonight. We might have a seat open up in an hour or two, but I can't guarantee anything. Though you're welcome to give me your number and—"

"I really have to eat here tonight." My voice came out high and shrill, so much so that the group behind me all stopped talking and stared at me at once. Embarrassment squirmed in my stomach, and I lowered my voice. "Is there really nothing you can do? Please?"

"I'm sorry." Though she sounded less apologetic than

bewildered. "As I said, you're welcome to give me your number, and I'll let you know if—"

"She can eat with me."

Both the hostess and I jumped; I'd been so immersed in our conversation I hadn't noticed someone approaching behind her. And not just someone.

Bennett.

Maybe I hadn't noticed him because he looked so different without those wire frame glasses. Those blue-gray eyes looked somehow bigger and smaller at the same time; I could see the thick fringe of brown lashes around the edges, where before they'd been blocked by the frames. He looked somewhat awkward in a plain black T-shirt and jeans, both of which hung on his frame. It was like he didn't know how to stand in something that didn't button down.

"Sir, are you sure?" the hostess asked.

"Yeah, are you *sure*?" I said doubtfully. Our last time dining in the same restaurant had gone terribly, to put it lightly, and now he wanted to sit at the same *table*?

"I'm sure," he said, and then, the shock of all shocks, he held out his arm for me to take. I stared at it for a moment, mouth hanging open, and briefly considered smacking it away before deciding I really didn't want to be kicked out of a restaurant again. So, I took it gingerly, my fingertips finding warm, bare skin. His muscles tensed as I touched them, though his voice wasn't tense but gallant as he said, "Let's go. My table's in the middle."

"Enjoy your meal," the hostess said, even more doubtfully than I'd sounded. Like what she was really saying was, *Good luck*.

I hissed into Bennett's ear as soon as we were a few steps away. "Do you really think this is a good idea?"

"No," he whispered back, and even though I was the one who'd raised the subject, somehow his confirmation still stung a little. "But from what I heard, you weren't going to be eating here tonight, and the whole point of this collaboration is that we have to eat at a restaurant at the same time." He bumped into a chair. "Sorry," Bennett said, looking down at it. The chair was empty. He looked back up and blinked at me owlishly. "Also, I followed your voice to the entrance, and now I have no idea where my table is. Everything is a blur."

A smile tugged at my lips. "I assumed you were wearing contacts." So that was why he was holding my arm. It wasn't gentlemanly at all; it was functional. Which made it a lot easier to focus with his warm skin beneath my fingertips. I gripped it a bit tighter, guiding him carefully between tables and around potted plants.

"I assumed I would be wearing contacts, too," he said. "My table should have my blue jacket hanging on the back of the chair. Did you know that contacts expire after a few years and are no longer safe to wear?"

"I did not. I don't wear contacts. Twenty-twenty vision, baby." I spied a navy blue blot. There. The jacket. I took us those last few steps and put his arm on the back of his chair, allowing him to pat around it and take his seat himself. "Is everything really a blur?"

"You're very lucky," he replied. "I'm nearly blind without my glasses." He pulled the menu closer to him, squinted at it. Then sighed. "I'm not sure why I thought that would help."

I frowned sympathetically at him, then frowned for real. *Don't sympathize! He's your enemy!* "Well, you read through the menu and ordered things Monday," I said coolly. "As did I. So we can just order the same things."

"That'll be a lot of food."

I shrugged. "So what?" It wouldn't be any more expensive than one of my usual trips, since we'd be splitting the cost between us. It would probably be less expensive, actually, since many of our choices would likely overlap. "I'll have the leftovers for lunch tomorrow."

"Fine."

Our waiter stopped by for a quick, distracted moment on his way to somewhere else, eyes flitting over us and around the room as he apologized for the wait and let us know he'd be with us shortly. Before we could even thank him, he was gone. Not that I was going to thank him. I was too busy panicking. Well, *panicking* was a strong word. It was more of a baby panic. "Bad news," I said. I leaned in toward Bennett, avoiding the golden pumpkin candle flickering merrily away, and lowered my voice. "The waiter is—"

"The same waiter who kicked us out last time," Bennett said grimly. "I might be nearly blind at the moment, but I can recognize voices."

The waiter had been so busy that he'd barely noticed us, but that could change when he came back. I knew he had tons and tons of customers in any given week, but how many were distinctive enough to be kicked out of the restaurant? (Hopefully, for his sake, not too many.) "Well, we might be getting kicked out of a restaurant twice in one week."

"Don't be so dire," Bennett said. "There must be something we can do."

"Of course," I said. "Well, I've got my wig. I wonder if you look different enough without your glasses? Or you can put on an accent?"

"An accent? How about this one?" he said in a fluently posh British accent. Then, in an Australian one, "It's difficult to recognize someone without their glasses, mate."

"I could recognize you anywhere," I said in a Cockney accent, the same one my grandmother used to do when we were reenacting scenes from *Mary Poppins* (obviously she always had to be Bert, because I had dibs on Mary). I almost felt as if she were here with me. What would she say? *Stop flirting with him using my voice,* I imagined. I hope you're picturing a squat, four-eleven woman with a legit mustache and boobs like watermelons, because that's what my nana looked like. *You are supposed to be a professional, and he is supposed to be your enemy. Do you remember what he said to you? He is not good enough for you, child.*

She was right. I made a mental note to call her and thank her. She'd have no idea what I was talking about, but that was okay.

He tapped the table with his fingertip. It clicked against the wood. "I'm not worried. The chances he'll recognize us are slim."

Of course, the waiter squinted at us as soon as he stepped back over and gave us his full attention, the same way I'd squinted at the hostess. "You look familiar," he said, squinting even harder.

Shit. "I just have one of those faces," I said at the same time Bennett said, "You're probably thinking of my twin brother."

I blinked at him, my mouth falling open a little bit at the sheer audacity. It was probably good he couldn't really see me, because he didn't miss so much as a step as he continued breezily on. "We're identical twins, and I know he was here the other night," he said. "He wears glasses. Does the guy you're thinking of wear glasses?" The waiter blinked, apparently lost for words. "He also dresses like a bit of a square. I'm always making fun of him, telling him to let his hair down. Figuratively, of course. We have the same haircut." Bennett tapped his fingers, harder this time, almost like he was trying to communicate through Morse code. Maybe signaling for help. "Open his collar a little. That's the expression I was looking for."

"I see," the waiter said doubtfully, and whether he believed Bennett or not, he turned to me, and that squint fell upon me so sharply it was like he was drilling into me with it. It was okay. I'd just double down on what I said earlier, that I had one of those faces everybody seemed to recognize, that—

"I have a twin sister, too," I blurted. My eyes went wide with panic. *Why did you say that, Julie?*

It was too late. It was out. Bennett's lips quirked in

amusement. So I doubled down on that, instead. "She's a brunette, though. And she hates his twin brother," I told the waiter, leaning in like I was confiding in him. "It's kind of ridiculous. They can't be in the same place together, or they start spitting and pulling hair."

Bennett made a sound kind of like a snort. I ignored it. "I certainly hope you don't recognize us, because that would mean you've met them," I said. "And you don't want to have met them." I leaned back, still kicking myself on the inside. We were definitely getting thrown out a second time.

"I see," the waiter said, even more doubtfully than before. And then he snapped his fingers. "Oh! That's how I know you!"

I began to stand so that he wouldn't have to ask me to leave more than once.

"You look just like my roommate's sister!" he said, eyes lighting up. "She has the same hair. Do you go to Alex at Metropolis Salon?"

"She absolutely does," Bennett jumped in. I turned a killer stare on him, but it was wasted since he was gazing up at the waiter. His lips twitched just the tiniest bit as he spoke, as if he were trying as hard as he could to hold back a laugh. "She and her girl Alex, they're the best of friends."

"I thought Alex was a man," said the waiter.

"My mistake," Bennett said. He buried his face in his hands, and his shoulders shook. For a moment I thought he was crying, and then I realized he had to be laughing.

Back to me. "I would definitely recommend going to

Alex next time you're up in the area," I said, and then my eyes settled on his gleaming bald dome. "Or, um, maybe not."

The waiter sighed through his nose and glanced up at the ceiling. I could practically read his mind through his bare, shiny skull. *Good Lord, what did I do to deserve this?* But his income depended on tips, so it wasn't long before he was back with his practiced smile, which looked very much like the one I wore every day for Mr. Decker. "Can I get you anything to drink?"

We ordered our tap waters, and our waiter skittered out of there: relieved, I was sure. Bennett lowered his hands, still laughing, and I found myself smiling. Like the waiter, I was pretty practiced in putting a smile on and keeping it there. But why was I doing that right now? I didn't care what Bennett thought of me. In fact, he didn't deserve my smile.

However, while I might have been practiced in pasting a smile on, I was a lot less practiced in peeling it off. Our culture really isn't invested in telling women *not* to smile. So it took a minute to flatten that smile into neutrality, then further turn that neutrality into a stern frown. By the time I'd finished with that, Bennett's laugh was dying a natural death. Good. I'd bury it. "Let's pick our food," I said nonchalantly, lifting up the menu and propping it up on the table like an elementary schooler putting up anti-cheating folder dividers on their desk. "I want the pulpo."

A moment of silence. I kind of wished I could see his face, but I didn't lower the menu. "Fine," he said at last, just as coolly.

I marked the octopus down on my phone to order. To be quite honest, octopus wasn't my favorite protein, but I was definitely going to feature it, if only because I knew Bennett definitely wouldn't. And then we haggled away. "There are a lot of potatoes on your list," Bennett said from behind the menu. "I'd like a little more variety."

I lowered the menu to respond. "There's plenty of variety. There's potatoes with cheese, and fried potatoes with sausage, and sautéed potatoes with ham on top of them."

"That's too many potatoes."

I wrinkled my nose. "There's no such thing as too many potatoes. That's like saying a dish has too much butter."

"I've definitely had dishes with too much butter," Bennett said. "Makes them greasy."

"Oh my God, that's blasphemy," I cried. The men at the table next to us looked over, askance. But I didn't lower my voice, just my menu, because blasphemy deserved volume. And eye contact. "There is no dish that isn't made better by more butter. *Nothing.*"

He opened his mouth, then closed it. Opened it and closed it again.

"See," I said triumphantly. "You can't think of anything, can you?"

"I wasn't even trying to think of anything," he said stiffly. "I want to try this orange salad with the olives. And the pan con tomate."

"Tomato bread? Boring."

"What you mean is that it doesn't photograph well,"

said Bennett. I curled my lip at him, then stuck out my tongue. He couldn't see it anyway.

"You know I can see that."

Oh well. "What I mean is that it's just tomato and bread," I said. "Boring."

"Pan con tomate or bust."

"Fine," I relented. "As long as I get all my potatoes."

"Fine. Get all your potatoes."

After we'd placed our order with the waiter, who interacted with us as if he were a chef asking for information on a guest who'd ordered French onion soup without the onions, we stared at each other in stony silence. Or at least, Bennett stared in my direction. I wondered what I looked like to him right now. Besides a blur. Could he see my hair? My eyes?

I considered taking out my phone and passing the time scrolling through social media, but he was just sitting there, staring. *Right. He probably couldn't see well enough to use his phone without really straining his eyes.* Maybe I should talk to him. Be nice. We were stuck here together, after all.

But his words filtered back through my mind. His derision. The way he looked down on what I did. I didn't owe him anything. So I pulled out my phone, ignoring the dirty looks shot at me by the men at the next table. Let them look. They were probably of the opinion that millennials were vapid youth who spent way too much time on our phones. In my own opinion, they were just jealous smartphones weren't around in their own youth. It wasn't like I was going to talk to Bennett anyway.

Soon enough, the food arrived, and I snapped prelimi-
nary photos of it all. (I could feel the judgment from those
guys next to us, warm like a fire.) The pictures didn't have to
look perfect—anything I'd feature I'd get again on a future
visit—but I wanted to have them for reference. "Don't touch
anything," I directed Bennett; he froze with his fingertips
on a patata brava. "Not until I'm done with my photos."

"Everything's going to be cold by the time you're
done," he grumbled. "No wonder people don't take online
restaurant reviewers seriously. How are we supposed to
judge cold food?"

The back of my neck prickled with annoyance. I bit my
tongue to keep from snapping back. Because he wasn't entirely wrong, was he?

"There," I said, putting my phone next to my plate. It
hit my knife with an extra loud *ting*. Those two guys looked
over at me again, frowning, and I had to bite my tongue
again to keep from snapping at *them*. "Go ahead. Savor
your lukewarm food."

Of course, the first plate he went for was the tomato
bread. He cut it carefully in half with his steak knife; he
didn't lose so much as an extra crumb on the plate. A true
skill. He closed his eyes as he bit into his half. It crunched.
A few drops of clear red juice dripped down his wrist to
the table. I watched their sinuous path for a moment, then
took my half and bit into my own piece with vigor.

It was good. Really good. The bread was earthy and
chewy, crunchy on the bottom and meltingly soft on top,
and rather than rubbing the bread with tomato as in a

traditional pan con tomate (yes, I'd done my research), the raw tomato had been shredded and mashed and spread on top, a cool, sweet, tangy contrast to the bread. A hint of garlic spoke up in the back of my throat; anchovies whispered somewhere underneath, the salt and the brine making everything else taste sweeter. I didn't know I'd closed my eyes, too, until I was swallowing and realized I couldn't place my next bite.

I finished my piece, then typed my impressions into my notes app, leaving wet tomato streaks on my phone screen. Bennett was still savoring his own half, a notebook or phone nowhere in sight. "Aren't you going to take notes?" I blurted, then looked around too late for the waiter. Fortunately, he was at another table listing off the specials.

Bennett shook his head. "I can't see enough to write. I guess I'll have to take notes in the bathroom." A wry smile twitched at his lips. "If I can find my way there. At least in the stall I can put my glasses on."

"I'll point you in the right direction," I said.

One by one, we went through the other dishes. The ensalada naranja, a salad of plump, juicy orange sections that were sweeter and sourer with the addition of green olives and olive brine. Chistorra con patatas fritas, one of the potato dishes I'd lobbied for that I was relieved didn't disappoint, a meaty chunk of sausage tangy with iron and rich with pork, wrapped up like a present in a crunchy, salty disc of potato. The paella, which was fine but not outstanding, the rice and seafood dish lacking enough of a punch from tomato and saffron.

"You're missing out," I told him when I got to the pulpo. I was pleasantly surprised in that it was actually one of my favorite dishes of the night; the octopus had been charred perfectly so that the outside was crisp and smoky and the inside was tender, and it had been paired with a green salsa that made me want to sing with its freshness and vibrancy. He just squinted at me skeptically.

Usually when Alice or another friend came with me on a review meal, we chatted the whole time, whether about the food or our lives or the women next to us who'd ordered nothing but a plain, unsauced, leathery chicken breast on an empty plate. Here, left with nothing but the taste of the food on my tongue and my own thoughts in my head and a burning distaste for the person sitting across from me, it was . . . different. Not better, not worse. It was as if, without hearing the person across from me talking, I could hear the food talking instead. Like, *Now that you're focusing, can you make out the hint of fish sauce running beneath the tomatillos and garlic for umami?* I could. *And did you know that octopi are really, really smart? Why are you eating me?* Was that Emerson Leigh's voice?

Okay, maybe I didn't always want my food talking to me.

Outside functional dialogue like, "Can you pass me the potatoes?" (to which I always had to specify, "Which potatoes?" the only way a question like that should be answered), Bennett only spoke when we were eating our dessert. We'd already eaten our churros, which had been delicately crisp and sparkling with cinnamon, and were now sharing a grapefruit granita. You couldn't exactly split ice onto two separate plates, so we were diving into the same dish with our spoons, each hoping the other one wasn't in possession of any communicable diseases. "Grapefruit isn't usually my favorite fruit, even in the citrus family," he said, thoughtful. "But this is something else."

He was right. It should have been a simple, maybe even boring dish: grapefruit shaved ice, with thin slices of candied grapefruit and mint leaves on top, all heaped into a frozen grapefruit skin. "I think the word you're looking for is *transcendent*." Somehow the dish was a thousand times greater than the sum of its parts. Each bite of ice literally melted away in my mouth, transforming into something luscious and concentrated, something that brought me right back to being a little kid in my mom's lap, asking for a spoonful of the grapefruit half she'd sprinkled with sugar.

But even better. And it was beautiful, too. I was already imagining the way the miniature shards of ice would glitter in my photo, the way the crystallized grapefruit slices would shine like jewels, how the green shreds of mint would keep it from looking too much like something you'd want to wear around your neck.

"Impressive vocabulary," Bennett said, his voice snide.

"Believe it or not, sometimes I *do* read books," I told him, just as snidely. "You can use it in your review, if you want. Free of charge."

He just sighed. "Whatever." And then pulled his glasses case out of his pocket, slipped them on, blinked a few times. "That's so much better."

"You're totally killing your disguise."

He shrugged. "The night's over, anyway. And I have to take my photos of the restaurant for the *Scroll*'s social media page. We'll come back on a different night to get official photos of all the plates, but . . ." He trailed off at the sight of my stormy expression. It would sure be nice to have the budget for that. "It doesn't matter. Smile?" He raised his phone.

I did not smile. "You want me to be in your photos?" I asked. "I thought we were just going to share pictures of the food."

He opened his mouth, then closed it, then opened it again. "I just wanted a . . ." He stopped and licked his lips. "I just thought you looked . . ." He sighed. "No, we don't need to take pictures of each other," he said. He rubbed at the side of his face, his eyebrows scrunched. "I'll just get the decor."

I folded my arms across my chest. I wasn't cold. I didn't feel like he was staring at me. I just . . . I don't know. I felt like I needed to guard myself against something. "I already got mine."

Even though he wasn't specifically taking a photo of me, the flash hit my eyes anyway. For a moment, I saw stars.

8

PEOPLE MIGHT LIE, BUT NUMBERS DON'T. SPECIFI-
cally, my engagement numbers and follower count. After
Bennett and I posted our reviews of Calabaza, they both
jumped for the sky. People loved our differing takes on the
same meal, and my new followers loved my association
with the *Scroll*. I wasn't just some random girl out trying
new restaurants anymore; the *Scroll* had varnished me
with a veneer of legitimacy.

I've been skeptical of food influencers before, but she's the real
deal. Thanks, random Internet guy, for making me feel
validated.

I liked Julie's better!! Bennett didn't pick up on all the nooances
of flavor that Julie did. So what if she couldn't spell *nuances*?
The sentiment was clear enough. I'd continue doing my
usual restaurant reviews, too—maybe once per week instead of twice, with some extra stuff mixed in to make up

for it—but my focus would be on this collaboration for a bit.

I sent Mr. Decker off to lunch with a reassuring pep talk about how his new hat didn't draw too much attention to his ears (it didn't; what drew attention to his ears was all the hair sprouting out of them), and then my phone buzzed. I picked it up and yelped. Jadaknoxeats has followed you. And, just a moment after that, while I was still staring gape-mouthed at my screen, jadaknoxeats has sent you a message.

I felt like I might vomit from happiness, the way I did as a kid when my parents would take me and my brothers to the fair and we'd compete to see who could eat the most fried Oreos and cotton candy. (The twist was that it was always my parents who lost because of all the vomit in the car.) And even more so when I swiped it open. Hey, Julie! Congrats on all the buzz! Let's collab sometime—maybe we can do a joint neighborhood crawl?

I had to fight myself not to write back *YES YES YES* immediately and risk looking too eager. Instead I set my phone on the desk, face widening in a smile so big it threatened to split my cheeks. Ironically, I realized a couple hours later that I'd actually forgotten to reply. I apologized for the delay as I told her how much I'd love to team up with her. But Jada didn't seem to mind. She wrote back immediately. Yay! Let's talk dates?

The afternoon passed in a blur of validation and busywork. Between scheduling meetings for Mr. Decker and coordinating a new office-cleaning service, I snuck peeks at my phone. Every so often I'd click over to Bennett's social media teaser that linked to the paper's official review, which dampened my enthusiasm slightly, because his number of likes was three times mine.

I emailed him before I could help myself. Your bosses must be happy about how well your review is doing on social media.

His answer came immediately. About as happy as I was when I got the level seventy Blood Sword of Death and Blood!!!

I blinked. Before I could formulate a coherent response to the *Blood Sword of Death and Blood*, another message popped up. I apologize. For some godforsaken reason, I allowed Penny to come visit me at work. Rest assured, it will never happen again.

His pink-haired twin sister. Of course. After the way I'd turned her orange dress into a red wine bloodstain, I had no doubt she wouldn't mind using the Blood Sword of Death and Blood on me.

And yet something about a level seventy Blood Sword sounded familiar . . . I dug deep into my memory, searching for that combination of syllables. And landed upon Marcus, shouting so loud one night from his room he'd woken me up. *You wizardy motherfucker! You think you're so hot because you're level seventy? Don't you dare snatch that Blood Sword out from under my nose, you motherfucking asshole!*

I'd found out the next morning that Marcus had missed out on his Blood Sword; it was apparently a very exclusive, very rare, and very-difficult-to-obtain reward from a raid boss in his favorite video game. My curiosity piqued, I emailed Bennett back. You play *Dark Avengers*?

He replied, I will neither confirm nor deny that.

Then, Why? Do you?

And then, Never mind. I don't care. By the way, I noticed your numbers have been looking good, too. At least, as far as I can tell, as someone who rarely uses social media. I rolled my eyes, but kept reading. It seems like it's working out well for the both of us. Where should we review next?

I set a timer on my phone for twenty-two minutes and twenty-two seconds—as not to look too eager, but also not to forget like I just had with Jada—then responded, I guess. Did you have somewhere in mind?

He didn't set a timer. He wrote back immediately. Are you familiar with Wander in the West Village? It just opened up a month or two ago.

Wander! My heart leaped. Yes! I've been dying to go there for ages. Good choice, when should we—backspace, backspace, backspace. I would not show him a hint of happiness. He didn't deserve it. Yes, I'm familiar with it. That sounds fine. Send.

The rest of the day, I couldn't get the picture of Bennett hunched over his computer, bright reflections of virtual battle reflected in his glasses, out of my head.

WHEN I MET Bennett at Wander the next week, it was with a smug sense of satisfaction and also an epic set of cramps. (Thanks, copper IUD!) We didn't technically meet at Wander but on the sidewalk outside; I'd gotten there early and decided to stroll down the narrow sidewalks, stepping occasionally onto the cobblestoned sections of street to admire the quirky little shops that had been driven out of so many other neighborhoods by Starbucks and CVS and bank chains. A cigar shop. A hatter. A shop that seemed only to sell dusty teapots and was almost certainly a front for the mob.

I was lingering in front of the teapot shop, wondering if I went inside what percentage chance there would be that I would stumble upon a murder and be shunted into witness protection and if that percentage was worth it for that porcelain beauty shaped like my childhood beagle, when a figure appeared next to me. "Are you a collector?" Bennett asked. From this close, he smelled like soap and something a little spicy, like he'd just come from a noodle shop.

"No, I just like that one." I pointed at the beagle. His snout was the spout, his long, floppy ears pinched together to create the handle. It was the cutest thing, except maybe for my actual childhood beagle, Snoopy. "Unfortunately, it doesn't look like they have any Blood Sword of Death and Blood–based teapots in stock."

"Ugh." He actually said the word, not exhaled it in disgust. "That's the last time I let Penny come to see me at the paper." He waited a moment, then added in the most begrudging tone, "And just so you know, it's not actually called the Blood Sword of Death and Blood, as Penny called it. That would be absurdly redundant. Its actual title is the Blood Sword of Destiny and Fortitude."

"Ah yes, much less absurd," I said. "Shall we?"

Inside the restaurant, the space was small but bright

and open, with modern tables of light wood and abstract
woven tapestries in bright colors hanging from the walls.
I was pleased to see the place bustling, all the tables except
for one packed full. A window open in the back showed a
shiny silver slice of the kitchen, people bustling around
inside, pots clinking.

A cheerful hostess led us to our table. I slid into the
booth side, letting Bennett take the chair, and wiggled
around a bit to see how comfortable it was. Very. "Thanks,"
I said to the hostess.

She nodded, consulting her tablet. "And I see it's your
anniversary. Happy anniversary!"

Bennett let out a strangled sound that might have been
him choking on something. The noise that escaped my
throat probably didn't sound all that different, but I was
the first one to respond. "What?"

She blinked and looked down again, as if double-
checking, then nodded to herself. "Yes, that's what it says
here. I'm glad you chose us to celebrate your special day!"
She winked. "We'll have a special surprise for you later on."

I blinked back, but she was marching away before I
could grab her tablet away and consult it myself. "She must
have been looking at the wrong reservation, because . . ." I
trailed off as I turned to find Bennett wearing a knowing
grimace.

"I'm going to fire my intern," he muttered. "Unless
this was the only way she could get us this reservation,
then I'll commend her. But otherwise, definitely fired."

I glanced over my shoulder. The hostess was staring at

us. "We don't want her staring at us or paying us any extra attention," I muttered back. "Do you want her remembering your face? Or thinking something is suspicious?" I swallowed hard. "We'll just have to pretend to be out for our anniversary. It won't be that hard. It's not like they're expecting us to, like, have sex on the table."

The moment those words came out of my mouth, I could feel my cheeks glowing. Bennett's face had gone red as a fancy heirloom tomato, too. He swallowed a couple times, his throat working, before he replied, "No, I imagine not." His voice was all strangled again, but this time I couldn't blame him. Not if he was also picturing what it might feel like to stretch out on this smooth surface, press our bodies against each other until there was nothing but sweat and heat between us, gently removing his glasses and placing them to the side before I grabbed his face and brought it to mine . . .

Good Lord. I nearly had to fan myself with the menu. Abort fantasy. Stupid fantasy that I didn't even want to come true. "I hope there's octopus on the menu," I said, pulling my menu closer and *not* fanning myself with it. Because I was fine. Totally fine. I definitely did not need to distract myself by thinking about the food. I skimmed it quickly, then clicked my tongue. "Darn."

"I don't think of octopus as a particularly Jewish food," Bennett said dryly, because of course, Wander was a Jewish restaurant. At least he didn't sound like he was choking anymore. Good. We could just proceed normally. Just two people celebrating an occasion out for a nice dinner.

"I don't think of pork as particularly Jewish, either, but there's a pastrami-rubbed pork shoulder on the menu," I said. "Definitely getting that." I was Jewish but not observant, much to the chagrin of my mother's family. I liked to use it as an excuse to eat lots of bagels and lox, mostly.

"Pastrami-rubbed pork shoulder sounds good to me," Bennett said. "And how about this kimchi chopped liver?"

We bargained our way to a truly enormous number of dishes. "My stomach might explode by the time we're through," Bennett remarked as he handed off his menu to the waitress.

I told him, "Well, I hope none of your stomach explosion gets on me." And then I pulled out my phone so I didn't have to keep talking to him or thinking about him, taking a quick picture of the menu before giving mine back.

I expected him to sit there silently as I scrolled through my social media, liking Jada Knox's new video even though I wouldn't have a chance to watch it all until later (We were mutuals now! We had to support each other!), but he spoke up. Probably because a couple on their anniversary would be speaking to each other, not because he actually wanted to talk to me. "So, what's your secret?"

I forced myself to look up and put down my phone. "I have many secrets, and I'm not sharing any of them with you."

He sighed. "No, I mean your secret to engaging your followers. Our social media intern is doing all he can, and we've been getting help from the cooking department, whose pages do really well, but I'm not doing well enough. How do you do it?"

Should I share anything? I was saved from having to provide an immediate answer or refusal by the arrival of our amuse-bouches. I sat up extra straight from excitement. I loved these little teasers before a meal, things I didn't have to order but just came to me like gifts from heaven.

These amuse-bouches actually *looked* like little gifts; they were small pouches of dough that twisted at the top and came to a gleaming golden-brown ruffle. They actually looked kind of familiar. "These were on *Chef Supreme*!" I said. I took a quick picture. "I wonder if they've got a sauerkraut and potato filling, like the ones that Chef Sadie made on the show." I bit into it. The wrapper crunched and then relaxed into a nice doughy chew, almost like a very thin pizza crust. Sure enough, the interior was plush and buttery with a smooth potato puree but also zingy with fermented cabbage, the sour shreds of leaf providing a perfect contrast to the richness of the potatoes and the crust. "Remember when I told you there was no such thing as too much potato?" A mustard seed popped between my teeth, spicy. I finished with the ruffle on top, brown and shatteringly crunchy. "It's still true."

"You may have a point." Bennett closed his eyes as he chewed, as if he were concentrating so hard on the taste and texture that he had to block out the outside world. He pulled out a notebook—a real notebook, with a real pen and a fancy black leather cover!—and scribbled a few notes in it.

"You know, you can take notes on your phone now," I said. I craned my neck, peering over the table. I'd expected perfect little blocks of letters, totally legible probably from across the room, but no, his handwriting was a messy scrawl. I swore half the letters were upside down.

"I like the feeling of actually writing something with a pen. It helps me remember things better." He capped the pen and stowed it away.

"It's also a lot more obvious to waiters or hosts that you're a food critic. If you're taking notes on your phone, you might just be texting, like your typical rude millennial."

He chuckled dryly. "So, you're looking out for me and my job, not mocking me for using an outdated mode of note-taking?"

I blinked, because I *had* been looking out for him. When had I started caring? *I don't*, I told myself firmly. "Whatever."

The waiter returned to clear our knish plates away. In the extra space, Bennett folded his hands on the table before him, steepling his fingers to a point. "So. Are you going to answer my question?"

"Both," I said promptly. "I was both trying to help and mock you. You're very mockable."

"Always wonderful to hear," Bennett said even more dryly than before, collapsed in the middle of the desert, a cry for water on his cracking lips. "But not that question. If you had any tips for making our social media succeed. My subscriber base is supposed to be what makes the *Scroll* different. What keeps us going in an age where the medium I love is slowly dying out and being converted to digital this and that." He lowered his gaze, but not before I saw his eyes go soft. Vulnerable.

Insecure.

"So," he continued, staring at the table. The waiter had missed a tiny piece of knish ruffle, nearly the same brown as the table's wood. "How do you do it?"

It came to me like a flash. He hadn't been dismissive of my work because he was a cruel person or he thought less of me for doing it. He hadn't made fun of me because he sneered down at my work from his print pedestal.

He'd done it because he was *afraid*. Because he felt threatened by me and Jada Knox and all the others, because we were moving in on his territory. Because his medium was dying, with fewer and fewer mostly old people still subscribing to print publications every year, while ours was booming.

Let's not get ahead of ourselves, I lectured my inner monologue. *Who even knows if all that is true? You're just starting to like him and looking for a reason not to hate him.*

"It's a lot of hashtags and search engine optimization and cross-promotion and things," I said. "Not that hard to learn. Especially if you have a dedicated social media guy."

"He's helping, but not enough," he said gloomily.

Just then our appetizers arrived, meaning I could change the subject before I started feeling bad for him. "Who would've thought you could combine kimchi and chopped

liver and have it taste good?" I mused, definitely not because I was feeling bad for him. It was hard to feel bad with
something this good in my mouth, for real. The chopped
liver was smooth but just a little grainy, rich but with just a
slight iron tang. The kimchi was sour and tart and crunchy
and a little fishy, clearly the real thing. Piled together on a
toasted slice of baguette and with a little extra richness
from homemade mayo, it was an excellent bite.

But not one that photographed all that well. Sure, the
kimchi was bright red and pretty, splayed out like phoenix
feathers, but the chopped liver was brown and mushy. I
didn't think liver would get me all that many hits. Something that also tasted good but didn't photograph very
well: the bite-size orbs of gefilte fish, the puree of who-
knows-what soft and smooth, its pearly grayness flecked
with orange bits of carrot. At least the vibrant beet and car-
damom pickle on top, reminiscent of horseradish, looked
nice.

"The *Scroll* isn't going anywhere," I told him. "It's been
around forever, and it's going to be around forever." I
pulled over my half of the latke appetizer. It seemed pretty
simple, a lacy-edged potato pancake fried until plush in
the middle and golden-brown around the crispy edges.
Like nachos, the toppings were what really made it. The
chef had played off the traditional latke toppings of applesauce and sour cream (#teamapplesauceforever), pairing
her potato latkes with a spicy apple chutney, with chunks
of both meltingly sweet cooked apples and crunchy tart
raw apples, and a thick cucumber raita that reminded me

of sour cream. "This is a really interesting dish. It's both Jewish and Indian."

"India has ancient Jewish communities, you know," he said, and though my hackles went up at the *you know*, he really didn't say it like he was condescending to me. He said it like he was sharing a piece of information that was interesting to him. "I went to India a few years ago and visited one of their old synagogues down south."

"That's nice that you got to go to India," I said, trying and failing to tamp down a flare of jealousy. I'd wanted to travel through Asia most of my life, sample all the incredible street food in Thailand and Vietnam, tour Japan's famous convenience stores that sold food as good as their restaurants, slurp cumin lamb hand-torn noodles in China. But vacation time was limited, and the cost of airfare was several months of student loan payments.

Bennett took a big bite of latke slathered in both toppings. "You're wrong, you know," he said with his mouth full. I tensed, assuming he was going to start talking about how his trip to India hadn't been all that, but he said, "The *Scroll* is in serious trouble. It's part of the reason they wanted to bring in a millennial as their new restaurant reviewer instead of someone more established. They thought it might get young people interested in subscribing."

"But the paper has five million subscribers," I said, after swallowing, because I had manners. "It sounds like you're doing fine to me."

Bennett hesitated, his eyes darting from side to side as if they might have tried making a break for it if not for the prison of his glasses. Then sighed. "It was at almost seven million a couple years ago," he said. I blinked and shoved another bite of latke down my gullet to disguise the shock. It didn't work. I choked, coughing it up, which just made it more obvious. I half expected Bennett to just get up and stride out of the restaurant, leaving me with the bill.

But he didn't. He actually kept talking. "We're bleeding subscribers at an alarming rate, losing them to digital publications and social media. And our most avid, most loyal readers are dying." He noticed my look of surprise and added, hastily, "Not because we're killing them off. At least, I'm not killing any off."

"That would be quite the plot twist," I said seriously.

His cheeks flushed. "I'm not a murderer, I swear."

"That's exactly what a murderer would say," I told him, and he only got redder. I grinned. "Relax. I know you're talking about your subscribers dying off from old age."

"Exactly." He was still rosy as he went on. "So many magazines and newspapers have shut down or gone digital-only in the past few years. If I can't turn things around . . ."

"Bennett." This might have been the only time I'd said his name without wanting to spit it out. "I can't imagine they hired you assuming you were going to turn the entire fortunes of the paper around."

He swallowed one last bite of latke. Somebody laughed in the background. Like magic, the waitress showed up to whisk our plates away. "Of course not. But I'm part of it, and if the paper fails while I fail, part of that is on my shoulders."

Your very broad shoulders, I did not say. I didn't say anything else, actually. What was I supposed to? That I felt sorry for him? Or for the paper? I didn't, not especially. The paper had made one bad decision after another, probably because they kept hiring a homogenous group of rich white dudes connected in some way to their board. And it wasn't like this job was Bennett's lifelong dream, the way it had been mine. He'd just stumbled into it.

Or so I'd assumed based on the stereotype. I didn't actually know for sure. "Why did you want the restaurant-reviewing job there?"

There were two ways this question could go. He could respond with something like, *I was bored after gallivanting around the world on a trip paid for by my trust fund and thought it might be fun to get paid to eat out every night*, in which case that would be it; I'd lose whatever respect for him I'd gained over the past week or two. Or he could answer with something like—

"I've just always loved food," Bennett said. "Always. My parents . . . weren't together, so . . ." His lips thinned slightly. "Usually, whenever my dad would come visit and take me and Penny out, he'd take us to a restaurant. All kinds of restaurants, French and Italian and New American, sure—I was fascinated by molecular gastronomy as a kid, how you could turn juices into foams and oils into edible sand—but also Ethiopian and Chinese and Japanese and Peruvian and Indian and . . . and I just loved all of them, how they were similar and how they were different." He pushed his glasses up his nose; he'd been talking so animatedly that they'd slid down. "I couldn't picture myself doing anything but writing and learning about food. So when this opportunity came up at the *Scroll* . . . it was the most exciting job application I'd ever sent."

I couldn't trust myself to speak, so I nodded. I hated that I understood. Because if my mom happened to be best friends with the CEO of a major paper like the *Scroll* (she was most certainly not; the most interesting person she was friends with was the owner of a tiny and not un-creepy museum of old puppets situated in a decrepit for-mer barn) . . . wouldn't I take the opportunity, too? Wouldn't I have done the same thing?

"Coming through!" The waiter appeared with our food, spreading our plates over the table with a bright smile. All thoughts momentarily fled from my mind as I took in the smells drifting from every plate. They made my mouth water.

"Where do we start?" I said, mostly to avoid having to respond to what he'd said.

This time, as we ate our way through the table, I kept an eye on him. Sure, I made certain to take clear photos of everything on the table, both pre-bite and mid-bite, and I took good, thorough notes on my good, thorough thoughts, because I was a professional.

But I also watched him closely, waiting to see that love of food. The surprised delight on his face when he took his first slurp of the brisket ramen, enjoying the tender shreds of savory meat, the chew of the crinkly noodles, the light but complex broth that hid the reveal of a plush matzah

ball with a thick corn flavor. The concentration as he tried
to place the flavor of the rub on the bowl of shredded car-
nitas that we portioned out ourselves and wrapped in mar-
bled rye tortillas with tiny sour pickles and thinly sliced
red onions and shreds of Havarti cheese. ("It's a pastrami
sandwich," he murmured as he took the first bite.) The
sheer pleasure as he closed his eyes while chewing the
duck, rosy and meaty in the middle and crispy-skinned on
the outside, in one perfect bite with pickled and fresh
beets.

I didn't have to look hard. It radiated out of his very
soul.

"Julie—" Bennett started, maybe ready to ask about
why I was staring at him like I was attempting to cook him
with my eyes. Neither of us found out, because we both
jumped as the waiter came to clear our plates.

Someone save me from that look in his eyes, I prayed, and it
was then I learned that God has a hilarious sense of humor, because the kitchen door swung open. Out marched
a woman carrying a plate. I didn't see what was on the
plate at first, because I knew this woman. She was short and
dark-haired, with rosy cheeks and shiny gold Converses
that sparkled beneath the ceiling lights. I'd seen her wearing those same gold Converses on TV.

My brain short-circuited a little as she kept on marching toward our table, and I saw what she was holding on
her plate. It was some sort of twisted pastry with cherries
and a chocolate sauce forming . . . hearts all over the plate.
And just one dainty fork.

Oh. Oh no.

She set the plate on our table with a wide smile. "I hear it's a special day for you, and I wanted to bring you this babka beignet on the house. Happy anniversary!"

Oh my God. I couldn't believe I had to lie to Chef Sadie Rosen.

"Thanks," Bennett was saying, so I went with something that was actually true.

"The food here is outstanding," I said. She turned to me. "I swear I'm not just saying this because you're here, but I rooted for you your whole season of *Chef Supreme*."

"Thank you, that's so sweet," she said, cheeks splitting in a wide smile that drilled dimples into the rose. She reached up to push a curl out of her eye, and my own eyes widened at the pear-shaped diamond glittering on her ring finger. She noticed me eyeing it and chuckled. "Luke— yes, Luke Weston, the judge from *Chef Supreme*—proposed a couple weeks ago. We're very excited."

"Congratulations!" I said. I *thought* they'd had chemistry on the show. "Could we take a selfie?"

"Of course!" She bent toward me as I held out my phone. I smiled extra wide as I took the photo; yes, I was excited to get it for myself, but my readers would love it, too. It might draw some extra attention to my page, especially if I dropped the news about the engagement. A lot of my followers were also big fans of *Chef Supreme*. Though, to be fair, a lot of people in general were big fans of *Chef Supreme*.

"Thank you so much," I said after a quick check to

make sure neither of us had our eyes closed or were angled so that you could see up our noses.

"No problem," she said, then gestured at the babka beignet. "Go ahead, try it!"

Bennett reached for the fork first and scooped up a perfect bite of everything, which was a relief. A relief that turned into panic when he held the fork out toward me. Not for me to take—for me to take a bite. "For you, sweetheart." His eyes sparkled behind his glasses.

I squared my shoulders. I could not believe this was happening. "Thank you, darling," I forced out, and let him feed me.

My lips closed over the fork, Bennett watching the entire time. My face warmed again at the intentness of his stare on my mouth, but surely he was just watching to see when he could remove the utensil.

The babka beignet was spectacular, light and fluffy and buttery, the chocolate filling dark and sweet against the tart brightness of the cherry. I parted my lips so that he could pull the fork back. His face was red again.

Fortunately, he didn't make me feed him, just took a bite himself.

Sadie asked, "So? What do you think?"

"Delicious," he said, but he wasn't even looking at the dessert. He was looking at me.

I couldn't even bring myself to answer. I could still feel the insistent push of his fork against my lips.

Sadie clapped her hands together. "Wonderful! Well, I won't keep you any longer. Happy anniversary again." I thanked her for the dessert, and she moved back toward the kitchen. Just before she passed inside, she looked back and called out, across the entire restaurant, "You two make the cutest couple, by the way!"

I was saved from having to respond by the door swinging shut behind her. I took another bite of babka beignet, keeping my eyes averted from my nemesis. Who let out a short laugh. "It's good she didn't go back to judge *Chef Supreme*, because she is *not* good at judging people. Right? We must have done a really good job at faking it."

My own laugh came a moment too late. "Yeah. Right. We must have."

I kept an eye on him as we finished our "anniversary" dessert. At the way his eyes narrowed the tiniest bit right before he laughed, the thoughtful way he chewed, eyes fixed upward as if he were writing about it in his head, the clean lines of his jaw. When one bite left behind a smear of gleaming crimson cherry sauce on his cheek, I had to fold my hands in my lap to resist reaching over and brushing it off with my thumb.

I was in trouble.

9

I HADN'T BEEN OUT TO A BAR SINCE I'D BEEN ghosted by the taxidermy enthusiast (a phrase that became sadder and sadder the more I thought about it). Though this bar was nicer than any of the bars he'd taken me to. The Dead Squirrel played at being a grunge bar, sure—the lighting was dim, the walls black, the music loud—but the floors weren't sticky, and the beers all cost at least twelve dollars.

No way I was paying that much for something that made me grimace when I drank it, no matter how cool it helped me look. I didn't need to look cool tonight. My followers wouldn't be seeing any of this. They didn't need a window into me serving as Alice's moral support during trivia night. Nothing against Alice or moral support; I was just terrible at trivia.

"Hey!" I waved over the bar until I caught the bar-tender's attention. "I'll take something fruity, please. Ide-ally where you can't taste the alcohol." I'd sip it slowly all night so that I didn't have to pay for a second drink. Which meant it should be . . . "But strong, please."

"If you're looking for something strong, maybe you should look this way," said the guy next to me. Or shouted, really, to be heard over the guitars clashing through the speakers. Which kind of ruined the suave effect I thought he was going for.

I rolled my eyes, then felt bad, because I knew how hard it could be to stick your neck out like that. I didn't want to put him down, but then again, I was definitely not inter-ested in anyone who would use a pickup line that cheesy. Unless the person was literally offering me cheese. That would actually be the best pickup line somebody could use. "Sorry, but I have a . . ." I trailed off as I turned and saw who the person was. What were the odds? "Oh, it's you."

Bennett's friend Ryan's thick blond brows furrowed in surprise. I couldn't believe it, but he was wearing another polo shirt with a rhino emblem on it. Maybe his entire wardrobe consisted of polo shirts with rhino emblems. He'd be cold in the winter, I bet. "Do I know you?"

I hesitated. I could explain that we'd met briefly at the Central Park Food Festival, where he was a giant douche-bag to me and didn't even have the decency to remember my face, and then probably argue with him for a half hour about who'd been right and who'd been wrong.

Or I could just . . . not do any of that. "What?" I said, turning away and pretending to spot someone coming in the door. I waved at nobody, which turned into waving at somebody when Alice pushed her way in. Filled with relief, I grabbed my drink, shoved a twenty across the counter, and hustled to her side.

Her lips twitched into an exhausted-looking smile when I reached her. "Our usual spot's over here," she shouted, and I followed her and a small group of what had to be her coworkers to a long table in the corner with a RESERVED sign on it. They all took a stool, so I took one, too. It was wobbly, one leg shorter than the other.

"Julie, this is Kelsey," Alice yelled at me across the table, nodding to the stocky blond girl next to me. We nodded and smiled at each other. "And that's . . ." She shouted the names of the four guys on the other end of the table. Were they all named Rob, or could I just not hear her? Probably the latter, but I chose to believe the former. Somehow each one looked like a Rob.

"You brought a friend, Alice?" one said. "Now we're at seven people. Teams are six."

Alice scowled. "You encourage me to bring a friend every week because we don't have enough people."

"It's fine," I said. "I can just watch—"

One of the Robs sighed, cutting me off. "Aren't you the 'influencer' friend? You're right, it's probably best if you just watch. Maybe you can take some pictures of us for the company newsletter."

Rage filled me. I placed my hands on my lap so that they didn't fly off my wrists and strangle someone. "You know what, I changed my mind," I said. "I want to do it after all."

Some discussion among the guys, and they decided on a complex system of us all rotating in and out. "The categories tend to go from easiest to hardest. Why don't we say ladies first," the Rob who'd called me an influencer said, nodding at us in what he probably thought was a generous way.

I was ready to punch him.

All four went up to grab drinks for the table. Kelsey followed, maybe to make sure they didn't pull any funny business. I gaped at Alice once they were out of earshot. "You weren't kidding."

"What?"

I leaned over the table, hoping they'd lower the music when it came time for the game. "You weren't kidding about what dicks they are!"

She leaned back, looking affronted. "Of course I wasn't kidding. Did you think I was?"

The rest of her team came back, spreading beers over the table, along with a glass of wine for Alice. They were all slapping one another's backs, splashes of beer sloshing over their rims. The long table next to us, which had also been empty with a RESERVED sign, was now filling up.

"That's one of the companies we're playing against," Alice explained. "They're in finance. A hedge fund, I think."

I looked over just in time to lock eyes with Ryan the Rhino. He blinked at me in response, maybe not sure whether to hit on me or ask me who I was. I smirked as he turned to look past me and waved toward the door. *Nice trick.*

Only the trick was on me. Because someone walked over to his wave. Someone I knew. All of my insides seized up as he turned to look at me.

Bennett.

Was it my imagination, or had the music suddenly quieted?

He looked just as surprised to see me as I did to see him. To his credit, he quickly lowered his eyebrows and gave me a little wave. I waved back only a moment too late. I would say he seemed out of place in this faux grunge bar in his usual button-down (green-and-yellow plaid today), but at that table full of hedge fund bros, he fit right in.

I sat back on my stool, trying to get out of his eyeline, and just managed to catch myself before sliding off. Stools don't have backs, as it turned out. One of the Robs cracked, "Whoa, I think someone's already had a little too much to drink," and was rewarded with guffaws and backslaps from the others. If only they'd slapped him a little harder.

I realized then that it hadn't been my imagination: the music volume had lowered. At the front of the room, near the bar, a man stood beside a chalk wall. He'd already divided it into a scoreboard between our team, Bennett's team, and three others spaced out around the bar. Apparently our team was named Walt Quizney. "Welcome to the

Dead Squirrel Trivia Night!" he announced. "Hopefully your teams will be better than they were last week. You were all so dead, we could've named the bar after you."

Dead silence. One uncomfortable titter. The announcer scowled. "Anyway, our first category tonight will be world history."

Rob One turned to the rest of us. He was white, tall and skinny, with long dark hair and a smattering of pimples on his cheeks. "Alice, Kelsey, or New Girl, one of you will need to sit this one out."

Alice scowled. "Why us?"

"We know a lot about history. Leave it to us," said another Rob.

"I thought we were up first," Kelsey said. Her voice was low and raspy. "I read the world section of the paper every morning, and I know a lot about—"

The bros laughed loudly, interrupting her. "The blonde can read!" one crowed, clapping. "Okay, Alice's friend, you sit it out. Kelsey and Alice, you can join in."

They were totally dicks. Sexist dicks. But I didn't mind sitting out this category. It gave me time to study Bennett's table, where they only had six people, meaning they all got to participate. He sat all straight-backed on his stool, an example of perfect posture—unlike me, who was slumped over in a way that would make a chiropractor cry—except when he'd lean in to debate some point or other with Ryan and his coworkers. He had a habit of tapping his fingers on the table erratically, as if trying to pound out some kind of rhythm. Or run and jump in a video game.

Their table was a lot more harmonious than ours. The announcer had asked for the last British prime minister to hold office while a member of the House of Lords. "Anthony Eden was an earl, wasn't he?" said one of the Robs.

"Maybe, but he wasn't the last one," said Alice. "I read in this book that—"

"It's got to be Eden," another guy said, talking over her. "Remember him from *The Crown*? Great show."

"I'm pretty sure it was Alec Douglas-Home," said Alice, but now even she sounded unsure of herself. Which was unusual for Alice. "It was a big deal because he gave up his title and—"

"So, we're going with Anthony Eden?" said the first guy. Without waiting for the others, he scrawled the man's name on their little chalkboard, just in time for the announcer to ask them all to hold up their answers.

"I'm looking for Alec Douglas-Home," said the announcer. Alice pursed her lips and cursed under her breath. I looked to the guys for an apology to her for blowing her off when she was right, but they were only laughing at themselves for getting it wrong. Should I speak up? My lips opened . . . then closed. Alice hadn't told me to say anything. I didn't want her getting mad at me.

But I couldn't listen to them talk about how it had been such a *hard* question and *nobody* could have gotten it. I rolled my eyes and shifted in my seat, looking back over at Bennett. Only to find him looking back at me. He half smiled in my direction. I waited for that swoop of dislike to come over me, remind me that he was the enemy, a jerk . . .

And waited . . .

And stopped waiting, because if it hadn't swept me off my stool by now, it wasn't going to. He was still staring at me. My eyes flickered to his lips. They were slightly parted, and I could imagine . . . imagine . . .

Imagine them telling me, over and over, how he didn't use social media because it was dumb and vapid, them speaking to the waiter at Calabaza and deliberately trying to bait me by ordering expensive wine they knew I'd hate. Brick by brick, I did my best to convince myself I hadn't started to like him at Wander.

"The next category will be food," the announcer stated.

Bennett flew out of my mind as I spun back to the table. "I can do this one."

"Me, too," said Alice. She'd accompanied me to enough restaurants, listened to me ramble about enough food stuff, and skimmed through enough articles I'd texted her that she probably knew as much as I did.

"Great, you three should do great with this category," Rob One said, and the others grunted with laughter. *Because women belong in the kitchen, amiright?* Skin prickled all over the back over my neck. *Do it. Say something. Don't explode and get Alice in trouble; just say something polite but firm.*

But then the announcer started talking. All my nerve trickled away into focus. "Question one," he said. "What is the only fruit to wear their seeds on the outside?"

Fruits swept through my mind in a dizzying, colorful

array. I cast aside their sorbet forms, then any fruit with peels. "I think strawberry?" They had their seeds on the outside, right? "Unless there's something rare and obscure I'm missing."

"We'll go with that," Kelsey said, and handed me the dry-erase marker. I scrawled **Strawberry** on our board just in time for the announcer to call for answers.

I held ours up but didn't look to the announcer first. Instead, I looked to Bennett's team. Sure enough, he was the one holding up his team's board. Which said **STRAWBERRY** in his nearly incomprehensible scrawl.

"I'm looking for strawberry," said the announcer. One of the other teams behind me groaned. Bennett flashed me a grin. Before I could think about it, I grinned back.

The questions became progressively harder from there. Thanks to a documentary series on Netflix, I knew that nachos were called nachos because of their inventor's name (Ignacio, nicknamed Nacho). Croissants originated in Austria, not France, a tricky question that knocked all the other teams down . . . except for Bennett. Thanks to a paper I'd written in college on the history of the celebrity chef, I knew that the first TV celebrity chef was Fanny Cradock in England, not Julia Child, which three of the other teams thought.

Not Bennett, of course. I wondered how he knew about Fanny. She wasn't exactly a household name. At least, not here. If I asked him, he'd probably expound upon a teenage trip to England, where he'd visited the former set.

The first food eaten in space? Applesauce. The first

sushi restaurant in New York City? Nippon. I kept waiting for Bennett to miss one, but he didn't. So, by the end of the round . . .

"Our top two teams are tied, which means we have a sudden death tiebreaker round!" the announcer said. He sounded very pleased with himself. "Walt Quizney and Very Stable Geniuses, please send up one member each to participate."

I was standing before Rob Two said casually, "I can go if nobody else wants to."

"I want to," I said back, and not just because Bennett was already walking toward the front and I *had* to take him down. Because I'd gotten most of the freaking answers. Okay, maybe Rob Number Two had known that the first fast-food restaurant founded was In-N-Out Burger, but that was *one* question. I didn't wait to hear his answer before stalking off, leaving my drink on the table, but I did hear him complaining loudly behind me about how pushy I was. Good. Let him think I was pushy.

I met Bennett up at the front of the room in the hot spot. In that it literally felt warmer up here. Sweat trickled down the back of my neck as I met his eyes. "What are the odds?" I said.

"That you and I would both have a friend attending the same trivia night and that we'd both agree to attend?" Bennett said. I hoped he wasn't about to calculate the actual odds of such an event, but then he said, "Pretty low. This is the first one I've ever gone to with Ryan."

I wrinkled my nose. "He tried out the cheesiest line on

me at the bar before you got here. I don't think he remembered me from the food festival."

Bennett laughed, taking a sip of his drink. I couldn't tell exactly what it was, but it was pale brown and in a small square glass, meaning it was probably something fancy. Should I have brought my drink up here, too? I suddenly wished I had something to do with my hands. "He can be a bit of an ass. I know. We were roommates freshman year at Dartmouth, and he was one of the only people I knew when I moved here. Besides Penny, of course. Though she practically pushed me out here tonight."

Curiosity nibbled. "Why?"

"Why did she push me?" He scratched the back of his neck. Maybe he was sweating, too. He had gone awfully red. "She says I need more friends here to take out dining since most of my friends live elsewhere." His lips twitched self-consciously. "She was not amused when I said I had her. I think she's a little wary of going out with me ever since *somebody* doused us in wine."

"I hope you told her I apologized for it. And that it was an accident."

Before he could answer, the announcer interrupted, "Sorry, guys. I'm having trouble finding my files. It's been so long since I did one of these in this category." He squinted down at his tablet. "Be right back. I'm going to go see if I can find a printout in my office."

Bennett sighed as the announcer walked away. "Is it extremely hot up here, or is it just me?"

"If I were Ryan, I'd make some kind of double entendre with that," I said. "But I'm not. So I won't."

Bennett snorted, taking another sip of his drink. "Okay." His high swoosh of hair was beginning to wilt. Bar noise, chattering and clinking and laughing, swelled around us. "Well, can I go get you something to cool down while we wait? Maybe a glass of wine? This place has surprisingly good—"

"Seriously?" I bristled. Almost like he'd attacked me. It felt kind of like he had, actually. We'd been getting along so well. I'd even thought I might be starting to kind of a little bit like him. And now here he was, back with the wine. "Again with the wine?" I deflated, shaking my head. "Never mind. Let's just wait for the guy to come back. Quietly."

I waited for him to smirk, but his face twisted into a storm of confusion. "'Again with the wine'? What are you talking about?"

I glared at him. "You know I hate . . ." I trailed off, because I couldn't exactly say aloud that I hated wine, even if he already knew. What if somebody overheard? Or what if he told somebody exactly what I said, and they leaked it online? "I don't like the wines they have here. Or the kind you sent me at Calabaza."

His mouth gaped, big enough to fit a whole fist in there. "Oh, sorry. I didn't realize." He closed his mouth. "I didn't like that we got off to such a bad start. Penny convinced me to send you something as a peace offering, and I thought a nice glass of wine would be a good way to show you I didn't want war."

So . . . he hadn't overheard me at the food festival. He didn't realize I didn't like wine.

Well, now I felt terrible. My shoulders softened from where they were bunched high around my neck. "I didn't know."

"Now you do." He stared down at me. I stared up at him. I swallowed, and it was like all the bar noise quieted down around us and all I could hear was the sound.

"I guess I should apologize," I said. I expected the words to be harder coming out, more reluctant, but they actually felt . . . good? "I'm sorry I jumped to conclusions like that. Maybe I could"—I scrunched up my forehead, mentally calculating how much I could spend tonight— "buy you a glass of apology wine? Once you've finished whatever you've got there?"

Bennett took a step back. "Not if it's going to be that painful."

It took me a moment to realize what he was talking about. "No, my face isn't like this because it's painful! It's because . . . well . . ." I couldn't exactly tell someone like Bennett Richard Macalester Wright that a fifteen-dollar glass of wine might very well tip me over the edge into insolvency. "It's something else," I finished lamely. "But trust me, nothing to do with you." I raised an eyebrow. "Maybe we're both reading too much into what the other says."

He shrugged. But then he cracked a tiny smile. "Sounds like what you're really saying is that you care about what I say."

"Definitely not," I replied automatically, but . . . well. He wasn't wrong.

The announcer chose that moment to come bustling back up, a crumpled packet in his hands. "Sorry it took so long," he said. "Let's begin."

The sudden death tiebreaker round would consist of a series of clues given to us one at a time, all pertaining to a celebrity chef. "Shout out the answer when you know it," the announcer directed. "The first one to say the correct name—full name, first and last—wins. Is that clear?"

When I nodded, it was at Bennett. And he was nodding at me, too. We were at war again.

Only this time I didn't hate him. As if he could read my thoughts, his lips quirked in a small smile. I felt my own lips smile back.

"Clue Number One: this chef began as a dishwasher at the famous Chez Dupont," the announcer said. Chez Dupont had been in Midtown Manhattan before its much heralded closing a few years ago. I'd never been; my chief knowledge of it was that it was extremely fancy and even more extremely expensive. "Within five years, they were running the kitchen."

Think, Julie, think. Who did I know who had classical French training? I had no idea who this chef might be, but I threw out some names anyway. "Lenore Smith. Geoffrey Zakarian."

Bennett clearly had the same idea. "Thomas Keller. Tyler Florence."

The announcer cleared his throat. "Clue Number Two: this chef has been married three times, though they may be most famous for their affair with movie star Naomi Kriss."

"Bobby Flay," I called.

The announcer shook his head. Bennett tried, "Daniel Boulud?"

"Daniel Boulud is French, like from France," I said. "Why would he have gotten his start at a restaurant in New York?"

Bennett shrugged sheepishly. "Because he really loved Broadway?"

The announcer didn't even dignify that with a response. "Clue Number Three: this chef's signature dish is a crepe filled with—"

"John Waterford!" Bennett and I shouted at the same time. We caught each other's eye and, for the first time, I grinned free, with abandon. Almost forgetting that we were in competition, I raised my hand for a high five. He raised his to me, too, but it was the one with the drink. Something I didn't fully register until my own hand was hitting it.

"Sorry!" I yelped before the drink had even spilled. Which it did: all over him. The jump he made when the liquid hit his shirt didn't help matters, either. What was left of the drink sloshed over the rim and drenched his button-down, turning the green and yellow into olive and mustard. "Sorry, sorry!"

Bennett cracked a smile. "You didn't have to attack me just because I said it first."

"One, I didn't attack you, and two, *I* definitely said it first," I said, but I did feel bad. He was totally soaked and now stank of whatever strong alcohol had been in that glass. Bourbon? Whiskey? I had no idea.

The announcer disagreed with me, sadly. "I heard the gentleman start a split second first, so I'm going to give this one to Very Stable Geniuses," he proclaimed. A chorus of cheers went up from Ryan's table, and boos erupted from Alice's, but none of them were very serious. The announcer leaned closer to us. "I have some extra bar T-shirts in the back office if you want one, man. I'll even give you a discount."

Bennett looked down on himself, lips twitching as he set the empty glass on the nearest bar. "Yes, I think that's a good idea."

"I'll be right back with a round on literature!" the announcer called over his shoulder before motioning for Bennett to follow him.

I probably should have just gone back to my seat, but my feet didn't want to move. Bennett had been kidding about me attacking him, right? He didn't think this was a repeat of the wine throwing at Calabaza, or that I was some kind of serial thrower of alcohol when the mood hit me. Right? I mean, he hadn't acknowledged my apology, but surely he knew I'd made one?

Something inside me *needed* to be sure he knew this was an accident. That I didn't hate him or anything. I could wait for him to come back, but what if the T-shirt was so hideous that he felt the need to leave through the back, unable to bear the thought of going to the bathroom to change into it? I couldn't picture the man in a Dead Squirrel T-shirt. He might be too embarrassed to show his face to his friends in anything that pulled over his head.

My feet scurried after him, back behind the bar, the bartender too busy to notice. Then down a long, dim hallway, closed doors on either side, and to the end, where the announcer was backing out of the room. He gripped a handful of cash, which he was tucking into his pocket as he noticed me. "Oh, hey, your boyfriend should be out in a sec."

"Thanks," I said, moving past him and stepping inside the dark room cluttered with file cabinets, where I found Bennett without a shirt.

Bennett. Without. A shirt.

My breath hitched in my throat, jaw dropping the way Bennett had dropped his wet button-down on the scuffed linoleum floor. He had his arms over his head, preparing to put them through the sleeves of the T-shirt, which left his long, lean torso on full display. A thin coating of soft brown-blond hair dusted his pecs and traveled down his stomach in a line. At least it looked soft. Obviously, I wouldn't know without running my fingers over it, following the line it made down his stomach and into his jeans, over his . . .

My jaw was still open. I shut it with a snap as Bennett finished pulling the T-shirt over his head. He blinked at me, glasses askew. I had to hold my hands down at my sides to keep myself from reaching out and fixing them. "Julie?"

"Sorry," I said hastily, then realized it was unclear what exactly I was apologizing for. "I mean, sorry for surprising you here like this. I didn't realize you were changing. I assumed you were just coming back here to get the shirt and that you'd be changing it in the bathroom or something. I didn't mean to walk in on you like that. On your naked torso."

His cheeks went red again, or maybe it was just because it was so hot in this room. Had it been this hot all along? "We're good," he said. "I mean, not we. Us. It's fine. I mean, I don't mind. It's okay. I'm not mad. Or anything. Am I making sense?"

"Yes!" I shouted. I would've shouted anything in response just to stop the awkward rambling. I couldn't believe I'd said naked torso. *Naked torso.* It made the whole thing sound so dirty, which it definitely was not. My mind was certainly not still with the soft-looking trail of brown-blond hair and how it would brush against my fingers as I unbuttoned his jeans and—"And sorry again!" For what my mind was doing to him. "Um, for spilling the drink on you! It was an accident!"

He pulled the front of the T-shirt down. It was slightly too small on him, clinging tight to his shoulders and making them look even more wide and square. "There seem to be an awful lot of drink-spilling accidents around you, Julie."

I swallowed. My throat was dry. "It's just a coincidence. I—" Focused in on his shirt and let out a surprised laugh. "I can spill another drink on you to get you out of *that* if you want."

Bennett stared down his front with a wry grin. "Can you believe he charged me thirty-five dollars for this?"

Upon the black cotton background was printed a drawing of a dead squirrel that appeared to have been created on Microsoft Paint by a below-average seven-year-old. In case anyone might have trouble discerning that the squirrel was dead, the artist had helpfully replaced the squirrel's eyes with Xs.

I could not believe that the shirt was worth anything more than the cost of materials. I could, however, be grateful for it distracting me from that naked torso. My mind began to clear. I took a deep breath. "Our friends are probably missing us," I said. "Especially yours. It's the literature round, right? Can your friends even read?"

"Good point."

Back into the crowded bar, the air thick and sweaty. I followed closely behind him until we got to the juncture of our tables. "Well, congratulations for winning our round, I guess," I said.

"Thanks," he said. "It was close. I don't know if I would've gotten it without your priming me at the food festival to think about crepes and John Waterford together."

I sighed theatrically. "I suppose I deserve that," I said, looking away. Right into Ryan the Rhino's face.

He was laughing at me. As I watched, he shaped his pointer and thumb into a big fat zero. "That's for costing us our shaobing. How does it feel to be a loser?"

I scowled at him instinctually. What a dick. I was a lot of things, but not a loser. My mouth opened wide to tell him just that, only before I could, Bennett said, "Shut up, Ryan. No need to be a dickhole." He looked faintly scandalized for saying that, and I was so tickled by that look I completely forgot to look at Ryan to see his reaction.

"Julie!" Alice called from behind me. "Come on! The next round is starting!"

Bennett and Ryan were now in some kind of discussion. Maybe about Bennett's hideous shirt. I had no place in it, but I lingered anyway. Should I, like, say goodbye? Or anything?

"Julie!"

"Coming," I called back to Alice.

With one last glance at Bennett, I beat it back to my table in time for the announcer to say, "The next round will be technology."

I was more than happy to sit this one out. I half tuned out the round, keeping my eyes on Bennett's table, where, I was pleased to see, they were absolutely tanking. I waved over the waitress. "I'd like to send that guy a glass of red wine," I said, pointing at Bennett. Aside from our discussion earlier, it was the least I could do after spilling his drink. "Yeah, the one in the Dead Squirrel shirt. Um, I don't know. Do you have any that are good but that aren't too expensive?"

We reached a fine equilibrium, but I still winced handing over my credit card. I tuned back in time for an argument at my table. "I'm telling you, it's Ethereum," Kelsey was spitting, wisps of blond hair going wild around her face. "I am absolutely one hundred percent certain. I was just reading about it literally this morning."

"Ehhh, I still think it's Bitcoin," said Rob One. "I'm invested in a lot of cryptocurrency, so I know. Do you even know what cryptocurrency is?"

If Kelsey were a snake or a vampire, all the Robs would have twin puncture wounds in their throats right about now. "Of course I know what cryptocurrency is," she bit out.

One of the other guys snorted. "Just because you bought a Bitcoin when they became famous doesn't mean you know a lot about it. Go with Bitcoin, guys."

I pounded my palms against the table. All our drinks jumped, and all eyes turned to me.

I didn't even care. "Hey, it's pretty obvious she knows what she's talking about," I said. "Stop being—don't be a dickhole."

"Yeah," said Alice.

The guys were silent for a moment. They didn't know what to say. Kelsey took advantage of their stun to grab the whiteboard, write *Ethereum,* and hold it up.

"I'm looking for Ethereum," the announcer said. Kelsey laid the whiteboard down on the table with a snap that felt somehow triumphant. Alice cheered and slapped Kelsey a high five over the table.

I grabbed for my drink before anyone could knock it over and took a sip. The fruit juice had been watered down since I first got it, and now it tasted mostly like ice.

I felt Bennett's eyes on me before I saw them. He was raising a wineglass to me. I'd almost forgotten I'd sent him wine. I raised my half-full, watered-down drink to him, then drank.

Somehow, this time, it tasted sweet.

THE SWEET TASTE lingered until the next morning, when I woke up on Alice's couch. Figuratively, obviously, since I'd brushed my teeth with my finger when we got home, and now my mouth literally tasted like morning breath. I covered my eyes, squinting at the glare coming in through the window. Well, filtering palely through the window, which faced the brick wall of an air shaft. How much had I drunk last night? I really should have stopped at that one drink, but after our team won the Technology round, the Robs had insisted on buying us all more, and it went on from there . . .

I widened my fingers, peering with one eye toward Alice's empty bed. Her studio was pretty small, not much larger than her queen bed, the couch I slept on, and a desk, but living alone in Manhattan was an achievement. I could hardly blame her for it, even if it had stung when she first told me she wanted to do it rather than hunt for an apartment with me. As much as I would have liked living with her, it would be nice to be able to walk around naked or sing loudly and badly during an early morning shower.

The bathroom door opened with a creak and a gust of humid, flowery air. "It's about time," Alice said, already dressed in jeans and a T-shirt with a cartoon character on it. It hardly seemed fair that she got to dress like that when I got paid so much less and had to dress in business casual. "You'd better run. I saw the six is delayed."

The six train was always delayed. I suppressed a sigh. A mad rush of brushing my teeth with my finger and trying to steam the wrinkles out of yesterday's skirt and blouse ensued. One was a success; the other was not. So I was cursing under my minty-fresh breath as I arrived at the office to find Emerson Leigh sprawled out on the office couch. Which was, incidentally, much more comfortable than Alice's couch; my neck still felt cricked, my shoulder aching from keeping myself from falling off all night.

Emerson Leigh sat up as I applied my big fake smile. She stretched her arms overhead with a yawn. "Good morning, Julie." Her eyes widened a bit as she took in my pink plaid. I could practically see the thoughts scrolling over her forehead: *Did she find that outfit crumpled up under a bench in the park?* "You look nice," she said brightly.

"Good morning, Emerson Leigh." I took shelter behind my desk, feeling more confident with less of me on display. "You're up early."

She beamed at me. "I am! It's been ages since I've gotten up before nine. The world feels so fresh and clean and bright this early."

It was bright. Too bright. "Is there something I can help you with? I don't think your dad's coming in today; he's doing something with Maisie up in Connecticut."

"I know. I was invited, but I told them I had waaay too much to do to be able to spend time playing golf," she said. "Dad told me I could use his printer and his fancy stationery to print out some poems I wrote about how yoga makes different pets feel to circulate at my launch party coming up, but I couldn't figure it out, so he said you could help."

Wonderful. Because I didn't have enough to do today. I jiggled my mouse to wake my computer up from sleep and could already see a screen of emails demanding my attention. Including one from Bennett. My heart did a funny sort of flutter at his name.

Not. Good.

"I hope I can handle getting everything done. That's why I got here so early, so I'd have the rest of the day," Emerson Leigh was saying. "Like, I have to pick my color scheme for the party."

I waited for her to go on, but she didn't. "What else?"

She gave me a disgruntled look. "That's a lot. I have to pick colors that not only match my dress without being too matchy but also flatter my complexion *and* reflect the themes of my business while not clashing with any of them."

"Right," I said, but my mind was already back on my email. Or really, back on Bennett. Hopefully, that flutter just meant I was going to have a heart attack and not that I was developing anything worse, like feelings for him.

Though really . . . would that be the worst thing in the world? Maybe we were from different places, maybe even different planets, but that didn't mean we couldn't be . . . couldn't be . . .

I didn't know where I wanted that sentence to end up. My thoughts were as mixed-up as the apple, hard-boiled egg, goat cheese, and steelhead trout salad I'd gotten once at Sweetgreen when my brain short-circuited in front of the make-your-own options. (The salad barista—is that what they're called?—had asked me if I was *totally sure* twice.)

That unsavory thought salad continued tossing as I helped Emerson Leigh format a few of her poems for the printer and then print out a shit ton of copies, all in color. I'd probably need to replace the printer ink. Fortunately, she didn't seem to notice anything was amiss. "I'm trying to decide which one to read first, but it's like Sophie's choice," she said, reclining against the counter and pressing the back of her hand to her forehead like she was about to swoon from the effort. "What do you think? Should I read this one about dog yoga, since dogs are really popular, or fish yoga, since it's the most different out of all the pets?"

I couldn't resist, especially because I'd asked last time and hadn't gotten an answer. "How does a fish do a yoga class?"

She blinked at me, frowning like I'd asked her the main ingredient in apple pie. "It's not *that* complicated. You know, Bennett asked me the same thing. You just—" She squinted at the stationery I was inserting into the printer. "Julie, is that upside down?"

It was, probably because she'd raised the subject of Bennett. I turned it the right way, then took a deep breath, licking my suddenly dry lips. "Hey, so Bennett dated your sister, Maisie, right? Just curious, but is he dating anyone now?" He'd mentioned needing more people to go out to eat with, but that didn't mean he wasn't dating anyone. He could be dating someone on a cleanse or a vegan or whatever.

"Why do you want to know?" Her eyes were wide but pleasantly interested.

Because if he is, I can stop these thoughts right in their tracks. "Just curious. I've been spending a lot of time with him lately, and he hasn't mentioned anyone. And I'm seeing him again tonight for another review and wanted to see if . . . um . . . I should order something extra for him to take to his girlfriend?" *Weak.*

She shrugged. "I wouldn't worry about it. The girls in our circle don't typically eat all that much."

"Oh." I wanted to make a snarky comment about that, but it was just . . . so sad. "I see." The printer chugged away in the background. "Well, do you know if he's coming to your party?"

"Why?"

Good Lord, she wasn't making this easy. "Because if

he had a girlfriend, he'd probably be bringing her, right? So did he ask for a plus-one?"

Emerson Leigh grabbed one of the printouts and stared down at it. "No."

I sighed out some of my tension. I hadn't even realized I'd been tense. "Then he probably isn't dating anyone. Not anyone serious, anyway." My mind whirled. I imagined showing up at Emerson Leigh's party, which for some reason had a winter theme, sparkly faux icicles (fauxcicles?) dripping from the ceiling, in a glittery blue dress like Elsa's from *Frozen*. Bennett would be there, and somehow he'd have known ahead of time to wear a matching sparkly blue tie with his dark gray tailored suit. He'd extend his arm, and I'd take it, and—

"I wonder where I could get a dress like that." I didn't realize it was me who'd spoken until Emerson Leigh turned to me, thick blond brows furrowed in confusion. I blinked, then tried to clarify. "I just want to make sure to look really nice for your party. For . . ." I couldn't say for Bennett. "I mean, I just want to look really nice."

Emerson Leigh stared at me. Squinted. Cocked her head. I was about to ask her if she was okay when she finally said, "Well, your outfit has to figure into the color scheme. So if you have any input on what colors look good on you, you should let me know before I pick them out."

I blinked. The printer whirred impatiently, asking for more paper. "There's a dress code?"

Emerson Leigh grabbed a stack of stationery and shoved it into the tray. Upside down, but I didn't correct her. "Obviously, the people working the party will need to look uniform."

"Working the party?" I thought back to the e-vite she'd talked about, but I hadn't actually dug it out of my email and read it.

"Of course. Dad said you'd be happy to help serve drinks and hand out printouts and things." Those green eyes widened innocently. "I'm sure he'll pay you for it, or whatever, since I know that's really important to you."

Her words settled over me with a cold clarity. She hadn't invited me to her party as a guest. As a friend. I was an employee. From a whole different planet than her and her other guests.

It would do me good to remember that.

I forced a smile as I yanked her printouts free from the machine. "Here you go."

"Thaaaanks!" Emerson Leigh trilled. "You're the best, Julie!" Then she actually looked down, and she frowned. "Oh wait. These are upside down."

I ground my teeth. "I'll fix it. Would you go out to my desk and hit print in, like, thirty seconds?"

"I guess," she said. "But what if I hit the wrong thing?"

I ground my teeth harder. I hoped dentures were included in my fancy health insurance. "You just have to hit print."

"Ooookay." She looked way too nervous for someone being asked to hit a button.

It took her longer to hit print than I expected. It got to the point where I almost went out there myself to make sure she hadn't gotten stuck between the couch and the armchair, but then she popped back in, her cheeks rosy red. "Okay. I think I did it?" The printer roared to life, and she beamed at me expectantly, as if she were waiting for praise.

Because that was my role. I worked for her family. Bennett probably had people like me who worked for his family, too. "Nice job," I said, and she beamed even harder. She even gave me a spontaneous little hug as she left. "Don't worry," she said into my ear. Her breath smelled like cinnamon. "I'll make sure to pick colors that make your eyes pop."

For when I'd be working the party. Serving her and Bennett drinks as they laughed and talked to each other, to the real party guests, to most of whom I wouldn't even exist.

10

AS IT TURNED OUT, BENNETT'S EMAIL WAS FIZZING and sparking with so much enthusiasm that I was surprised it hadn't short-circuited my computer. He'd sent two follow-ups to make sure I'd seen it by the time I made it back to my desk chair. I clicked on the most recent one before I even kicked my shoes off and dug my toes into the plush carpet, which is how you know it was serious.

> Hello, Julie. You didn't respond to my previous messages, so I went ahead and booked the table. If you object, then . . . well, then I suppose I'll just go without you, because I would not just kill to eat at this place but kill something I loved. Like a puppy. Okay, I wouldn't kill a puppy to eat here, but I'd at least think about it.

I quirked an eyebrow with amusement, and then, as I

scrolled down to the original message, my jaw dropped. Bennett had scored a reservation tonight at one of the hottest new restaurants in town, booked solid even for those of us with professional connections (him, not me): West. The unassuming name stood for West Africa; the restaurant explored West African cuisine and the food of the West African diaspora scattered throughout the world. Forget the Nordic restaurant we were supposed to go to tonight.

I messaged back, I would kill YOU to eat at this restaurant, so it's a good thing the reservation's for two. I hesitated, then added the crying-laughing emoji to be absolutely clear that I was kidding.

Mostly.

I spent the rest of the day dreaming of tuna tartare scattered with benne seeds, which Jada Knox said tasted like coffee in the most pleasant way. At least, until it came time for me to gather the contracts I had to messenger to Mr. Decker for his signature. They'd come in yesterday, and I'd been waiting to send them out until end of day, when he'd be back at his apartment in the city. I'd left them in a manila folder on the other side of my desk, except . . . the manila folder was gone.

I blinked hard at the empty swath of desk, like that might make the contracts suddenly appear. Nope. Shockingly enough, it didn't work.

Shit. They'd already been signed by the other party of the business deal Mr. Decker was doing, so it wasn't like I could just print out another copy for him. I lifted every book and paper on my desk, paged frantically through the filing cabinets in case I'd had a brain fart and stowed them away, even got down on my hands and knees to peer underneath. Nothing there but dust.

Shit shit shit. If I didn't get these contracts off to Mr. Decker by end of day, he'd be furious. He didn't like leaving things hanging. So everything else flew out of my mind, replaced only by the steps I needed to take to not get fired. Call the business partner's assistant on her office phone and her cell phone until she finally picked up, an after-six surliness in her voice. Beg her to hang around long enough for her boss to sign and then messenger the copies over to us at our expense. Assure Mr. Decker when he inquires about where the contracts are that they're on their way, the messenger must just be held up.

It took almost an hour to get it all done. By the end, I was sticky with sweat all over, panting like I'd just raced my brothers to the jingling ice cream truck for the last SpongeBob pop, the one with neon-colored gumballs for eyes. I leaned my knees onto my elbows, lowering my head into my hands . . . only to catch a glimpse of a manila scrap stuck behind the desk against the wall.

I cursed as I sat up, but it was too late to go back. To distract myself from what an idiot I was, I grabbed my phone. Six calls, missed while on silent. I froze. Someone had gotten into a car accident and died. A troll was wreaking havoc on my page, being so foul and crude that my account had gotten suspended. I'd left the stove on in Alice's apartment that morning and burned her building down. It had to be something that bad to merit—

No. They were all from Bennett. And just like that, I remembered our reservation at West. The one that was set for—I glanced at the time—five minutes ago.

Shit shit shit shit shit shit shit.

The idea of actually calling someone on the phone was loathsome, but I didn't think twice before returning Bennett's call. He picked up on the first ring. "Where are you?"

I didn't even bristle at the impatience in his tone. I deserved it. "I'm so sorry." The words tumbled out of me. "Work stuff killed me. I'm running out now, be there ASAP." I hung up before he could say anything else and literally ran out the door. It was a good thing the office door locked automatically, because I thought I might otherwise allow random thieves to pillage our computers and Mr. Decker's ovarian cancer charity merch rather than take the fifteen seconds to lock it.

The rush to the restaurant—I splurged for a cab and, with a thrill like I was in a movie, told the driver to "step on it, please"—kept me from dwelling too much on my resentment. On the point that of course Bennett could get there on time; getting there on time was literally his job. While I had to balance getting there on time and writing my review with another job.

Okay, maybe I was dwelling a *little*.

West was housed in the lobby of a fancy hotel in Chelsea, and when I burst into the lobby, my eyes wild and my hair taking whatever opportunity it could to match, the host behind his sleek stand widened his eyes. But I had no attention for him—only for Bennett beside him, who was polishing his glasses on his blue-and-green plaid sweater in what I could only describe as an agitated way.

"I'm here," I cried, and he shoved them back onto his head only half cleaned. He spun back around to the host stand so fast I worried they'd go flying off.

"My entire party is here now," he said. "Can we still—"

His shoulders wilted as the host shook his head. "I'm afraid we only hold tables for fifteen minutes, sir."

My eyes strayed over the host's shoulder as Bennett argued—okay, begged. They landed upon a table, upon a small plate mounded with glistening dark pink cubes of tuna, threaded throughout with dark green leaves, dotted with the benne seeds Jada Knox had said tasted almost like coffee . . .

Jada Knox . . .

Jada Knox had been here. That might mean . . . Maybe I could . . .

I stepped up beside Bennett, squaring my shoulders, trying to ignore how close I stood to him, the warmth that radiated from that blue-and-green sweater. "It's all my fault. I got tied up at work. Bad boss," I lied, gambling that the host would have some experience with a bad boss.

His eyes did soften. Just a little.

Time for phase two. "I know my friend Jada Knox ate here recently. You know Jada?" I didn't wait for an answer. I wanted it to seem like the answer was assumed, because who didn't know Jada? "She's actually my colleague more than my friend. We're doing a collaboration together soon."

Jada and I had been going back and forth, trying to figure out when and where. The girl was *busy*. "I'm Julie Zimmerman, also known as JulieZeeEatsNYC. I have almost seventy thousand—"

I stopped as he held his palm up toward me. "I'm sorry, but we don't offer free meals to influencers."

"I'm not looking for a free meal," I said. "Just a table. Please. We had a—"

"As I said, I'm afraid we only hold tables for fifteen minutes past the reservation time. We gave your table away already." The softness had leached out of his voice. "And we don't cater to influencers here. If you were the food critic for the *New York Times* or the *New York Scroll*, that might be different."

I glanced at Bennett, then at the floor, worrying I'd given him away. Or was it to hide that shame bubbling up inside me again? Because that was all I was to the host. An influencer. Someone who took pretty pictures in exchange for free meals.

Bennett thanked the host politely and stepped away. It took me a moment to follow him; if I dared to look up, I was afraid I might burst into tears. But I focused on taking deep, even breaths and thinking about the cutest thing I possibly could (the baby who'd waved at me on the subway this morning, that beagle teapot in the window of the mob front near Wander) until my insides stopped roiling so much. By the time we made it outside to the sidewalk, where we kept to the side near the brick wall of the hotel so that we wouldn't get trampled by herds of businesspeople fleeing their offices, the tears had receded and I could speak normally again.

"I'm really sorry," I said, and now my breath hitched for a different reason, because what if he was mad and didn't want to review restaurants with me anymore?

I hated that I cared so much. "I had to send these contracts out for signature at the end of the day, and somehow they slid behind my desk and got stuck, and I couldn't find them, and—"

"It's okay," Bennett interrupted. "I don't blame you." He sighed, tipping his head back so that the lights of the city above reflected off his glasses, making him look for a moment like a skyscraper himself. "I just really wanted to eat here."

I nudged him with my elbow before I could stop myself, and then I had to stop myself from holding it for an extra moment against the hard plane of his waist. "Too bad you couldn't tell him the truth."

"Too bad," he echoed. He sighed again, so long and drawn out he might have been letting out all the air in his body. "And we already lost the reservation at the other place. I can definitely get another one, but probably not for a few weeks."

More sweat bloomed in my armpits. It took me a second to realize why, to put a word to the tingles in my stomach. Nervous. I was nervous. But why? We'd tried to get dinner. We'd failed. We could try again in a few weeks. Even if that meant I wouldn't see him until then. "I'm worried that we'll lose momentum if we don't give the people something," I said. I'd still been doing my regular reviews—I had material queued up on an excellent Thai restaurant I could put out instead of this one—but people loved our collaborations. My engagement numbers were highest on them. "There's got to be something we can eat together. Something good that we can feature."

Bennett scoffed. "All the hot new restaurants the *Scroll* would want me to do are booked up for weeks."

"And God forbid we do anything other than a hot new restaurant," I needled. "Why not . . . that diner?" I pointed at the nearest twenty-four-hour greasy spoon. I'd gone there plenty of times for a postmidnight drunken burger and fries, or omelet and fries, or just an enormous plate of fries. "Could be a fun angle. Mix it up a little."

Bennett rolled his eyes. "I don't like paying for food I could make better myself."

Of course. Of course he'd be that insufferable. I'd dated a guy in college who was convinced he could cook better than any restaurant nearby. He would've needed to use salt for that, though. "Yeah, okay."

His back stiffened. Behind me, somebody laughed loudly. I turned to see a guy ride by on a unicycle, a rainbow clown wig puffed all around his head. I turned back, unimpressed. Clearly, the laugher hadn't been in New York very long. Bennett clearly hadn't noticed him at all and was in the middle of a diatribe on how excellent a cook he was: ". . . will have you know that my skills may not be up to par as compared with a high-end restaurant chef, but they're certainly better than the standard cook's."

The words shot out of my mouth before I knew what I was saying. "Not better than mine." *What about that time a few weeks ago when you utterly destroyed rice and eggs, two of the simplest things you can make?* But I ignored that little voice. I hadn't asked for its opinion. "I used to make these lamb burgers with yogurt and mint for barbecues that my friends and family would beg for. Sometimes they'd say I was only invited if I brought them."

Bennett snorted. "That says a lot about the desirability of your company."

"Stop trying to change the subject," I said. "You're a food snob. I can't imagine you've made many burgers."

"So many burgers, and all better than yours." He raised an eyebrow at me. A challenge.

I took it. "Fine, then. Prove it."

"Prove it how?"

I crossed my arms. Overhead, the sun was just beginning to go down, bathing us both in an orangey glow. I hadn't actually thought this through.

Bennett crossed his arms back. The pose accentuated his forearms, made the rangy muscle bulge and the light dusting of fair hair glow in the dying light. My cheeks warmed, or maybe it was that they'd just figured out what was coming before my brain did. "Burger cook-off," he said. "My apartment isn't far from here. We'll document it for our social media, have it be a fun special event behind the scenes."

If I thought through the number of *shit shit shit*s that truly applied to this situation, I'd be standing here silently until the sun went all the way down. *Backpedal this situation. Figure out a face-saving way to get out of this. Fake an emergency call from your landlord. Your apartment's flooded. With mice.* "I don't know," I said. "I, um, I think I might have a . . . thing."

Nice.

He raised an eyebrow, then the second eyebrow. "Are you chickening out?" He shook his head. "What a shame. But I guess it's okay if you can't handle the heat."

How.

Dare.

He.

I straightened my shoulders, then inhaled deeply. If I breathed out right then, I thought I might actually exhale fire. "Of course I'm not chickening out," I said. "I was just thinking . . . um . . . it would suck to have burgers without fries. But as long as you also want to make fries, of course I'm in." Fries were easy—all I had to do to make oven fries was chop up potatoes and toss them in oil and throw them in the oven, right? I could definitely do that.

Somehow his eyebrows went up even higher. If he wasn't careful, they might jump right off his head. "Good," he said. "Then it's on."

AS SOON AS we got to the grocery store, I ran ahead of Bennett so that I could surreptitiously consult Chef Google without him seeing—I hadn't been lying about my famous lamb burgers, but I'd neglected to mention how long it had been since I'd fired up that skillet. Unfortunately, Manhattan grocery stores, especially this fancy little gourmet one Bennett frequented, didn't leave a lot of room for hiding. Whenever I went back to suburban Pennsylvania to visit my parents, I treated going to the grocery store kind of like I treated going to the zoo. *Oh my God, I didn't realize there were so many species of cheese. Look at all the baking goods roaming this sprawling plain.*

The first obstacle: the grocery store did not have ground lamb. They had regular lamb at the butcher's counter that could be ground, but the butcher had gone home for the day. "Sorry, it's almost closing time," said a worker in an apron, not sounding sorry at all.

"Well, that's a shame," I said to Bennett as we stood in front of the meat cubby. Or at least it felt like a meat cubby compared to the meat warehouse in other grocery stores. "I guess we'll have to—"

"Both use ground beef, I know," Bennett said. Was it my imagination, or had he rushed to get those words out before I said *cancel*?

Of course he wants to do this, I told myself sourly. *He probably got cooking lessons from Bobby Flay as a child.* "I'm not as experienced with ground beef," I said, setting the groundwork so that it wouldn't be as embarrassing when I lost.

He shrugged and tossed the two most expensive packages into the cart. I wondered if it would be gauche to take one out and switch it for a cheaper one. Probably. "I have salt and pepper and all the basic pantry items at my apartment already," he said. "But we'll need buns."

Obstacle number two: the bakery section had also been cleared out for the night. "We donate everything right before closing," said the same worker as before, not bothering to apologize this time. And of course they didn't have those squishy preservative-filled rolls that could last for weeks on the counter.

I heaved a sigh I hoped sounded more disappointed than relieved. "Well, we can't make burgers without buns." I hoped he wouldn't suggest stopping at a bodega. Would someone like Bennett even set foot in a bodega? Would someone like Bennett even know what a bodega was?

Bennett scoffed. "You can't make your own buns?"

Julie. No. Don't bite this time. But he looked down on me, those blue-gray eyes already gloating, and they lit that spark in my belly. That, or maybe it was how close he was standing to me all of a sudden, so close I had to crick my neck to look him in the face, and I didn't want to say anything that would make him back away. No matter how embarrassing it might be for me. But really, how hard could baking hamburger buns be? Baking was basically chemistry. Right? You just combine the right amount of the right ingredients and pop it all in the oven and—poof—hamburger buns.

"I assume you already have the ingredients we'll need in your massive pantry," I said, and this close, I could see Bennett's Adam's apple bob up and down.

"Of course," he said. "What self-respecting cook wouldn't?"

He stared down at me. I stared up at him. He could cook me with those eyes. I could already feel my insides heating up, melting . . .

I tore my eyes away, cheeks flushing. "I should get the potatoes."

He followed me to the produce section, where, together, we sorted through the russet potatoes, turning them over and examining them carefully for any rotten spots. I couldn't stop glancing over at his slender fingers running over the potato skin, wondering how they might feel on mine.

11

I'D MOSTLY GOTTEN AHOLD OF MY TRAITOROUS body by the time we made it to Bennett's apartment. For one, I'd insisted on paying half the grocery bill—I wasn't going to be in anyone's debt—and the number on the screen had been like dunking myself under a cold shower. I didn't have time to calculate in my head before handing over my card, so I had to settle for a silent prayer it wouldn't overdraft me again.

My jaw dropped open when Bennett stopped in front of a building I thought was a fancy hotel and led me into the lobby. Which also looked like a fancy hotel: the floor was white marble, polished so finely I could clearly see my reflection and the hairs that had escaped my ponytail, and a glittering silver chandelier spun high overhead. "Good evening, Mr. Wright," said the besuited doorman behind an ornately carved wooden desk.

Bennett smiled back and nodded. "How are you, Mr. Woods?"

The doorman chuckled as Bennett and I stepped into the elevator. The mirrored doors closed before us, and as we started rising, so smoothly I could hardly feel it, Bennett said, "Everybody else calls him Fred, but it feels weird to me for me to call him by his first name when he calls me 'mister.'"

"I get it," I said. I did not; I'd never had a doorman, or anyone who worked for me, really.

At least the fancy lobby prepared me for Bennett's extremely fancy apartment, so I didn't gawk like I'd never seen floor-to-ceiling views of the sparkling city lights before. His kitchen was as big as my living room, all the appliances sleek and chrome, and the connected living space had a ceiling that stretched high above us, the walls lined with bookshelves. I didn't see a TV.

Because I was actually curious and also because I wanted to delay what was going to be a sure humiliation in the kitchen, I stepped up to the closest bookshelf and let my fingers trail along the spines. "Bourdain!" I exclaimed, and felt the dagger of sorrow through my heart I always felt when reminded he was dead. Anthony Bourdain had introduced me to the idea of sharing my love for food and good restaurants through his TV shows. I was so sad I'd never get to meet him, and even sadder that his love was gone from the world.

"I love Bourdain." He stepped up beside me. "They're all first editions. And signed." Of course they were. "I've got A. J. Liebling over there, and Jeffrey Steingarten. Clementine Paddleford, James Beard, Ruth Reichl. And of course there's M. F. K. Fisher."

"Oh!" I moved over to squint at the spines but didn't dare touch them. I'd read many of the famous food writer's books in college. Back at home, I still had the editions I'd picked up in secondhand shops, the bindings tattered and page corners worn away nearly to nothing. "She's my favorite. She broke so many barriers."

"'There is a communication of more than our bodies when bread is broken and wine is drunk,'" Bennett recited. "'And that is my answer when people ask me: Why do you write about hunger, and not wars or love.'"

When I looked at him in amazement, the tips of his ears had turned red. He said, "That's my favorite M. F. K. Fisher quote."

I became aware that I was holding my breath. I didn't want to breathe out, though. It felt like it might make this moment end. This moment where he was standing so close to me, those words on his lips, those lips slightly parted, telling me that food stood for love, and war stood for love, too, or maybe it was just in my own mind that I was mixing the two of them up, because I knew Bennett and I could never be together, knew that our positions meant we were at war, and yet . . . and yet . . .

My lungs begged for air. I sucked in a deep breath and broke eye contact, broke the tension that had been hanging between us. "That's a good quote. Do you want to know my favorite?"

"Sure." His voice was rough. In the corner of my eye, I saw him lick his lips.

Like most normal people, I didn't have any M. F. K. Fisher quotes memorized. So I selected one of her books at random—well, not random, the one that looked the least valuable—and flipped to a random page. Hoping I'd find something beautiful but decidedly unsexy, maybe about the smell of a mushroom farm or boxes of durian.

Where my eyes landed: *Sharing food with another human being is an intimate act that should not be indulged in lightly.*

Thanks a lot, Mary Frances Kennedy. I shut the book with a snap. "Never mind, I forgot it."

"The book's right there." It felt almost like he was studying me, his arms crossed as he leaned against the bookshelf. How could something so simple as a lean be so sexy? It was like he was mocking me.

I brushed past him. I couldn't watch him lean if my back was to him. "It's late. We should probably get cooking."

I remembered once I was in that giant stainless steel kitchen that, *Wait, I definitely do not want to "get cooking."* But it was too late. I was in it now.

At least the fact that we'd volunteered to make our own buns meant that I could consult my phone. "I haven't memorized the ratios of flour and yeast and . . ." What else went in hamburger buns? *God, I'm in trouble.* ". . . all the other things we need for baking. It's not like I'm making hamburger buns every day," I said, while covertly googling How do I make the best hamburger ever?

"Fine. But phones go on the counter. To make sure

we're not looking up anything else." He gave me a pointed look. I rolled my eyes, mostly to hide the guilt, and quickly switched over to googling How do I make the best hamburger buns?

"Whatever." But I propped my phone on the counter up against the iridescent blue-and-pearl backsplash, the kitchen's only pop of color. "But don't try to cheat by reading my recipe. It's the best one." I knew that because the recipe creator had called them "The Best Hamburger Buns," and obviously, she wasn't biased at all.

"I don't need your recipe."

Panic swelled inside me as he went back and forth between his pantry, which was about the size of Marcus's walk-in closet, which was the prize of our apartment and something I'd sacrificed for the bedroom with the better view (aka the street and not the sad "courtyard," where you faced the backs of other buildings). He strode purposefully, like he knew exactly what he was doing, and he didn't have to stop and rummage around to make sure he had something—again, like he knew exactly what he was doing.

I swallowed hard, pushing my shoulders back. Trying to project confidence. "I guess I'll start my burgers while you're doing that."

He didn't answer, just gestured at a cabinet over the stove. I opened it to find what appeared to be every bowl or cutting board or rack that a cook could ever possibly need. What did I need to make a burger? I should chop some onion, right? And I'd need a mixing bowl for the beef. I pulled down a cutting board and big bowl—which still had a label in it, odd—and grabbed a knife from the knife block, laying it gently on top before realizing that I'd picked a knife almost as big as my head. Big knives scared me, but it wasn't like I could chop with a paring knife here the way I sometimes did at home. It would immediately mark me as an amateur.

I've done a lot of things in my life that have freaked me out. For one, purchasing and eating gas station sushi coated with Cheetos dust as an attempt to get attention in one of my earliest reviews (#badidea). But chopping that onion with that giant, extremely sharp knife was definitely up there. It took all of my focus, first trying to cut it in half while it rolled merrily around the board and then chopping it into irregularly sized, probably too-big pieces, to keep myself from chopping off at least part of a finger. I'd broken out in sweat by the time I finished, my heart beating like that time I'd downed a caramel macchiato without realizing I'd accidentally ordered four espresso shots in it.

Bennett paused in his mixing of hamburger bun ingredients to glance over his shoulder and judge me judgily. His eyes slid down to my pile of onions, then back up to me. I said, defensively, "I like it rustic."

He said nothing, just turned back to his bowl. I dumped my package of hamburger meat into the bowl with the onions, then went for my phone, then reconsidered and washed my hands thoroughly before touching it. I opened up the camera function in selfie mode, smoothed down some of the escaping hairs from my ponytail, and fixed my big fake smile. "Hey, everybody! So, change of plans. Your favorite *New York Scroll* reviewer Bennett and I were supposed to go out for another joint meal tonight, but, long story short, the reservation gods were not on our side. So what are we doing instead?"

I explained our plan to the camera, leaving my face for only a few seconds to show them the bowl of meat (with just a few of the prettier onions poking out from underneath). Another hank of hair fell free with the motion. I tucked it behind my ear as I turned the camera back to myself, in the process catching Bennett's eye . . .

. . . because he was openly staring at me while I spoke. Fortunately, I was a professional. My cheeks heated up, but my viewers would pass that off as a healthy glow and probably ask me for my skin care routine. "Anyway, stay tuned for my post later when you'll get to see by just how much I kick Bennett's ass."

It is to my testament as a performer that I managed to wink into the lens without dissolving into embarrassment. I watched it over once quickly to make sure I hadn't flubbed anything—listening to the sound of my own voice used to make me cringe, but I was used to it by now—and hit post. Which freed me up to set my phone back down and demand, "What?"

"Nothing." Bennett's lips quirked in amusement. "It's just funny watching you work."

I bit my tongue so that I wouldn't retort something about how it *was* work. "Weren't you going to post, too?"

"Oh. Right." Bennett reached with flour-crusted hands for his phone, then hesitated and went to wash them off, just like I did. Which somehow made me relax a little, enough to return to my bowl of meat and onions and add a good flurry of salt before mashing it all up. I was supposed to mash it, right? Mash it good?

Now I was starting to get in my own head. I finished mashing the meat and onions and salt together, then clumped them into patty size and packed them all together as tight as I could so that they wouldn't fall apart when I went to cook them. Once done, I stacked them up on the cutting board while I worked on the buns.

"Switch places?" Bennett asked. I stole a glance into his own bowl as he passed. It was full of white gloop, which was not helpful as far as snooping went.

At least I could look up my recipe now. I opened my phone, which took me automatically to my social media, where responses were pouring in. I didn't like looking at feedback while I was in the middle of something, but I couldn't help scanning a few pieces of it while I switched over to the recipe.

Don't pack it too tight!

Touch the meat as little as possible!

Don't add salt until the end!

Make sure to salt throughout!

I took a deep breath, trying not to let it all worm itself too deep into my thoughts. The salt thing was contradictory. I literally could not salt throughout *and* not salt it until the end. Or could I? Was I missing something totally obvious?

"You okay?" Bennett was watching me again with that infuriating look of amusement. "Want to give up? We can just eat my delicious burgers."

Yes. "I would rather eat my own foot," I said. "Just figuring out the best way to start these rolls."

The rolls started great. I dumped some yeast in with some warm water and sugar as the recipe specified, then mixed in the flour and salt and everything else. I mixed it all together, and it got nice and sticky and looked like dough.

You know what's extremely therapeutic when you want to punch somebody in the face? Kneading dough. I slammed and punched and slapped that dough until it turned soft and pliable. By the time I was ready to divide it into round chunks and let them sit for a bit on a baking sheet, I felt *great*. Maybe I should bake more often. Or start a bakery where I got to do this every day. Annoying troll trying to ruin your morning? Don't stress, just go beat up some bread.

With ten to twenty minutes to kill—that was the range the recipe gave me, but I had no idea what I was waiting for—I tiptoed over to Bennett. He was forming his patties into big hunks of meat, pressing on all sides and then squishing them flat between his hands. "Need any help?"

I said loftily. "I just need to cook everything. Don't worry, it's okay if you're a little slow."

"Is it?" he said dryly, not missing a beat. "Thank you, so much. I feel validated."

I couldn't help grinning. "Step aside so I can turn the oven on."

I set the oven to preheat at the temperature the recipe had told me, then pulled open the cabinet Bennett directed me to for a burger pan. "This apartment doesn't have a grill?"

"There are grills up on the roof-deck," he said. Of course there were. "But I think somebody's having a party up there tonight, so unless you feel like shouldering your way through a bunch of drunk twenty-one-year-olds . . ."

I shuddered. "That wasn't fun even when I *was* one of those drunk twenty-one-year-olds."

"You aren't a big party person, either, huh?" He bent down and pulled out a big, heavy pan for himself. Cast iron, I was pretty sure. But that appeared to be the only cast-iron pan, and there was no way in hell I was going to ask him to share, so I pulled out a regular stainless steel pan instead and set it on the stove.

"Not so much," I said. "In college, a bit. I assume you're not a big party person, because you own a Blood Sword of Death and Blood. You can't earn that if you're out partying all the time."

He didn't answer that, only stared seriously down into his cast-iron pan. Had I struck a nerve? He'd seemed fine the last time we discussed it.

Then again—who cared? *I'm not here to make friends.*

Before putting my burgers into the pan, I took a look at my buns. They looked exactly the same as they had when I'd put them there. Was something supposed to happen in those ten to twenty minutes? Weren't they supposed to rise or something? I poked at one dubiously.

"Problem over there?" Bennett asked.

"Not at all," I said. I'd put them in the oven and hope for the best. What was the worst that could happen?

Approximately twenty minutes later, I was staring at the worst thing that could happen. Well, maybe not the *worst* worst thing that could happen. I hadn't lit the kitchen on fire or singed my eyebrows off. But my burgers looked gray and dense and unappetizing, and my buns may as well have been matzah (the dry, cracker-like, worst part of any Jewish holiday. Yes, even the ones where I had to fast).

Maybe I shouldn't have teased this on social media, I thought with a wave of nausea.

Bennett, meanwhile, had taken over the stove. His burgers hit the cast iron with a sizzle that could probably be heard in the neighboring apartments, and he slid his buns into the oven with a flourish. "If yours aren't living up to expectations, don't worry," he called over his shoulder. I'd retreated from the kitchen and was examining his bookshelves again, awed by his collection of cookbooks. He seemed to have every cookbook that had ever been printed. I pulled *Coconut and Sambal* off the shelf and opened it up, surprised by the crack of the spine—he must not cook much Indonesian food—and inhaled the new-book smell. "We can dine on mine."

His grandiose statement was kind of ruined by the "oh shit" he let out when he turned back to his cast iron, and it only took me a moment to realize why he'd cursed: the pungent odor of overly charred meat. I sauntered closer to see him frantically attempting to flip one of the burgers, which, by the edges I could see, was burned black on the bottom. It seemed to be fused to the metal. "Did you not season your cast-iron pan?" I said smugly. I knew all about the seasoning of cast-iron pans thanks to the yelp Marcus had let out the one time I tried to be nice and do his dishes and almost washed his in soap and water. Apparently, that would have washed away the level of hard-earned season-ing, which prevented things from sticking and the pan from rusting.

Drops of sweat rolled down Bennett's temples, damp-ening the sides of his hair so that it curled over his ears. "I . . . must have forgotten. It's been a while since I've used this pan," he puffed. He jammed the spatula under the patty as hard as he could, and finally it flipped over—though it left a layer stuck to the pan. "It's fine. I'll just put it in the oven and let it cook through without burning." He managed to repeat the process for the other patties, then shoved it all into the oven and turned back around, wiping his forehead with the kitchen towel.

"Gross," I said amiably.

"Shut up," he said, just as amiably. "I need a drink. Do you want one?"

Drinking with Bennett in his apartment while his hair curled over his ears and he recited M. F. K. Fisher to me? That was a decidedly unwise idea.

But that didn't mean I didn't want to do it. I pushed the thought off. "Shouldn't you get started on the fries?"

He looked at me with such pleading that I couldn't help but burst into laughter. Over my cackles, he said, "Don't you think we've done enough for one night?"

I wiped tears from my eyes. "Sure. If you admit I'm the better cook."

He slung the kitchen towel over his shoulder, as if he were a soldier heading off to war. "I'd rather die."

The oven punctuated his statement, rather dramatically, by bursting into flame.

Not the entire oven—that would've been too dramatic. But the cast-iron pan had clearly ignited, maybe from all the grease from the charred burgers, and by the time either of us had unfrozen to shriek for help (me) or run for a fire extinguisher (Bennett, who responsibly had one beside the kitchen door), the fire had died down on its own. Bennett stepped forward gingerly and turned the oven off with a beep.

Both of us just stood there for a moment, staring at the now-smoky glass of the oven door. "Well," I said, breaking the silence, "I think we can safely say I won. Considering my burgers are at least edible."

"If not especially appetizing," he said.

I shrugged. Couldn't argue with that.

He sighed. "I suppose we were both more out of practice

than we thought. Which isn't surprising, considering how much we eat out. I was trying to remember the last time I cooked. I definitely haven't baked in a while, given how dead that yeast was."

I gasped. "So, I can blame my terrible buns on you and your dead yeast!"

He raised an eyebrow as I realized how that sounded. I snorted back a laugh.

Bennett did, too. "Well, now I *really* need a drink." He stepped around me to the fridge and pulled out a bottle of wine. "You want some? It's probably better than what they had at that bar that you didn't like."

That wine had probably cost at least a hundred dollars. Maybe more. I actually had no idea how much expensive wine cost. I did know that I didn't want it because, no matter how fancy and expensive, it would taste like motor oil to me. "Sure," I said. Because it didn't matter if it would taste like motor oil to me: I couldn't let anyone know.

Together, we moved from the kitchen into his combination living room and dining space, since the smoky smell was not exactly appetizing (not that anything could make wine appetizing). His dining table and chairs were clearly antiques, made of some shiny wood with high, stiff backs and cushions that were plush but not so plush I sank into them. I took a seat facing the floor-to-ceiling window, the city lights sparkling before me. What a view. What it must be like to see this view every night.

I couldn't look away, not as the trickle of wine pouring sounded beside my ear, not as Bennett took the seat next to me. That pleased me, for some reason. Not because we'd be sitting next to each other. It was something about how he wanted to take in the view of the city, too, that even if this apartment had been given to him by his rich parents or whatever, at least he didn't take it for granted.

He pushed one of the goblets of wine in my direction. The crystal stem sparkled in the light, and suddenly, I felt a little bit like I was living in a movie. Me, the view, the glittering glass of wine. The handsome guy next to me. That polished smile on my face, the composure I kept up for my subscribers and my boss and the rest of the world.

Bennett picked up his glass and whirled the wine around (pretty sure that's a technical term). Then stuck his nose in the goblet. "Mmm," he said. "I'm getting earthy notes, like the soil after a rain."

Why would I want to drink that? Still, I obediently picked the glass up and whirled the wine around myself, then stuck my nose in, too. Motor oil. What could I say that matched up with soil after a rain? Maybe flowers? Tea? Bugs?

I set the goblet down, feeling almost like I'd already downed a few. "I actually hate wine," I said, and it was out. A laugh bubbled up after it. Free. I felt free.

Bennett set his own glass down, too, though he looked concerned. Maybe because my laugh had sounded a little deranged. "Oh, I'm sorry, I didn't realize. You talk about liking wine on Julie Zee Eats NYC," he said. "I have beer, too, or vodka and juice, or just juice, or—"

I was still laughing when I interrupted him. Definitely

verging on deranged now. It just felt really good not to have to choke down this wine, have to keep my smile up the whole time, have to pretend that I just loooooved it. "No, it's okay. You wouldn't have known because I'm a big fat liar online." And then his words caught up to me. "Bennett Richard Macalester Wright. Did you just admit to following JulieZeeEatsNYC?"

"Wow, you remember all four of my names. I suppose I should be honored." Bennett took a long drink of his wine. "Yes, I've checked out some of your reviews and watched some of your videos. They're quite . . ."

He trailed off, and all those good feelings went away. I felt my whole body tense. "Quite what? Vapid? Tasteless?"

Surprise flashed over his face, and he took off his glasses, rubbed the lenses on his shirt. "No! Quite the opposite. I was going to say that they were really . . . great. No, that's a terrible word for a writer to use, isn't it? Impressive. I was really impressed by them."

The tension drained away, joining the still-present odor of burned meat lingering in the air. "Oh. Thanks."

But he wasn't done. "It's different than what I do in that you're approaching the food and the restaurants from another angle, but ultimately, it's all the same, isn't it? We love food. We want people to go out and eat the food that we love." He slid his glasses back on, blinked owlishly in my direction, then set his hands on the table, the right one resting only a few inches from my own. I could practically feel the heat of his skin radiating onto mine. As if attracted to it, my hand, also on the table, drifted closer to his. Now

I could definitely feel the heat. "Only you built your operation up from scratch, which is even more impressive than me, because I jumped in with a ready-made audience. Your hustle is amazing."

I rubbed the back of my neck, which forced the angle of my face away from his eyes. Which I definitely didn't do on purpose. Definitely not because I couldn't handle the admiration in his eyes and what it might make me do. "Oh. Thanks."

And you know, I'd just loosed some truth, and even though it was just about wine, it had made me feel lighter in the best possible way. He'd just admitted something true, too, bared a little piece of his soul. Maybe I could do that as well. "One of the reasons—really, the main reason—that I played that trick on you at the Central Park Food Festival was because I was jealous of you," I admitted, staring at the table as my cheeks heated up. "That should actually be present tense. I *am* jealous of you. I love what I do, but I want the clout and the prestige that you have. Sure, my followers value my opinions, but the food world as a whole doesn't, not really. You have a name behind you. I just have *my* name."

The silence that fell after the last word left my lips somehow felt different than the silence that had fallen between us before. More comfortable. More open. Like I could say anything into it, and it wouldn't come back to bite me.

And, like that feeling had given permission to my body to be just as honest, my hand reached out and covered his on the table. His hand beneath mine was warm, large enough where mine didn't cover nearly all of it, his skin soft and his bones hard ridges that tensed at the touch of my skin.

What are you doing? I thought furiously at it. My lips opened to say *sorry*, and I went to pull my hand away, but before I could do either of those things, his hand flipped over, our palms meeting as he threaded his fingers through mine.

It was like when I was a freshman in high school and held a boy's hand for the very first time. The touch of his skin on mine made me tingle all the way up my arm, and the way he squeezed my hand, reassuringly but also firmly, as if to say, this is the way I'd squeeze around your nipple or cup your ass to press you up against me.

I had to get out of here, or I'd be squeezing way more than his hand. And that would be a disaster for both our careers. I cleared my throat and yanked my hand away. "So," I said brightly even as his eyes dimmed. Should I tell him I hadn't pulled away so abruptly because he was gross or something? No, then I'd just get into that storm of apologies again and make things weird. "I'm starving."

Twenty minutes later, we were at Shake Shack, surrounded by bright lights, white furniture, and a cheerful combination of drunk college students and working people grabbing a bite at the end of the day. The smell of fried food was salty and crunchy, somehow, in the air. We ordered our food, paying separately, and then I staked out a table while Bennett waited with the buzzer for our order to be ready.

Alone at the table, after wiping some crumbs off with a napkin, I had a moment to think about how I should handle tonight's debacle on my social media. I'd already posted that stupid live video, after all. In the future, I'd better wait to post anything like that until I was done and certain of success. I could just delete it and pretend it never happened. Or post an update tomorrow looking cheery and confessing that I'd had a little too much wine and forgotten to take pictures, but the burgers were incredible. It might make me look relatable, but still an expert in my field. Or I could ask one of my brothers if they had any good burger photos they wouldn't mind me swiping and claiming as my own.

But then Bennett approached with our ShackBurgers and cheese fries on a red plastic tray, and I remembered what it had felt like in his apartment to tell the truth about the wine. To not stress about it.

I held up a finger as he went to grab his burger. "One sec."

He sighed dramatically as I smiled into my camera. Not my big fake smile. A smaller smile, one that was a little abashed. "Hey, folks. So . . . I am indeed about to eat some of the best burgers and fries of my life." I quickly switched the camera and panned over the tray, wishing my viewers could smell it, then turned it back to my face with a smile. "Let's just say that I might be a little out of practice when it comes to cooking. I'd love any tips on cooking accounts to follow to get back up to speed! In any case . . . I'm hungry."

I gave them an embarrassed little wave, then shut it off. Time to dive in. I teased the palate with a couple of fries first, their crispiness just barely starting to wilt under the thick, creamy layer of cheese. And then the burger. I moaned as my teeth sank through the soft bun, the crunchy fried portobello mushroom oozing with cheese filling, the meaty burger itself.

Because of the food, and definitely not because of the way Bennett and I laughed at ourselves as we ate it— definitely solely due to the food—it was one of the best meals of my life.

12

MARCUS WOKE ME UP THE NEXT MORNING WITH his laughter. Which I suppose is preferable to being woken up by screaming or crying, but still much less preferable to not being woken up at all.

I cracked a bleary eye in the direction of my phone. Which said eight forty-four.

Shit.

I shot upright, rubbing my cheeks. I hadn't gotten to bed until late last night because of our Shake Shack dinner and a subway ride home that had lasted an extra half hour thanks to a sick passenger in the train ahead. (Bennett had tried to call me an Uber, but I'd lied, saying that I'd get my own downstairs. Ubers from Manhattan to where I lived in Brooklyn cost a fortune—I didn't want him paying for that for me.) I must have forgotten to set my alarm. Now I was going to be late to work unless I really hustled.

I ran out to the bathroom past Marcus—still chortling—to brush my teeth and wash my face. No time for a shower. Ran back past him—what was the man laughing at for this long?—to throw on the first dress I found, then whipped it off and pulled on another one after I remembered the reason the first one had been hanging in front had been to remind me to do an extra-intensive cleaning because of a salad dressing stain I couldn't get off.

A hair tie pulling my hair into a high bun—lopsided, I'd redo it in the office—and I was ready to go. I grabbed my satchel, shoving a new library book in as I walked out into the living room, and finally had a moment to ask Marcus, "What's so funny?"

"You," he responded, and I realized he was holding his phone up to his face.

"You mean my videos from last night?" On my subway ride home, during the delay, I'd gone on and done a little live Q&A. It had been a lot of ignoring the people asking me my bra size or what color panties I was wearing and a lot of describing the disaster of the night's cooking, my journey from being a pretty good cook in college to a current mess. I'd gotten a lot of great tips, too. Now doubt seized me, made me nervous. "Was it that bad?"

He lowered his phone. "No, it's great," he said, and it took me a moment to realize he was being sincere, not sarcastic. My shoulders relaxed. "You came off really funny and authentic. I'm not the only one who loved it."

"Really?" Tight schedule be damned, I pulled out my own phone and quickly scrolled through the top comments. Marcus was right. They were overwhelmingly positive, full of encouragement and sympathy and stories about how they, too, had overcooked the pork chops until they were dry and tough, or accidentally served their vegetarian sister-in-law beef stew. I smiled. "Wow."

"There's only one thing that's unfortunate," Marcus said, sighing dramatically. I braced myself for the one troll who had ruined everything or how I hadn't noticed the glob of cheese sauce clinging to my chin. But he said, "I wish I had something to share, too, but I've never made a single cooking mistake."

It was my turn to laugh my way out of the apartment.

THE FIRST THING I did when I got to work was not to lay out Mr. Decker's papers or check his messages. The first thing I did was email Bennett.

> My followers reveled in our disaster. We might have to make this a regular thing.

Bennett responded immediately. Maybe without burning down my kitchen?

I'll consider it, I wrote back, grinning. Next time we can try flooding it. I'm open to various sorts of disasters.

Well, obviously. You need some variety in your disasters, or disaster just gets boring. Do you still want to try West again next week? I miraculously got another reservation but also

managed to book a backup at Lima, which is supposed to
be excellent.

A warm glow swept through me. Gross. Sure. As long as
you don't light their kitchen on fire.

I never light a kitchen on fire before my second visit.

Bennett and I bantered for most of the morning. But I
couldn't focus entirely on our back-and-forth, because
Jada and I had *finally* connected on a date and a time and a
plan. Honestly, I didn't care what we did; I would've traveled out to Far Rockaway if that's what she wanted or reviewed all of the city's different salad chains. But what
she'd ultimately emailed me as her suggestion actually
sounded really fun. I haven't done a crawl of my own neighborhood in a while. Why don't you come along for a day of filming? I'll
show you my favorite places and we can take turns recording. I'll
probably do live videos all day and then an edited compilation video
that I'll actually post.

I unscheduled the post on that Thai restaurant that
had been languishing in purgatory. Which was unfortunate, because its fried whole fish—cut into cubes before-
hand, all then battered in rice flour, fried, and reassembled
onto the crispy brown carcass before being drenched in a
bright, tangy lime-and-chile dressing strewn with fresh
green herbs and sharp, crunchy slices of red onion—was
probably one of the best things I'd eaten in a long time.

Count me in. I'd be meeting her this weekend in Morning-side Heights.

And then came the email. When my phone lit up, I figured it was Jada confirming, but it was actually a message from a self-described "boutique feminist small-batch wine company." A bit of a mouthful. The gist of their message was shorter than their self-description: they wanted me to promote their wine.

My first instinct was delight. Sponsorship money was always a delight. The more people I could get to pay me to post, the more of a chance I had of someday getting to quit my day job.

But the second was doubt. I flashed back to last night, how good it had felt to hold Bennett's—no, how good it had felt to tell him the truth about my wine-related feelings. How good it had felt to be honest with him and then with my followers.

If I shilled this product I knew I didn't like without even tasting it, that would set me back. Even if it made me good money.

I could respond to them later. I set my phone aside, and not a second too soon, because just then the door flew open and Mr. Decker rushed in, trench coat flapping, hat nearly slipping off his impressive head of silver hair.

I jammed my shoes back onto my feet and leaped up. "Good afternoon, Mr. Decker!" I could count on one hand the number of times he'd shown up at the office without me knowing it first. Today he was supposed to be attending a director's board meeting for one of his investments down-town, then heading back up to Connecticut to have dinner with his wife. "Is everything okay?"

"Everything is not okay." His eyes were wild. "It's my fortieth wedding anniversary this weekend."

Maybe I was misunderstanding his mood. Maybe he wasn't panicking but was just that excited about being in love with his wife. Which I could get behind. I didn't have much contact with Mrs. Decker, but she'd always been kind to me and was unfailingly fashionable in a glamorous Jackie O sort of way. "Congratulations!" I'd always thought old people in love was more romantic than young people in love, because that love had stood the test of time. "That's great. What are you doing for it?"

"I don't know. That's the problem." He turned those wild eyes on me, and for a moment, I felt like a rider who was about to be bucked from her horse. "Why didn't you remind me?"

Aaaaand I went flying. I had the power in the next split second to determine if I landed with a thud that only bruised my tailbone or if I'd break my neck. "I wasn't told of the date, but I'll make sure to put it on my calendar for next year. In the meantime, it's not too late to plan some-thing," I said soothingly. His shoulders relaxed a little. "What do you think? I can get you into dinner at a place like Daniel or the Four Seasons, have them send out a spe-cial dessert for her. Maybe a show or a concert first? The New York Philharmonic is always reliable, or is there a show she's been wanting to see on Broadway?"

His shoulders popped right back up around his ears. "No," he said miserably. "I may have panicked and hinted that I would be throwing her a surprise party."

I blinked. "Oh."

"But I assume you can help with that." He straightened, and just like that, he was self-assured again. "Nothing too big or flashy. Send invitations only to our closest friends and family, maybe rent out a fun restaurant for Sunday brunch. Order something parrot-related for her parrot collection. Maybe a Swarovski crystal parrot? Do they make those?" He stared down at me. "Are you going to write this down?"

I grabbed for a pen and a scrap of paper and did my best to scribble along with his train of thought, which was plowing right ahead. "And maybe a Peloton? She's been talking about wanting one, but would that be an insulting gift?"

He went on for what felt like the rest of the workday—but was really only about fifteen more minutes—before the door opened again behind him. He nearly jumped out of his suit, and actually did jump out of his fedora, which finally went sliding off. Emerson Leigh caught it neatly as she entered, hoisting it high above her head like a trophy.

"Emmy!" I only ever heard Mr. Decker's voice go that gooey when talking to one of his daughters. "How are you? Are you having fun with your animal yoga?"

Emerson Leigh plopped her dad's fedora on her own head, then grinned at him. He smiled indulgently back. "It's not fun. It's a business."

"Of course it is," he said. His tone was both loving and patronizing at once. "Julie, did you hear that Emmy here has already booked her first client?"

"Daaaaaad," Emerson Leigh drawled in that way that on its surface meant *stooooop* but that in reality meant *go onnnnnnn*.

"Maisie's chihuahua is going to be so calm after his session," he said. "I have to run now, dear." He reached for his hat but stayed his hand. "You can hang on to that. It looks much better on you anyway."

They both laughed as he rushed out, then Emerson Leigh turned to me. Mr. Decker's old man fedora did legitimately look much better on her than it had on possibly anyone else, ever. "Did you hear that, Julie?" she chirped. "Maisie booked me to do a yoga class for her dog!"

"I heard! That's great!" I left off the fact that Maisie was her sister and that she'd probably been threatened into it by her father, who was funding Maisie's boutique. (There just weren't that many people to buy her artisan perfumes and hand-woven tapestries, even on the Upper East Side.) "Do you need anything, Emerson Leigh? I have a ton on my plate."

"I'm just grabbing something from my dad's office," she said, but she didn't move. "What's going on?"

I took a deep, calming breath. I couldn't make it look like I was unhappy or stressed-out. Not in front of the boss's daughter. Also, I couldn't tell her that her dad forgot his anniversary. What if she went back and told her mom? I'd definitely get in trouble. "Your dad asked for my help planning a surprise anniversary party for your mom. I just . . . I have a lot to do for it, and I'm not entirely sure where to start."

Her eyebrows popped up, and her mouth widened into a perfect O of surprise. "Where to *start*? Julie, planning parties isn't as easy as people sometimes think it is! You should've gotten started earlier!"

I gritted my teeth. "I know."

She glided to my side, the scent of her flowery soap filling my nostrils. "Don't stress out. Stress only makes things more difficult. Here, let me help."

Help from Emerson Leigh? I couldn't help thinking of my five-year-old niece asking to help when my mom cooked lunch for the family. Yes, it was adorable watching her mix up her bowl of ingredients, but there was usually twice as much flour flying all over and sticky things stepped on and tracked everywhere.

But before I could tell her I didn't need her help, Emerson Leigh was pointing at my list with one polished pink fingernail. "For the restaurant, I'll call Haversham's on the Upper East Side. My mom loves their brunch food, and they have a nice private room in the back with this parrot portrait she just adores." She picked at the finger. "And she already has a Swarovski crystal parrot, but I know this hot up-and-coming artist who would rush-paint a parrot picture for her in exchange for my dad buying a big piece later on. Everyone will love that."

I goggled at her for a moment before remembering

that, right, she'd been her sorority's party planner. "Wow. Thank you."

She beamed at me. "You're very welcome." Then plopped down on my desk, treating me to an excellent view of her crotch. "It's going to be tough to get good invitations printed at this short notice, but here are some ideas . . ."

Over the course of the next hour, Emerson Leigh tackled basically the entire party. The things she said she was too busy to do or couldn't handle, she wrote down in a color-coded list for me. I estimated that it would take me maybe a couple more hours. "This is amazing," I said. "You're so good at this."

She hopped up and dusted her hands together. "Why do you sound so surprised? I'm good at a lot of things. Like making actual dogs do downward dogs."

"Right."

She disappeared into her dad's office and emerged a few minutes later with a stack of framed photos in her arms. I'd looked at them enough times while in Mr. Decker's office to know that they featured him with all sorts of prominent figures, from Joe Biden to Hillary Clinton to Mitt Romney to George W. Bush. (Mr. Decker played both sides of the aisle.) I didn't ask, but Emerson Leigh explained anyway. "I'm doing research on celebrities and political figures to see who has pets so I can try and get one of them interested in my business."

For once, I was kind of sorry that she didn't hang around a little while longer.

13

SUNDAY MORNING FOUND ME WAKING UP AT
eight o'clock even though I didn't need to leave my apartment until eleven. As Marcus snoozed away in the other
room, I rubbed my usual tinted moisturizer on my face
and some highlighter on my cheekbones. Usually after
that, I didn't do much more than sweep some mascara on
my eyelashes. I liked to tell myself—and sometimes my
followers—that I didn't want to distract from the food,
but really I just didn't like the feeling of too much stuff on
my face.

But today I darkened the outside of my eyes with eye-
liner, swept what I hoped was a complexion-flattering
gold eye shadow up to my brow bone and dotted on a little
bit of white at the inside corners of my eyes (the video I
watched said it made your eyes look bigger), and pursed
my lips for a rose-colored lipstick. Nerves jangled in my

stomach as I regarded myself in the mirror once I was all done. My face looked like an accentuated version of its usual self, every feature highlighted, but it didn't look like art. Not like Jada's face did.

My worry was interrupted by Marcus banging on the bathroom door. "I'm going to pee in the kitchen sink if you don't hurry up in there."

The makeup had taken longer than I thought it would, but I'd fortunately done the hard work of picking the perfect outfit the night before. Jada tended toward floaty, feminine, sparkly clothes, and I had quite a debate with myself out loud (and with Alice over text, who could not have been more clear about how much she didn't care) about whether I should try to imitate Jada or do my own thing as usual.

I looked down at my blouse and dark jeans. Admittedly, my blouse was a little fancier than my usual sweaters, with a cinched waist and puffed sleeves. But maybe I'd gone in the wrong direction. Would I look good enough next to Jada Knox? Did I feel good enough? Did I *ever* feel good enough? Did *anyone* ever feel good enough?

I sighed. *This is not the time for existential questions.* But my phone beeped, reminding me that I had to leave right now if I didn't want to be late, so good enough it had to be.

I didn't spend a lot of time on the north edge of Central Park. But as I sat there trying to read my book without being able to focus and just people-watching instead (for the first and probably only time ever, the subway had actually delivered me somewhere ahead of time), I got to see firsthand how beautiful it was. The flowers and elaborate statue fountains of the Conservatory Garden. The turtles sunning themselves on the shores of the Lake. The Frederick Douglass statue standing majestically in the middle of traffic. So, when it came time to meet Jada beside that statue, I actually had something to say besides *Oh my God, thank you.*

She was easy to spot in her long gauzy white skirt and sparkly red crop top. Diamonds winked at me from her belly button and her ears, which, since she'd pulled all her braids back into a high ponytail, were on full display. They were delicate, shaped like seashells.

Julie, stop being so weird about her ears. No matter how beautiful she is.

She was already talking and smiling at the same time, something that had taken me ages to be able to do without looking like I was constantly grimacing. "Julie, so nice to meet you!" she said, coming in for a hug. She smelled a little bit like the ocean. "Thanks for coming out with me today."

"I should be the one thanking you!" I said, then remembered that I'd planned to start off with something else. "It's beautiful up here. I walked around the Conservatory Garden before we met up, and it was like being on an old English estate."

"I'm glad you like it up here!" She smiled at me. "I love that collaboration you've been doing with the reviewer at the *Scroll.* I've pushed for ages to do something like that with one of the major critics, but they snubbed me."

I gaped at her as we began walking. I had no idea where we were walking to, but I'd follow her anywhere. "They snubbed *you*?"

She shrugged. "Yup."

"I'm just surprised," I said. "You're *the* big name in New York food reviews on social media. You have, like, four hundred thousand followers! You'd think they'd all be jumping at the chance to link up with you."

She laughed like the tinkling of bells. "That's sweet. But no, they always had some excuse for me, both for when I proposed collaborations and when I pitched them pieces. Our audiences were different. My idea wasn't deep enough. They don't take influencers seriously in that world. I've placed plenty of pieces in digital spaces or younger publications, but the old guard's been stubborn."

I frowned sympathetically. She went on. "Honestly, though, it all worked out for the best. I don't need them." She stopped short in the middle of the sidewalk. A guy behind her barely stumbled to a stop before bumping into her, but he actually smiled at her as he stepped around her instead of cursing. Magic. "Shoot, I meant to get an introductory video when we met up. Can we pretend we're just meeting up on the sidewalk now and film it?"

I will do anything you tell me to do, I didn't say. Instead I just went with "Sure."

A few minutes later, we had videos on each of our phones of the other one walking toward us, smiling and waving. I wondered if anyone would be suspicious of how staged it was, then decided I didn't care. If anybody following me didn't realize how staged everything was, this could be their introduction. "Great, I'll do a quick little explainer of what we're doing and then post a snippet to get people checking in all day," she said, her thumbs already flying over her phone. "The others I've done this with started gaining followers pretty quickly."

Most of my followers were probably already following Jada. What did she have to gain from this? "Thanks. Also, I don't know if I mentioned this already, but this was so nice of you to reach out. I owe you one."

She raised an eyebrow. "Don't mention it. We've got to stick together, you know?"

"What do you mean?"

"Your boy at the *Scroll* has a whole team behind and around him. He's got a network at papers and publications all over the city," she said. I had to speed walk to keep up with her as she deftly wove her way through the crowds on the sidewalk: people sipping drinks outside a bubble tea joint, a woman having a very animated phone conversation beside a Laundromat, delivery drivers zipping past on their electric bikes. There was so much to focus on that I didn't have the mental space to protest her calling Bennett "my boy." "We've only got each other. So we have to be there for each other."

I pressed a hand to the general region of my heart, touched. Even as she went on to say that wasn't strictly true, because now she had a small team to manage her sponsored content and arrange her schedule. My mouth opened to joke that being on her team sounded a lot like

what I did for Mr. Decker but snapped shut before anything could come out. I didn't want to risk sounding silly.

Jada and I continued chatting as I followed her. She
could've been escorting me to an alleyway to murder me,
except that Manhattan didn't have alleyways as such. (A major pet peeve of mine in movies that ostensibly took place
here!) I told her about my older brothers, that we'd grown
up in the Philly suburbs but were now scattered all over the
country, here and Philadelphia and San Francisco and Aus-
tin, about the first mean comment I'd gotten that made me
cry. She told me about how she'd begun reviewing food for
the student newspaper at Spelman College, that she was
considering starting a fashion blog showcasing the finds she
scrounged in thrift and vintage stores and redid herself, that
she had a twin sister who was (gasp) a picky eater whose
favorite foods were white rice and plain chicken.

By the time I was sympathy-cringing at a story of how
Jada baked the most basic vanilla-on-vanilla cake as a surprise for her sister's master's graduation only to have her
sister spit it out because it tasted "too much like vanilla,"
we'd arrived at our first stop. "It's called Brother Rabbit,"
Jada said of the small but sleek storefront, the hanging
sign with rustic lettering upon a silhouette of a very long-
eared critter. "The chef is from New Orleans and her family is from the Caribbean, so it's like a Cajun menu with
Caribbean influences."

A bell over the door rang as we walked in together.
The hostess smiled at her and greeted her by name before
ushering us to a table neatly tucked away in the back. "In-

teresting," I said to Jada as the hostess walked away. A small leafy plant bloomed in the middle of our table; I assumed it was fake until I brushed against it reaching for the menu. "You have a different method than me. I try to be as incognito as possible when going somewhere I'm going to review."

"I respect that," Jada said. She unwrapped her napkin and let it flutter neatly onto her lap. "I just figure at this point, why bother? It's not like they're going to totally revamp their menu for me. I'm not reviewing service. I'm reviewing the food. And I never let them give me free food, because I don't want anyone to think I'm being bribed. I always pay."

"Interesting," I said again, for lack of anything else to say.

She slipped me a half smile. "You don't have to copy what your boy and his friends are doing. We're a whole different thing."

What did she mean by that? Before I could ask, she had her phone out and was speaking into it. "Friends, I have been meaning to come to Brother Rabbit for so long, you don't even know. But I'm so freaking thrilled to finally be trying the . . ."

Should I also be making a video? I went to pull out my phone, then realized I couldn't be talking at the same time that Jada was talking, then re-realized that she was holding her phone out, prompting me to look into it. I instinctively pasted on my biggest smile and gave it a wave. When she nodded almost imperceptibly, I launched into my own spiel, only a split-second pause at the beginning when I realized I couldn't just echo her. "Ever since I started following Chef Brenda, I've been intrigued by . . ."

I was glad the hostess had put us in this little back nook shaded from the stares of the other restaurant-goers. I didn't say that to the camera, though. Jada lowered it and tapped her fingers on the screen. "I'm posting it to my story. You can share it. It looks good if we do a mixture of shared content and filmed content, so you can do the next update."

"Okay, thanks," I said. The waiter came by to take our order. I reached for the menu, realizing as I read it through that Jada was only giving hers a cursory look over. "Do you know what you want to try?"

"*Do* I." Jada's entire face lit up as she went over the dishes she'd heard good things about or that seemed particularly exciting or novel. I found myself agreeing with everything she said. So she ordered, and as the waiter went away, I returned to our conversation from earlier.

"So what you were saying before, about us being a *whole different thing* than the traditional publications . . ."

She stared at me patiently, waiting for me to go on. I kind of hoped she'd take over from where I'd trailed off and elaborate on what exactly she'd meant. Instead, I fumbled. "Because I feel like I do my best to be like one of their food critics. Like, staying as anonymous as possible, all of that."

Jada grinned at me. "If you really wanted a dog, you wouldn't get a fish and expect it to walk on a leash and cuddle with you, would you? No. Fish might look gorgeous in a tank and be interesting to watch, but they just won't do what you want from a dog. If a fish tries to do everything a dog can, it'll fail miserably. So let the fish be the fish."

And then maybe buy that fish a yoga class. "Are we the fish or the dog?"

"We're influencers," Jada said. She brushed a loose braid behind her ear. "And we have so many unique strengths in what we do. You'll miss out on what makes our job truly great if you spend all your time trying to be a pale imitation of something else."

I was saved from having to respond by the arrival of the appetizers. "Let's take our pics."

It was nice to be out eating with someone who knew the importance of getting just the right light and just the right angle, and didn't make me feel even a little bad for taking so long. Who didn't protest about having to stop mid-bite for a great shot and even suggested angles that looked better for each particular food. Honestly, it made me feel a little disloyal to Alice, because she was as great as you could expect a layperson to be. But I was willing to bet that she'd rather have Kelsey than me by her side when it came to . . . I don't know, debugging code or writing a new library or something.

Though being real, I would've eaten beside Mr. Decker if it meant this food. Even though we had ordered light, ordering light for a food reviewer meant ordering a roughly normal amount of food. We noshed first on flaky biscuits that melted in my mouth when slathered with a combination of sweet cream butter, smoky bacon butter, and a spicy drizzle of local honey infused with chiles. Then on a salad, crunchy chunks of iceberg and romaine bathed in a coconut-lime vinaigrette, studded with chunks of roasted squash, sunflower seeds, and crispy pork belly that melted into bacon fat on my tongue.

I sat back with a sigh as the waiter cleared our plates away. It had taken tremendous willpower, but I'd managed not to finish all of the food. "When you talk about unique strengths in what we do, what exactly do you mean?"

"We get to work for ourselves," Jada said bluntly. "Forge our own paths. Nobody's telling me that I can or can't cover a particular restaurant, or take a certain angle on a story. I get to run my own brand and my own look."

Which was great for her, considering she was probably making thousands of dollars a week. Me? Sure, the freedom was great, but was it worth it if there wasn't any security?

She was talking again. "I love being able to be who I am without having to filter myself. No pun intended," she said. I cracked a smile, because we definitely all used filters. "When I was working for the school paper, sometimes I felt like I was trying to be someone else, and it showed. My followers are there for me, not somebody else. If I want to be too real, I can. I can be clear about how much I hate cilantro and not have to worry about appealing to somebody else's readership. If somebody really loves cilantro, they can unfollow me." She cracked a grin of her own. "Or complain in the comments. Their call."

That made me think about my own dislike of wine and the sponsorship offer I still hadn't been able to bring myself to reply to. I opened my mouth to chime in . . . and hesitated. Was I really ready for that?

I could be hypothetical. "Do you ever promote products you don't like?" I asked. She cocked her head. "Like, if a company contacted you and wanted you to promote their . . . premium cilantro, and you really wanted the money but didn't technically need it, would you do it?"

I expected a long answer full of justifications or reasonings, but it ended up being one word. "No."

I blinked at her. She blinked back. "Just no? You wouldn't even think about doing it?"

"Oh, I've done it," Jada said. The corners of her mouth twisted wryly. "When I was first starting out, I shilled these breakfast bars made out of carob and coconut. I don't like carob. As soon as I posted my first one, I felt like such a phony. And people could see it. Every time someone posted that they'd bought them because of me and didn't like them, I felt terrible. I don't feel that way when I'm selling something I actually believe in. It felt wrong, and *I* felt wrong, and I haven't done it since."

It was easy for her to say that now, when she was a big name. Still, it resonated with me. It had felt so good to be real.

But also, the money . . .

She squinted at me like she could see into my head. To keep her from asking more questions, I said hurriedly, "What else do you like about influencing?"

Her eyes widened, but they lingered on me a moment too long, like she knew exactly what I was doing. "Well, aside from what I already said, you can't beat the flexibility. I can schedule reviews when I want, go wherever I want, take vacations whenever I want."

"That must be nice," I said wistfully. I technically got two weeks of vacation a year, but most of those days were taken up with doctor's appointments and things like that. When I had mustered up a week in Maine with a guy I was dating last year, Mr. Decker had the temp calling me twice a day asking for help. Sure, I could've just not picked up. If I wanted to make my boss grumpy.

Grumpy bosses maybe didn't want their assistants making them grumpy in their office anymore.

The waiter arrived with our entrées. Because we'd "ordered light," there were also only two of these. A firm whitefish with crispy skin that glistened under the light and shattered between my teeth, nestled atop a smooth, creamy carrot-ginger puree, luscious with just the right amount of butter (a lot). Roasted carrots, yellow and purple and orange but always caramelized on the outside added pops of sweetness and texture, and candied ginger was sprinkled on top, providing some spice and some chew.

I was sad when it came time to move on to the second entrée, but it cheered me right up. A pasta that had clearly been made here, thick strands that were tender but with a chew to them, bathed in a sauce of coconut milk and garlic and ginger and chiles. I could've slurped this pasta down all on its own, forever, but the buttery chunks of shrimp and crunchy bits of okra scattered throughout made for most welcome diversions. Okra seeds popped with relish on my tongue.

Jada and I got some quick photos of the scraped-clean plates to pair with appropriate drooling emojis, then a selfie of the two of us laughing together over them. I kind of wanted to make it my phone background but instead went to add it to my page, like a normal non-creep. Just as I was about to hit the key to make it live, my phone began to vibrate.

Mr. Decker.

I bit my tongue and sighed at the same time. "I'm really sorry. I have to take this." I hopped to my feet, wincing as my knees hit the bottom of the table. My phone buzzed insistently in my hand; I could practically hear Mr. Decker's impatience on the other side. "I'll be right back." Hopefully.

I wanted to take the call outside, where Jada wouldn't be able to hear and maybe judge me, but threading my way through the crowded restaurant would have taken too long, so I had to answer halfway through. "Good afternoon, Mr. Decker," I said, cutting myself off before I could automatically complete saying my traditional office greeting of *Good afternoon, Mr. Decker's office.* "Is everything okay?"

"You sound like you're out," he non-answered. A little suspiciously, like he was a kid who still thought his teacher lived in the school. Maybe he did think I slept under my desk, using an Ellen's Promise hoodie as my pillow. "I just wanted to tell you what a great job you did."

I cleared the crowd waiting by the hostess stand and made it outside, which really wasn't much quieter than the restaurant. I blinked at a group of guys smoking something that smelled a whole lot sweeter than tobacco. "What?"

"With my wife's party," Mr. Decker said loudly. His words sounded a little looser than usual—not a lot so, but enough where I, who was used to analyzing his words and his tone and inferring his mood and his needs from them, could hear it. Was he tipsy? "My expectations weren't very high because of the time limit, but you blew them out of the water. My wife is delighted. I don't know how to thank you."

How about with a big bonus? I didn't say. Instead, I told him, "Thanks." And then, a little bit reluctantly, "Honestly, Emerson Leigh was a huge help. I don't know if I could've done it all without her."

His laughter roared in my ear. "Good one." And before I could protest that it was true, he'd hung up. Without a goodbye.

I sighed as my phone swung back down to my side. I turned to go back in and nearly jumped out of my jeans. "Jada!" For someone wearing so many crinkly layers, she could move awfully silently. "Didn't hear you there!" Had she heard me? "Should we go back in?"

"I already paid up. Thought I would treat you."

"That's so kind of you, but really, you don't have to!" I blurted. "Do you have Venmo? Let me send you—"

She stopped me with a gentle hand on my shoulder. "Seriously, I wanted to. You'll pay it forward one day." I could do that. Okay. "Besides, it sounds like you deserve it if you're taking work calls on a Sunday."

I flushed. "You heard me?"

She slapped me on the back so hard I actually stumbled forward a step. "*Yes*, I heard you. You sounded like me a couple years ago! I was in marketing until I quit to do this full-time. At a start-up, which meant my boss felt like he could bother me any day, any time."

She'd been where I was. I had to fight the urge to reach out and give her a hug.

"Now I hear from him occasionally, sucking up to me, asking me to do an advertisement for one of his products or talk about a client." Her laugh rang like the tinkling of bells. "It's the best. Ten out of ten, highly recommend."

I followed her to the next place with more pep in my step, dazzled by the thought of Mr. Decker or Emerson Leigh someday sucking up to me. All through our next meals of steamed rice rolls and Southern cuisine and an encore Ethiopian meal we could only eat half of because our stomachs were about to explode, all through the photos we took and videos we shared.

14

I WAS STILL RIDING HIGH WELL INTO THE WORK-
week. Not just because of how well Jada and I had gotten
along and how we'd traded numbers, how I thought we
might actually become real friends and not just social media "friends," but because of the boost our collaboration
had given my page. Thousands of new followers. Lots of
new engagement.

"I'm ready for you, West," I murmured at my desk to
my computer screen, where I was scrolling through the
West African restaurant's menu. I'd finally get to eat there
tonight. That was definitely why I was feeling those excited tingles in my stomach. Yup. The only reason.

I took a few calls for Mr. Decker—he was, for a change
of pace, up in the Hudson Valley today on an anniversary
getaway with his wife—and got back to considering the

menu. Right now my top choices were all meat-related, and we'd want to get some vegetables to balance them—

The office door sailed open, Emerson Leigh's bright laugh floating through a moment before the girl herself did. I fixed a smile on my face, but she was looking over her shoulder, talking to someone behind her. I sat up straighter, hoping she hadn't brought Maisie.

But no. It was worse. As the door opened all the way and Emerson Leigh stepped fully inside the office, I could see him: first a slice, the swooshy hair and pressed button-down (a deep rust-red today), then the whole thing, the long legs and broad shoulders and close-lipped smile.

"Oh, hey, Julie," said Bennett. Like he didn't expect to see me here.

"Hey, Bennett. Hey, Emerson Leigh," I said automatically. My stomach lurched as the door clicked shut behind them, trapping us all inside. My shoulders itched as I watched him watch me sitting behind my desk. It felt weird. All the other times we'd been face-to-face, I'd felt equal to him. Sitting across from him at a restaurant table. Burning his kitchen down beside him. Yelling at each other while standing on equal ground.

But this was different. It was like he had power over me here as a guest of my boss's family. He could ask me to make him some copies or order him some food from downstairs, and I wouldn't be able to say no. Just ask how many or what kind.

". . . so he *did* end up walking down the aisle with his kilt on fire, but nobody felt bad for him since it was really his fault," Emerson Leigh was saying, but Bennett's eyes were on me. He stepped forward, bypassing the front table covered with glossy magazines and copies of Mr. Decker's memoir, through the vacuum of empty carpet, where sometimes I did sit-ups if nothing else was going on, then stopped at my desk, resting his elbows on the ledge surrounding it. I'd always liked that ledge, since it hid the mess of my desk from anyone else in the office and also made for a convenient barrier between myself and some of Mr. Decker's smellier or handsier guests, but now I found myself wishing it wasn't there.

Where would he rest his elbows then?

"Are you ready for West tonight?" Bennett said, and something about his tone disarmed me. He might have been looking down on me—literally, since he was standing and I was sitting—but he wasn't talking down to me. He wasn't making this awkward.

I tilted my computer screen toward him. "I've spent the last hour obsessing over the menu."

Too late, I realized maybe I shouldn't have said that in front of my boss's daughter. She was looking toward me, her eyebrows pinched as if she were annoyed. Hopefully not annoyed enough to go running to her dad about how I was wasting time on the clock.

Bennett said, "I'm very much looking forward to it." Except he said it not while he was looking at the menu but at me. Which made me feel all flustered. Even though he obviously wasn't talking about seeing me but eating at the restaurant.

Right?

Emerson Leigh gave us a cheery laugh, her arms crossed over her designer sweatshirt. "From what you were just telling me about it, the food sounds so good. Hopefully, soon I'll be able to go with you! I wish menus were organized by color; I'm supposed to reintroduce green into my diet soon."

"I've always liked green," said Bennett. Still looking at me. And my green blouse. Okay, now he was *definitely* messing with me.

I went to roll my eyes, only to find out that my eyes wouldn't roll. I stared down into my lap instead, unable to raise them. Because if our eyes met?

I thought they might spark.

"Hey Ben, you know what?" Emerson Leigh said. "Julie makes the best coffee."

Aaaand now I was crashing down to earth. Back in my place. "I don't know if I'd say that," I murmured. "I just stick in the K-Cup and hit the buttons."

"Oh, but something about the way she does it is just magical," Emerson Leigh said to Bennett, speaking over my head. "Ben, do you want some coffee? Julie can go make you some."

My cheeks heated. Why did she have to do this right now? What if he said yes, and I had to obediently get up and trot off to the kitchen to bring him coffee like I was his secretary?

"I'm all right, actually," Bennett said. "But thanks."

Emerson Leigh scooted forward and finally looked at

me. "Julie, Bennett told you that he hates social media, right?"

"I've gathered that," I said dryly.

She paused and looked over at him, as if waiting for him to protest. He didn't say anything. She asked me, "And you're okay with that?" She was picking at one of her cuticles again. Once, Mr. Decker had asked me if I'd be able to make her stop, but fortunately, he'd forgotten about it. "Because your social media is really important to you! Doesn't it hurt your feelings?" She turned and stared at Bennett again.

My stomach flipped at how hard she was picking. She was going to draw blood if she wasn't careful. "I think everybody has their own thing." My voice was careful. If she'd asked me this question only a week ago, I probably would've taken the opportunity to go all in on Bennett, snarking about how he thought he was better than me and most of society, how pretentious he was being. Now? I didn't want to. "As long as he doesn't disrespect me or what I'm doing, he's allowed to like what he likes. For example, I think opera just sounds like screaming, but if somebody's a fan of opera, great! More power to them."

She stared at Bennett again—no, she glared. This time, Bennett sighed. "I don't think social media is stupid. And I have respect for influencers. Maybe I didn't a few weeks ago, but seeing all that Julie did, all she's doing . . ." He trailed off, making my cheeks prickle. "Anyway. I prefer to stay off social media thanks to something that happened in college, when a friend—well, 'friend'—posted pictures of me out partying, which got back to my dad, who was furious. After that, I decided it wasn't worth the trouble."

"I get it," I said. Once, I'd taken a picture with my arm around my (male) cousin, which my then boyfriend had seen and gotten super weird and jealous about. Which really ended up with me determining that social media was great, since I was rid of him after that. "It's cool."

Emerson Leigh sighed dramatically. "Well, *finally*. I thought I'd have to hint for ages to get him to say something to clear that up. Now you guys can get along, right?" She looked from him to me, me to him.

I opened my mouth to tell her that we already were getting along but stopped before any words came out. Maybe he'd been the one telling her we weren't getting along because I thought he looked down at what I did.

Aw. That was so nice of her.

And then she had to go and ruin it. "Julie, I think I left something in the copy room. Can you go find it for me?" She fluttered a hand and placed the back of it gently on her forehead, as if she were just *too* exhausted.

Irritating. Patronizing. But I worked for her father, and I couldn't say no. "What is it, Emerson Leigh?" I asked through gritted teeth as I rose.

She hesitated long enough that I had to hesitate, too, only a few feet away from Bennett. I didn't want to look at him, which meant looking down, which meant focusing in on his hands instead, on how it had felt to hold one, which ultimately was worse than looking into his eyes. "Oh, you'll know it when you see it," she said finally.

I hoped it wasn't one of her clients. I cursed wildly and creatively inside my head as I stepped inside the small, narrow copy room, filled most of the way by the giant copier and stacks of paper and miscellaneous office supplies and extra Ellen's Promise merch Mr. Decker didn't want cluttering up his office. Bennett had probably done this exact same thing before, sent some employee, someone just like me, in search of something he didn't even—

"Julie?" I spun around to find the man himself stepping inside the room after me. The door clicked shut behind him.

I was suddenly aware of how unbearably tight it was in here. Just by coming inside, he was only a few feet away. I crossed my arms over my chest, like that would increase the distance. Make him less likely to see me as an employee. "What is it?" I asked tightly. "Did I take too long? Did Emerson Leigh also want me to bring her a"— I cast my eyes around—"baseball cap with the Ellen's Promise logo?"

"She said I should come help, too—that you might not be able to see it by yourself." He glanced around the room gingerly. "I don't see anything that I recognize as hers, though."

To look anywhere else but on the counters right beside me or on the copier, I'd have to step closer to him. My entire body flushed at the thought. "It's okay, I think I got it. You can go."

"Okay." He twisted himself around and pushed at the door. Then pushed at the door again, jiggling the handle. "Uh-oh. I think it's jammed."

"You probably just didn't push it hard enough. The handle is finicky."

He stepped aside, leaving just enough room for me to push my way through. Not enough room for me to stand there without touching him, though. A lot of him. It was almost like we were spooning standing up, my back against the soft length of his front. I paused for a moment before jiggling the handle myself, luxuriating in the way it made me feel protected. Safe. Even though there was nothing in here I needed protecting from, except maybe myself.

I slammed myself against the handle. He was right: it wouldn't turn. So I banged on the door. "Emerson Leigh?" I called. No response. I banged again. "Emerson Leigh! Emerson Leigh, can you hear me?"

Still no response. Nerves prickled all over my skin, or maybe those were goose bumps, because Bennett was still touching me. "You could go over there, you know," I said.

"I can't," he said. "You're blocking the way."

I spun around, and now heat throbbed all through me from my chest down between my legs, because we were front to front, and my eyes met his with a spark that sizzled, and his voice was husky as he said, "We might die in here."

There are worse places to die, I thought, nestled against his chest, and then I said it out loud. I could feel rather than hear his laugh. And then I was looking up at him, and he was looking down at me, and he asked the question with his eyes, and I answered it, and he bent down, and I lifted my chin and then we were kissing.

Kissing. I was kissing Bennett.

His lips were soft against mine at first, gentle, exploring. But I craved more. I wrapped my arms around his shoulders and pulled him closer, kissed him harder, parted my lips and let his tongue slip inside.

I was kissing *Bennett*.

He made a little noise deep in his throat, a growl or a purr, as he slid his hands down my body to my waist. They touched the exposed slice of skin between my blouse and skirt and *God* that flash of tingly heat made me gasp. Made me want more. Made me want *him*.

"Julie." My name was a plea. I answered him with another kiss, curled myself into him so tight I didn't know if I'd be able to untangle myself from his warm skin and soft curls and the gentle flex of his biceps as he held tight to me.

I didn't want to, though. I wanted to wrinkle that pressed button-down, slip my hand beneath it and trace the divot running down his back, bite his earlobe and feel him shiver. I wanted to—

The door swung open. Emerson Leigh stood there silhouetted against the office, hands on hips. She was smirking, face satisfied like a cat who'd snagged a full salmon fillet from the table. "Found the key!"

She made no comment on our entwined state. An entwined state that was *extremely* unprofessional, considering I was currently at work. For her father. In his office.

What was I *doing*?

I sprang back, shoving Bennett's arms away, my rear hitting a shelf piled high with copier paper and various packages of stationery. I cleared my throat. "Sorry. Um, I couldn't find whatever it was you left in here, Emerson Leigh."

She was still smirking. "No, I think you did."

The words didn't register until I was sitting back at my desk, smoothing down my skirt, taking deep breaths to try and slow my racing heart. Had she set us up in there?

Deep breath in, deep breath out. *Whoooosh*. It wasn't like I could say anything to her. She was my boss's daughter.

"Julie?" Bennett was hovering over my desk now, and I could not deal. I could not deal with this now at work, with Emerson Leigh watching, with Mr. Decker smiling at me from all those copies of his memoir.

"Yes?" I said crisply, picking up a packet of paper from my desk and lining up the edges against the wood like it was the most important thing I had to do all day. Hopefully, he wouldn't notice that the papers were upside down. "I have a lot of professional work to do. In this professional environment."

His shadow moved away. I didn't dare look up until I heard his feet step back. "I see," he said. "Professional. Yes. Well. I should get back to the office. My boss will be looking for me." He cleared his throat. "I'll still see you at West later? I hope?"

"Can't wait," I said, and that was true. I couldn't wait for the food. And maybe there, away from my office and the offspring of my boss, I could talk to him about what had just happened. Emerson Leigh and I watched Bennett lope to the door, look over his shoulder to flash us a lopsided, uncertain smile and then leave.

Deep breath in. The door closed behind him. Deep breath out. Emerson Leigh picked at her cuticle.

I just forced my usual smile onto my face. "Anyway, what's up, Emerson Leigh? Did you need something from your dad's office?" *Aside from the fake thing in the copy room that I couldn't find?*

Before she could respond, the phone rang, the short pattern that meant it was a call from the front desk downstairs. I grabbed for the receiver. "Hello?"

"Hi, Julie? I've got two girls here for you, an Alice Wong and a Kelsey Courtney?"

I blinked in surprise. Had I told Alice we should meet for lunch and then forgotten in my post-Jada haze? No, it would've popped up in my calendar. Also, we never met for lunch, since my office was in Midtown and hers was all the way down in the Financial District. Also also, there was no reason Kelsey would be here, too. "Um, send them up, please? Thank you!"

Emerson Leigh was staring at me, wide-eyed, as I set the phone gently back into its cradle. I said in explanation, "Um, my best friend and her work friend are here? For some reason?"

Those green eyes brightened like a forest beneath the emerging sun. She clapped her hands together. "Oh, how nice!"

When I heard footsteps coming down the hall, I pressed the buzzer under my desk that automatically opened the door. Hopefully, the footsteps belonged to Alice and Kelsey and not two light-footed murderers, though to be real, if someone truly wanted to murder me, the door latch wasn't going to hold them off.

But the door indeed opened to reveal Alice and Kelsey. They rushed in, and everything else around Alice blurred, because her eyes were red.

I didn't think I'd ever seen Alice cry before.

"Who did this?" I said, jumping to my feet. "Say the word and I will murder them. It will be bloody." I paused and considered. "It actually probably won't be bloody. If I were to murder someone, I'd probably poison them, because it's harder to trace and also, hello, upper body strength."

Alice sniffled and swiped at her nose, and she turned her eyes in my direction. They blazed with the fire of the cast-iron pan filled with something bubbling the waiter warns you not to touch when he sets it on your table. "Please don't murder anyone on my behalf. I don't want to have to visit you in prison. It sounds stressful."

"I will do my best to refrain, then," I said. "But what are you doing here?"

"We quit."

"What?"

"Our jobs," Kelsey said, stepping forward.

I blinked. The words took a moment to wind their way into my brain, past all the Emerson Leigh and Bennett–related junk. "You guys quit your jobs? What happened?"

As Alice and Kelsey told their story, their words jumbling together and sometimes spilling over each other, Emerson Leigh and I sat on the couch together, our eyes darting back and forth. The story was one I'd heard from Alice several times before: their teammates being dicks and making their lives difficult.

Only today, Alice had snapped. It hadn't even been because of something "big": it had been the one pate a choux that made the entire pastry tower collapse. One of her teammates had come to her with a pretty basic question about something she'd been working on, then interrupted before she had a chance to fully answer with "that doesn't sound right" and then went to her subordinate dude, who had the same answer. Alice had snorted and rolled her eyes. The first guy had snickered and said, "Of course you'd get emotional."

"I realized I couldn't do it anymore," Alice said, sucking in a deep breath and holding it.

Kelsey continued. "We'd talked about wanting to stick it out to show them we were strong. We didn't want to give them the satisfaction of driving us out."

Alice exhaled long and slow. "But I realized I was dreading going into work. Why were we trying so hard when it's a booming job market out there for software engineers?"

So they wrote out letters stating exactly why they were leaving and posted them on the company-wide Slack channel. "HR's been calling nonstop," said Kelsey. "I had to turn off my phone."

"So now we're jobless," said Alice. She reached up to push her overgrown bangs out of her eyes and . . . Was her arm shaking? No. *All* of her was shaking. "And I'm starting to regret posting that letter for everybody to read. What if it goes around the whole industry? We might be unhirable."

"*I* think that it's badass," Emerson Leigh chimed in. Both Alice and Kelsey jumped, as if they hadn't noticed she was there. Emerson Leigh jumped, too, but to her feet. "So hashtag girl boss. I wish I had some of your nerve." Her lips wavered a little bit, then pressed up into a smile. "Actually, my starting a business takes a lot of nerve. I don't even have time to worry about anything else! Like my . . ." She trailed off, blinking, lips still frozen in that smile.

Alice blinked. "You must be Emerson Leigh."

Emerson Leigh pressed a hand to her chest, now full-on beaming. She was the only person in the room smiling right now. "You've heard of me! Is it because you have a pet and you've thought about signing up for my services?"

"No," Alice said. Emerson Leigh's smile faltered a little. "Julie's told me about you."

"Oh, I see."

"So now we're both freaking out," Alice said, turning back to me. Kelsey nodded in agreement. "Because we don't have jobs, and we don't know if anyone's going to want to hire us. I mean, I'm okay for six months or so if I have to be—I have some money saved up—but I really wanted to save that money for a down payment on an apartment one day."

Kelsey nodded again. "I'm okay for a few months, too. But I have student loans to pay. So many student loans."

"Solidarity." I held out my fist. She wrinkled her brow at it, like she wasn't quite sure what to do, but then gamely gave me a fist bump.

"That really sucks," said Emerson Leigh sympathetically. "But I think it's a good thing you're not there anymore. It sounds like a toxic workplace."

"It really was," said Alice.

"You should just get your parents to help you out," Emerson Leigh said earnestly. I suppressed a sigh. "Even if they just pay your rent for you and float you some extra cash for going out, that'll help a lot."

Alice and Kelsey blinked at her again, as if Emerson Leigh had just touched down from another planet and they were trying to make sense of her green skin, four arms, prismatic eyes. "Um . . . thanks," Kelsey said finally.

Alice did not thank her. "Okay, but in the real world, my parents can't help me, and I don't know what to do."

"It's all going to be okay," I said. "I bet there are plenty of companies who will look at this positively. I know sexism is rampant in the tech industry, but there have to be places out there who are run by or are at least supportive of women. Who knows? Maybe HR is trying to call you to offer you your job back because they fired the dicks on your team."

"I wouldn't want to go back even if they were," Alice said, then looked a little shocked at what had come out of her mouth.

"And it's true, there are so many places out there to work, big companies and small companies and everything in between," said Kelsey slowly. "And the demand is greater than supply right now when it comes to skilled coders."

"That's true," Alice murmured.

They were looking better already, which was encouraging to see. "So take a couple days, see how everything shakes out, then do some research and start sending résumés," I said. I might even be able to get them some good leads through Mr. Decker's contacts, but I'd wait to confirm that before making promises I might not be able to keep. "You'll get snapped up in no time."

Alice sank down into one of the squashy armchairs, propping her elbows on her knees and sinking her face in her hands. "Thanks," she said, her voice muffled. "I'm glad we came here. We stalked out and I just . . . I didn't know where else to go."

A lump rose in my throat. "I'm touched." So much so that I thought I might cry.

"Whatever you do, you should def go wild tonight," Emerson Leigh said. "Like, *wild* wild. If you wake up and remember everything that happened, you didn't go wild enough."

"Definitely. I'm taking you out," I said.

Alice lifted her face from her hands, and the shiny look of optimism on her face made me want to find her the best food, the best drinks, the best place to scream into the void and have nobody look at you. Maybe Times

Square? Probably Times Square, at least when it came to the screaming part. "Thank you, Julie," she said. "I think that's the only thing that could make me feel better."

"Anytime," I said. That settled it. Those expense reports I was supposed to file today could wait. I'd spend the next hour or two, or however long it took for Emerson Leigh to get bored and leave, doing research on where to take them, and then I'd tell Mr. Decker I wasn't feeling well and duck out early. Alice and Kelsey definitely needed the hot chocolate at City Bakery, which might as well have been drinkable fudge, and they closed at four today. So hot chocolate, and then later, for dinner . . .

Dinner.

Bennett.

I was supposed to have dinner with Bennett at West tonight. It had been so hard to get a reservation, and I wanted to eat there so badly, and we had to talk about what happened between us in the copy room, and my followers would love it, and . . .

And I didn't care. Today, my best friend was all that mattered. Oh, and Kelsey, who I'd almost forgotten was here, probably because she'd drifted off to the side and stuck her nose in a copy of Mr. Decker's memoir. Alice cared about her, so I cared about her, too. And she seemed cool. Even if she looked genuinely absorbed by Mr. Decker's detailed account of his extremely standard upper-middle-class upbringing.

"Let me just email Bennett—you know, the *Scroll* critic who I've been collaborating with—and let him know I have to cancel dinner tonight," I said. Emerson Leigh looked up at me from her phone, those green eyes keen.

"Oh, I didn't know—" Alice started, clearly about to demur and tell me to go on without her, but I waved her off.

"It's really okay. It's fine. I want to hang out with you guys tonight. I just have to let him know."

Emerson Leigh's mouth dropped open with what looked like dismay. "You can't abandon Bennett! Not after your—" Her mouth snapped shut. Our kiss. She was referring to our kiss. Which had been today. God, it felt like it had been ages already, like I'd always kissed Bennett. And she was right, partially—I did want to talk to him about that kiss. About how maybe it could be something more.

But my best friend was more important right now. No matter how magical that kiss had been, it could wait another day.

"I have to. Maybe you can take my place at West tonight." The idea gave my stomach an uneasy jolt. I didn't like the idea of Emerson Leigh and Bennett sitting on either side of a cozy table, laughing with their perfect white teeth on display as they shared tuna tartare off a single spoon. (I don't know why the restaurant only had one spoon, okay? Maybe the dishwasher broke.)

Emerson Leigh's forehead crinkled with a frown. "I can't, Julie. I'm still eating only white food. Remember?" How could I forget? "You'll talk to him soon, though, right? He's just . . ." She sighed.

"Yes." I could promise that much at least. "I will."

She nodded at me, then popped to her feet, flipping

her blond ponytail over her shoulder. "Good. Anyway, I should probably head out. I have *so* much work to do today. You guys are actually kind of lucky that you just get to chill for a bit!"

If it were anybody but Emerson Leigh, I'd think they were being mean, but she actually meant it. Still, Alice's nostrils flared. "Good seeing you, Emerson Leigh!" I as good as ushered her out with a hand on her lower back. As soon as the door clicked shut behind her, I hightailed it back to my desk to fake sick for Mr. Decker, grab my bag, and hustle out. "Have you ever had City Bakery hot chocolate?" I asked them as the door closed behind us. Hopefully, Emerson Leigh hadn't dawdled in the elevator or lobby; it would be awkward if we caught up to her.

Alice snorted. "I'm your best friend. Of course I've had City Bakery hot chocolate."

"I've never had it!" Kelsey said. I wrapped my arm around her shoulders as we walked. Her hair smelled a little like dried apricots.

"Kelsey Unknown Middle Name Courtney," I said solemnly. "I am about to rock your world."

SEVERAL HOURS LATER, I had both rocked her world and discovered her middle name was Eloise. "I can't believe that hot chocolate was a drink and not a drug," she said. "Something that good can't be legal."

The one sore spot of the evening was that I'd reached into my bag for my phone after the hot chocolate so we could figure out the best way to get to the K-Town restaurant I'd chosen for dinner and realized that my phone was not there. "Crap," I said. I could visualize it sitting on my desk, next to the work phone and the stack of expense reports I was supposed to file. Lot of good it was doing me there.

"What?"

"Left my phone at the office," I said. Thank goodness I hadn't left my keys behind, too. "But it's fine. You'll just have to look up directions."

My phone could wait until tomorrow morning. Still, even though I knew humans had survived without smartphones for thousands upon thousands of years, I felt unmoored without mine, like one of my hands had been bound up in an immovable cast. I kept reaching for it to check the time, if it was supposed to rain, what my latest comments said. *This is probably good for you*, I told myself. *You can prove you're not addicted.*

It felt weird, too, not taking pictures of my food. Critics of food influencers always said that food tasted better when you didn't focus on taking pictures of it. But as I ate the crackling hot bibimbap bowl piled with tender shreds of spicy beef and all sorts of vegetables, all brought together by the oozy fried egg on top, I didn't feel that way. Maybe it made me a stupid millennial, but I *liked* having pictures of my food. When I scrolled back through my photos, it meant that I got to relive this day, to think about how delicious each element had been instead of forgetting about it. The pictures made it easier for me to remember each experience than any number of words describing them could.

I raised my glass. The soju cocktail was sweet and spicy and almost gone. "To the crusty old men who give me side-eye every time I take pictures of my food!" I sipped before Alice and Kelsey could toast me, because this toast wasn't really for them. "Fuck you!"

This may have been my third soju cocktail.

Our last stop of the night was in Times Square, a place I usually did absolutely everything in my power to avoid. It was always loud and flashy, crammed with obnoxious tourists, full of places that insulted the New York food scene with their very existence in the city, like Applebee's and Olive Garden (even if I did have a soft spot for their breadsticks).

But it became a different place late at night. All the families had scurried back to their hotels to put their kids to bed. The big stores were closed, but the lights all still flashed overhead, blue and red and green and yellow, screaming neon into the night sky. There were still plenty of people milling about—it would get empty after midnight, but we were almost thirty, and I had work tomorrow—but there was enough room for us to stake out a clear spot in the middle of it all.

"Ready?" I asked them, tilting my head back so that the world spun crazily around me, flashing lights blurring and advertisements of beautiful women and men with guns in TV shows and skyscrapers rising impossibly high until they disappeared into the clouds.

"Ready."

We opened our throats and screamed all our frustrations into that sky. If it could handle all these lights every hour of the day, it could handle our screams, too, for a little while.

15

I ARRIVED AT WORK THE NEXT MORNING—EARLY, so early—with a squint and a feeling like somebody had smacked me over the head with a good-quality cast iron.

"This never happened in college," I muttered as I dragged myself into the lobby of Mr. Decker's office building. Even through my vintage cat-eye sunglasses, the marble floors gleamed so brightly they made my eyeballs ache. "What I wouldn't give for my twenty-two-year-old body. Not the brain, but definitely the body."

I pressed my palms together and prayed in the elevator to every god who'd ever existed, then breathed a long stream of thank-yous once I entered the office and found it blessedly empty. The cup of coffee I brewed up was much stronger than usual. Double strength so that I'd at least be reasonably functional by the time Mr. Decker got in.

Though really, nothing made me feel more functional

than slipping my phone back into my hand. Maybe I *was* actually an addict. I could worry about that later. For now, I immediately clicked into my account, made sure no major trolls had set up shop overnight (just one minor one, who I blocked immediately). Good. Then over into my texts. My mom had texted me; from the lack of response by now, the police might be showing up at the office any moment to make sure I was still alive. I texted her back to assure her I wasn't dead.

No other non-work-related messages, but I did have a bunch of missed calls. All from Bennett. I frowned thoughtfully at the screen. That was weird. Maybe he'd been so overcome by the meal at West that he had to rhapsodize about it right then and there? Or maybe his building management was charging him for the oven and he wanted to collect my half of the bill? That would suck.

Or was it about our kiss? Had he panicked?

I swallowed hard. It was kind of early to call him back, and also, that would have involved talking on the phone, so I turned to email. Hey there—saw all your missed calls. What's going on?

I then had to get into all the emails I'd missed yesterday afternoon and evening, and then Mr. Decker showed up, and I had to get him his coffee and brief him on the calls he had coming up today, so it was a while before I realized Bennett hadn't responded to me. Which was kind of weird, since he always got back to me so quickly. But he easily could've been having a busy day at work, or maybe . . .

Could he have been calling me over and over because something was wrong?

Sweat broke out on the back of my neck as I connected Mr. Decker to his noon conference call. I couldn't stop the images running through my mind: Bennett blearily stepping into the path of a speeding cab while hungover. Bennett slipping on clumsy feet and falling down a flight of stairs. Bennett reaching for his phone with a bloody, broken hand and calling me.

Bennett not injured, not dying, but realizing that he'd made a huge mistake kissing me. That he'd been terribly unprofessional and wanted to make sure I knew it right away.

I took a deep breath. I was actually going to make a phone call on my personal phone. A big day. I picked up my phone and hit the button to return his call.

It went straight to voice mail, which was anticlimactic.

I didn't bother leaving one, instead clicking back over to my email. Hey, not to pester, but just wanted to make sure you were okay! Please let me know. Ugh, I sounded so needy, but it couldn't be helped. I gritted my teeth and clicked send.

The response came immediately. I'm fine.

Two words. With a period and everything. I waited a few more minutes, in case maybe he was typing something more and had accidentally hit send too soon, but no. Nothing. If I followed up with that, though, I'd seem even needier than before. Pushier.

And then I realized that I didn't care. I blinked, surprised at my own daring. I was quite liking this new give-no-fucks version of myself. So I sent back, Sorry if I'm being paranoid or something, but you don't sound fine? Is it about what happened yesterday? When we kissed? I took a deep breath. Because you don't have to worry about it. We can just pretend it didn't happen. I grimaced as soon as the message left my inbox. Alice would shake her head, tell me I should never start an email to a guy with "sorry" unless I'd truly done something wrong.

Oh well. Too late now.

He wrote back with, Yes.

Wow. Rude. It was like he'd actually reached out and cut me; pain flashed across my abdomen. But Mr. Decker's conference call was ending, and then I had to run down and grab him lunch—turkey sandwich with provolone cheese and pickles, hold the mustard, salt and vinegar chips on the side but only if they're kettle-cooked—so it was a little bit before I could get back to Bennett. Which was good, because it kept me from writing back something charged and confused like, *What the fuck, you passive-aggressive jerk?*

So I sent back, Can you elaborate, please? I thought we were being professional, and this isn't very professional.

Another email popped up as soon as that one went out, but it wasn't Bennett psychically being aware of what I was going to send before I sent it. It was Emerson Leigh, an automated reminder for her party that was happening in—ugh, seriously? How had it snuck up on me so fast?—only a few days. She'd added on a personalized message. I decided on yellow for staff! So wear your finest yellow outfit. ☺

Naturally. I looked terrible in yellow.

"Julie?" Mr. Decker called from his office. "Come here for a second."

But I hesitated, because just then, an email from Bennett popped up. Long enough where I couldn't read the whole thing in the preview. I'd have to click on it. "Julie?" Mr. Decker called again.

I made a split-second decision. Picked up the office phone. "Good afternoon, Mr. Decker's office!" I said loudly and chirpily into the dial tone. That would buy me a minute or two, so I clicked on the email.

> You were a no-show at West last night. I called you over and over to see if you were going to make our reservation, but you never answered your phone. I understand that you want to keep things professional after what happened yesterday. That's entirely fine, and I agree with you that we should just pretend our slip of judgment didn't happen. But skipping our reservation due to our unprofessional personal matters is decidedly NOT professional. You could have at least told me you weren't going to show.
>
> Best regards,
> Bennett

I sucked in a breath. Somehow the most painful part of that email was the sign-off. I'd been relegated from a friend back to a business acquaintance. A laugh almost bubbled up. Imagine me thinking that only a couple weeks ago.

How had he not gotten my email? I remembered telling Alice and them that I needed to email Bennett to let him know I wouldn't be able to make it . . .

. . . and then I realized I had rushed out without actually sending the email.

Crap.

Well. At least this had exposed how Bennett really felt about us. About the kiss. That it was a big mistake and we should keep things professional.

Which was fine. It was what I wanted, too. Right?

Suddenly, the plastic of the phone was cold against my ear. I pitched my voice extra loud to make sure Mr. Decker would be able to hear. "Thank you, but we're not interested at this time." And I hung up. Took a deep breath. Forced my shoulders back. Pasted on my big fake smile and strode into Mr. Decker's office.

"What's up?"

Once I'd helped Mr. Decker figure out some travel options for later this year, I hurried back to my desk and opened my email back up. Bennett, I'm so sorry. I had an emergency situation pop up yesterday with my best friend, and I needed to be there for her. I seriously was about to email you but I got frazzled and caught up in the emergency and totally flaked, and then I accidentally left my phone in the office, because again, frazzled. No excuses, I'm sorry.

His tone had decidedly softened with his next message. I'm glad you're okay. And I hope everything is okay with your friend, too.

I think she'll be fine. I hope so, anyway. I paused, then added, How can I make this up to you? I shivered a little as I sent it with the unknown, because even if we were definitely keeping things professional going forward, anything could come back.

Anything.

What did actually come back made me pause. I'm scouting a fancy French restaurant for the *Scroll* tomorrow night for an updated review. Sebastian. Not the kind of place you typically review. In fact, the kind of place you typically scorn for being pretentious and overly expensive. I want you to come with me.

I was familiar with Sebastian, but I googled it just to make sure my familiarity was correct. A meal there came out to a few hundred dollars, easily. The *Scroll* review from one of Bennett's predecessors almost ten years ago extolled the cuisine as masterful, fine-tuned, classic. Photographs displayed big white plates with a few bites of food artfully arranged in the middle, waiters in tuxedos, exclusive bottles of wine. I sighed.

I'd probably overdraft myself again if I didn't move money around. I could probably delay my rent by a few days until my next paycheck came in, though Marcus wouldn't be happy. No eating out next week. I could keep my page updated with some flashbacks, or I could do a fun countdown of the best whatever type of restaurants each day. People loved countdowns and getting to share their own favorites.

The funny thing, I realized as I emailed Bennett back to confirm the time of the reservation, was that I hadn't even considered not going. I hadn't even considered not making it up to him.

EVEN THOUGH SEBASTIAN was located in a grand, stately former hotel in that border area between Midtown and the Upper East Side, the dining room was modern, light, and airy, with tables spread out beneath an atrium sparkling with chandeliers. I guess with a menu that cost as much as it did, they could afford to give diners a little extra space.

The white-gloved waiter actually pulled my chair out for me as I sat. I giggled self-consciously as he walked away. Thank goodness I'd gone for the dressier end of business casual today with the dark green Anthropologie dress I'd thrifted that tucked in at the waist and flared out at the bottom and made me feel really, really pretty. Especially thank goodness, considering Bennett had dressed up in a suit. A charcoal gray suit that had clearly been tailored specifically for him, considering the way it clung to his broad shoulders and followed the form of his body all the way down. The same body I'd pulled close to me, hard against me, ran my hands down as his mouth melted into mine.

I took a long sip of my water. Perfectly tepid, though for once I kind of wished it was ice-cold. *Professional. We're keeping it professional.*

"So what do you usually order here?" I asked, reaching for the menu. Which did not have any prices listed. Great.

Well, usually vegetarian entrées were cheaper than meat or fish, so I could order this risotto and hope for the—

"It's a tasting menu," Bennett said. "Which I love, because then we don't actually have to decide. We just get everything." He hadn't even bothered looking at the menu. Instead, he was gazing across the table at me, head cocked, like he was hoping to see my reactions to the listed food.

I ducked my head. He was a professional food reviewer. He really should be looking at the menu.

The first course arrived before we'd even ordered anything. A potato chip on a tiny plate, heaped with glistening black pearls of caviar, topped with a spoonful of something creamy and white and speckled with something else pale and yellow. I loved caviar. This would be exciting if this single potato chip didn't probably cost, like, twenty dollars. "Bottoms up."

Even though I wasn't technically reviewing this place— not my brand—I couldn't help but analyze the bite as I crunched down. The potato chip was one of the best potato chips I'd ever had, and let me tell you, I know my potato chips—it was shatteringly crunchy but not hard, still crispy beneath its layers of toppings, salty and savory and a little oily without being overly so. The white cream on top was rich and sour, the shavings of hard-boiled egg yolk on top softening its tart edges. But the star of the dish was the caviar, and it didn't disappoint. Each little bubble burst on my tongue with the essence of the sea itself.

I'd closed my eyes as I chewed so that I could focus more intently on the food without getting distracted by anything around me, so it wasn't until I opened them that I realized Bennett hadn't eaten his yet. "What?" I asked, because he was staring at me, a little smile playing on his lips.

"Nothing," he said. "You just . . . really looked like you liked it."

I licked a smear of sour cream off my lip. "I did."

He went in for his own bite then, popping it in his mouth with his eyes closed, head tilted to the side as if he were listening for some distant sound. He managed to get a smear of cream on his lip, too, and when he opened his eyes and the pink tip of his tongue darted out to retrieve it, my heart skipped a beat. "The amuse-bouche is always one of my favorite parts of the meal. It's like a little experiment every time. It's not on the menu, so the chef is allowed to take themselves less seriously."

I liked them, too. Amuse-bouche literally meant something like "fun for the mouth" in French. How could you not like something with that name?

"I really hope this place is as good as I remember it," Bennett said softly, leaning in. He paused as the waitress came by to collect our amuse-bouche plates. "I was scared to come do this review."

"Because of living up to the previous reviewer's take?" His elbows were on the table. I thought that was supposed to be rude, but it was comfortable, and if he was doing it, I could do it, too.

He shrugged. "A little. I mean, he gave it four stars. The highest rating you can give. But things have changed since then. And I don't mean the chef or the menu. I mean

the times. Of what people find important in their food."
He glanced at me, and I knew he was thinking about the
rise of people like me.

"Well, I'm not reviewing today," I assured him, but
that didn't mean much. Jada Knox had already come here
for a review. She'd rated the food highly, saying that it
wasn't stuffy like some of the other fancier French places,
but that it was overpriced and not as innovative as it could
be. She'd also noted that she was one of the only Black
people in the building, including among the staff.

Bennett's apprehensive expression didn't budge. "Don't
you remember the big fuss when Pete Wells at the *New
York Times* downgraded Per Se from four to two stars? It
was a huge deal. Like a bomb had gone off. People lost
their jobs."

"No, but I remember his review of Guy Fieri's Times
Square restaurant." He didn't laugh. I softened. "You don't
even know if you're going to have to downgrade it yet.
Why don't you eat the meal first and see?"

He nodded once at me, resolute. "You're right."

I tried to make small talk until the dishes started arriv-
ing, but my usual topics—the weather, the food ahead,
how terrible the subway was—didn't gain any traction.
Maybe he didn't take the subway. Maybe he took a chauf-
feured car around all the time. "The traffic in New York is
terrible," I said, but the food started coming before I could
test my hypothesis.

We ate a fish tartare studded with hearts of palm and
sparkling with yuzu, plush and meaty; a sweet, flaky salad

of king crab crunchy with apple and a fried apple chip; and seared scallops with a crispy crust served over braised fennel. "So?" I asked when I'd set my fork down. The first two courses had been good enough that I'd forgotten how much I was paying for this meal; the third one was good, but not that good. "Thoughts so far?"

His eyes were still closed as he chewed his last bite of scallop, but they opened at my question. "Extremely good," he said. "And the service is impeccable."

As if summoned by the praise, a duo of silent busboys appeared to whisk our plates away and clean up the piece of fennel I'd dropped on the tablecloth and hadn't noticed. One refilled my water glass without spilling a drop, then they vanished just as quickly as they'd appeared before I even had the chance to thank them.

"I was probably ten the first time my dad brought me and Penny here." Bennett's eyes had closed again, as if he were trying to taste the memory, too. "He said he hadn't wanted to bring us to a place like this before we were old enough to behave." Not to appreciate it, I noted. "I don't remember all the dishes we had, but I do remember there was this seared tuna with sesame and seaweed. Very rare in the middle, nearly raw. Perfectly cooked, of course, but that wasn't how Penny and I saw it back then. She refused to eat it, which made my dad shake his head and turn to me. The idea of biting into that tuna made me want to throw up, but the idea of disappointing my dad and making him shake his head at me like he had at Penny made me want to throw up even more.

"So I ate that tuna, and to my surprise, I liked it. My dad had only said that we should try one bite of everything, but I ate all of it, and for the rest of the meal we analyzed each dish the way I do in my reviews. It was fun. I was good at it."

"So this is where you realized your calling."

"In a way." He finally opened his eyes in time for the next course to show up. The white truffle risotto, creamy and fragrant and probably very, very expensive. The first bite literally melted into my mouth, coating it with velvety richness. I groaned out loud.

Because of all the groaning, actual conversation was impossible until the plates had been scraped clean. "Don't get me wrong, the food here is excellent," I said. "But the market's been trending away from restaurants like this. Do you think there's still a place for Sebastian and its ilk?"

His eyes lit up, and then they blazed, or maybe it was that his glasses magnified the light and heat. "Most of the people here aren't the ultrarich. They're people who save up and come out for a big birthday or an anniversary or another special occasion for the Sebastian experience. The food and the service and the ambience. They come to be treated like kings and queens for a night.

"And don't get me wrong," he continued. "I love what's trending right now. I love that chefs and cooks are bringing creative, exciting food to people for less money. I love that different styles of cuisine are getting more attention and that the major food scene is finally understanding that Chinese food and Indian food and Thai food are as intricate and worth as much money as French food or New American food. I love how innovative chefs are becoming with how they sell their food and how pop-ups and food trucks and things like that are allowing great chefs to share their food with people without the immense resources needed to open a restaurant. I think it's all great."

What he was talking about were the types of food I highlighted on my page. And as his eyes flashed at me, I knew it. He was talking about me.

"I just think," he continued, "that there is room for all kinds of food out there. Don't you?"

What he was really saying: there's room for both of us on the scene. The stodgy newspaper reviewer and the influencer.

I realized for the first time that I wasn't thinking of the former with envy. Because did the small restaurants producing that creative and innovative food, experimenting with all new things and all new styles, feel envy for places like this? Maybe for the financial security their name and reputation provided. But they wouldn't be able to experiment as much, try new things, with all these bills to pay and that reputation to uphold. Push come to shove, did I think most of them would throw away what they were doing to do this instead?

I didn't think they would. I didn't think *I* would. Jada had been right. We did have unique strengths of our own. We could be real and be great.

I jumped to my feet, nearly colliding with the waitress carrying out plates of venison with cranberry and apple and charred cabbage. The smells drifting off them were delicious, but I was more impressed by the fluid way the waitress managed to sidestep me without so much as a cranberry rolling off a plate. The training here really was amazing.

I noticed Bennett was staring at me, baffled, only once I was already standing. "I have to go to the bathroom," I blurted, and whirled around. The waitress somehow pointed the way for me with her hands full. I thanked her and rushed off, realizing too late that it probably looked like I was having some kind of gastrointestinal emergency. Wonderful.

But I really needed to collect myself. Take a few deep breaths of the fancy rose-scented candle burning sweetly on the sink. Luxuriate in the toilet paper that was thicker and softer than any of my hand towels. Slip a few complimentary travel-sized bottles of expensive hand lotion into my purse. And really let this seismic change in how I felt toward my life and my job roll through me while I wasn't expected to keep eye contact and make polite conversation.

I hadn't looked down on any of the restaurants or food trucks I'd covered on my page. I'd been more impressed by them than these fancy French places. (Though now, I did have to admit, they were pretty good, too, or at least this one was.) I shouldn't have assumed everybody was looking down on me.

Though let's be real, a salary and benefits for my food

stuff would be really nice. And maybe that's what my continued association with Bennett and the *Scroll* would get
me, if my follower count kept jumping up and up and up.

Or maybe it would keep going up if I was more honest
with my followers, like how they'd loved me and my cooking disaster.

Which meant I had an email to send. I pulled out my
phone and navigated to the message the wine company
had sent me. They'd checked in a couple days ago to make
sure I'd received their first email, since I hadn't responded.

I could do this. I could be myself. And I could feel
good doing it.

> Hi! Sorry for the delayed response. I really appreciate you
> reaching out, and your product looks great, but I don't think
> it's a good fit for me. (I'm not the biggest wine fan.) Best of
> luck, though! I'm sure other people will jump all over it. ☺

Send. Done. I smiled at myself in the mirror, and I
actually liked what I saw.

Hopefully, other people would, too.

I stayed there, blinking at myself in the mirror, until
another person came in and gave me an odd look. I headed
back out into the restaurant, where our table was clear. At
my questioning look, Bennett said, "They'll bring new
plates of venison out now that you're back." Sure enough,
it was only a few minutes before the waitress returned. I
waited for him to ask me if everything was okay, but he

didn't. I did catch his eyes lingering on me as we ate our venison, though. And our steak and the collection of pastries that came out with a surprisingly mellow sesame ice cream topped by a sticky caramel brittle.

I took a deep, fortifying breath as the waitress cleared our dessert plates, steeling myself for the check. No matter what, it was going to hit me like a sock to the stomach, but if I clenched up all my stomach muscles, it would hurt less.

So, I was surprised when the waitress showed up instead with our coats. Bennett stood and shrugged his on, hesitating when I didn't move. I cleared my throat, hating how awkward it felt to talk about money. "Um, the check? We haven't paid?"

"Oh, I, um . . ." The tips of his ears were turning red again. He rubbed at the back of his head, turning his elbow into a wing. "I paid the check while you were in the bathroom."

He'd paid for me. Like this was . . . a date. Maybe . . . he didn't actually want to keep things professional?

"Not like a date," he added hastily. "Um. Because I'm reviewing this place. I put it on the company card. They always pay for my meals. Um. That I review."

My cheeks heated the way I was sure his ears were. Of course. I always paid for Alice when we went out. This was a business dinner. A professional business dinner. For both of us.

But as he held the door for me, as I declined a nightcap (my body was ready to give out after that hangover), it didn't feel like one.

16

ALICE AND I USED TO TEXT EARLY IN THE MORN-
ing, but no longer. Now when I texted her, she wouldn't
respond until ten or eleven. Sleeping late. Which was good;
she deserved to get some rest after everything that had
happened. But I thought she'd want to know about the
exposé published on Jezebel that recounted the experiences of women in tech and that quoted her and Kelsey's
letter.

Thanks, Alice said. They asked to interview me, but I
declined. Now I guess my name's out there anyway.

Hopefully, it'll be a good thing, I texted back. I considered making a joke about how she was famous, but it didn't
seem like the moment. Dinner soon? There's this new Ha-
waiian place in the East Village I've been dying to try.

As long as you're paying.

"Julie?" Mr. Decker called from his office. I hopped to my feet before he even said, "Come in here for a second."

I walked into his office to find him surrounded by garment bags. I blinked in surprise. "How did these get in here?"

"Emerson Leigh must have stopped by late last night and dropped them off."

"I see." I girded myself. "What's in them?"

I imagined shapeless yellow sacks she'd sent over for me since she didn't trust my fashion sense, but if that was the case, she would've left them draped over *my* desk. Mr. Decker nodded toward them, meaning I should go ahead and open them up. I found an assortment of suits and ties, combinations I never would've selected in a million years. A white suit with orange trim and a glittery silver tie. A pale pink suit with a tie striped blue and green. A charcoal gray suit with a muted red tie I thought would be the least offensive of the bunch until he motioned for me to pull it up . . . which placed on display the frayed cutoffs it was paired with.

"What do I do?" Mr. Decker asked me. The pure, panicked helplessness in his eyes, that of a vegetarian brought for a birthday dinner at a barbecue joint where even the salad has bacon on it, almost made me laugh. I held my breath for a moment, forcing it back down.

"I assume she had these sent over for you to wear to her party?" I asked.

He nodded.

"Why don't you tell her that none of them spoke to you and you're just going to wear something from your closet that you're comfortable in?"

Mr. Decker, small behind that massive antique desk, pressed his lips together. Over his shoulder I could see all the way down into Rockefeller Plaza, the tourists swarming like ants. Well, ants with cameras. "I don't want to hurt her feelings."

"Maybe there's a compromise to be had." I turned to study the offerings. "Like, you could wear one of the ties she picked out with one of your own suits?"

He blinked at them and scratched his thick head of silver hair. "Maybe. That's an idea." He turned to eyeball me. My skin prickled. I was used to him looking over me or past me or through me, not at me. "Emerson Leigh told me about your side project, and I took a look at your . . . what is it? Social media page?"

I nodded, holding my breath. I didn't even know why I was nervous. I was a good assistant, even with only half my brain dedicated to the task. He wasn't going to fire me for having a hobby. Maybe it was that I cared what he thought of me or that I cared that he was finally thinking of me at all.

"I really need to try that . . . what was the place?" Mr. Decker gave me a tiny smile. It looked out of place on his broad face. "The one with the lobster and waffles?"

My shoulders relaxed. "Daily Catch." I leaned in a bit, as if confiding in him. Which didn't make any sense, since we were the only two people in the office, but somehow it felt like the right move. "And the lobster and waffles is truly excellent, but make sure you get the clam chowder. It's really special."

He looked down and reached for something on his desk, and for a moment I thought he was dismissing me, until I saw what he'd grabbed was a pen. I could read the words he scribbled upside down on his monogrammed stationery: *Daily Catch, clam chowder.* "Thanks. I'll have to get your recommendations for business lunches more often."

This time when he looked down, it *was* a dismissal. Even though he couldn't see me, I bobbed my head almost like a curtsy. A warm glow spread through me as I walked back into the main area and to my desk, and it took me a moment to realize what it was.

Pride.

But it flared into something else entirely when I noticed Bennett's name in my email inbox. This time, it didn't take me a moment to figure out what it was.

Bennett's words dampened it. As I read, my eyebrows knitted themselves together, the way my brothers used to say would give me wrinkles.

Julie,

I've received some news from my editor and our social media team this morning: they say that our two joint reviews did well enough, but that demand for them has quieted down and that it's time for me to return to my standard fare.

I hate to admit it, but I've quite enjoyed our work together and have learned a lot. I hope you'll say something similarly mushy in response, or else I'll feel like a fool.

Bennett

"No," I said out loud. To the email, to the universe, I didn't know.

"What?" Mr. Decker yelled from his office.

"Sorry, talking to myself!" I yelled back, then whispered, "Fuck."

I didn't want our professional time together to end, especially considering that was the only time he seemed to want from me. I didn't want to stop seeing Bennett.

And it sounded like he felt that way, too.

Emboldened by his confession of mush, I wrote back without thinking about it too hard.

Bennett,

I've enjoyed to the extreme making you feel like a fool, so I don't want to say anything in response. (Though, *cough*, I have learned a lot and MAY have enjoyed parts of it, too, *cough*.)

Surely the *Scroll* wouldn't say no to a grand finale at Alpaca House. I've already made the reservation. What do you say?

Julie

I knew he'd been wanting to try Alpaca House for ages. I had, too. Located out in Williamsburg, it was known for its Nikkei cuisine, the fusion of Peruvian and Japanese cuisines—Peruvian ingredients, Japanese techniques—that resulted when Japanese immigrants made their home in Peru. Two Nikkei restaurants in Lima, Central and Maido, were regularly listed among the world's best. I hoped I'd get to go south someday and try them.

His response dinged. I say yes. They will, too. We have to give our fans notice, after all. Ugh. Saying we have "fans" sounds so bizarre. When is the reservation?

One little white lie: I hadn't actually made the reservation yet. I clicked over to the restaurant site and, as expected, there were no open reservations for the next week. So I gave them a call and spoke (pleaded) with a very kind (patient) host, who found (descended from the heavens and blessed me with) a reservation that had just been canceled tomorrow night after I pulled out Mr. Decker's name. It was early, meaning I'd have to duck out before the end of the workday, but Mr. Decker usually didn't stay past four. Tomorrow at six. Is that okay?

See you then.

THE NEXT NIGHT at 6:05, I hurried beneath the expressway toward Alpaca House, cars zooming all around me. The light changed halfway through, and the cars honked, grilles and lights forming furious faces in the gloom of the underpass.

Bennett's face, fortunately, was not that furious when it caught sight of me outside the restaurant. "I'm sorry,"

I said hastily, a little out of breath. "The train was delayed, and—"

"Don't worry about it. You're here." He was already opening the door, pausing a moment to hold it for me. "Let's eat."

The inside was bright and cheerful, larger than it looked, with a long bar running down the center and jangling music playing all around us, probably to cover up the sound of the highway. The host ushered us to a table on one side, beside a bright mural of a red-and-yellow alpaca. He was licking his lips, eyes wide and excited. I glanced at him sidelong as we sat. "Do you think he's gearing up to eat us or eat our food?"

"Either way, I think we'd better gear up for a fight," said Bennett. "Butter knives won't be enough. I hope their steak knives are sharp."

"Do you think it would be too much to ask the kitchen for a cleaver?" I asked, and before I knew it, the two of us were snorting with laughter. "Just kidding. I'm kind of afraid of cleavers. I feel like I'd pick one up and it would immediately animate itself and chop off one of my hands."

"A common cause of injury," Bennett said seriously. "I myself have done away with some of my competition through mysterious cleaver accidents. The police didn't so much as bat an eye."

The alpaca only looked more menacing as our appetizers arrived. "I'm not so sure about this one," Bennett said, looking down into the salad that had landed before him.

"I know, me neither," I said. "But pretty much every review online called it out, so I figured we should give it a try."

We both went in for a bite, our spoons clinking against each other over the wide blue bowl. I understood his hesitation because the combination of ingredients inside just seemed so bizarre: soft pearls of earthy quinoa formed the base, mixed with chewy bits of slab bacon, avocado, bananas, and Brazil nuts. I popped the spoonful into my mouth and chewed, expecting these ingredients to clash with one another.

But they didn't. They sang together, the saltiness and chew of the bacon mixing with the sweet, silky banana and grassy, buttery avocado. The salty crunch of the Brazil nuts gave the dish texture, and the quinoa was a fairly neutral stage for all the rest to shine. The whole effect was unique, something I wasn't quite sure how to write about. How to put it all into words. *But*, I thought as I cocked my head, *it'll speak really well in a photo, where you can see all these different things mashed up against one another. It'll be beautiful, like its taste.*

I'd have no problem describing the ceviche in words. Raw sea bass, firm and gleaming and presenting just a little resistance to my teeth, marinated in an explosion of sour citrus and ripe garlic and crunchy onion, chile peppers sparking heat on my tongue. The fierce citrus cooked the fish in a way that allowed the essence of the fish to shine through along with the marinade, untouched by fire. To soothe the intense flavors of the ceviche, it was served alongside a simple mashed sweet potato and crunchy pieces of giant corn that tasted like a purer corn chip.

We also noshed on maki rolls filled with eel and cream cheese, a strange combo of fat and fat that somehow worked, a salad of pickled sunchokes, some charred octopus with yucca root. I pushed away the appetizer plates with a groan. Somehow we'd picked them all clean. "Okay, I'm full. Time to go home."

His eyes widened with alarm. "You don't mean that."

"Of course I don't mean that." Again, my superpower: I never really got full. I could probably eat forever, though I'd never actually tried. My stomach might explode, like a goldfish. "I'll fight you for the last fry."

"I'm a formidable opponent," he warned.

"Yeah, but I've got the alpaca on my side." I glanced over at the cartoony mural, where the alpaca was still staring greedily at our empty plates. "You might not have noticed, but I've been sneaking him pieces of ceviche."

Bennett smacked his forehead with his palm. "How could I have missed that?"

We both laughed as the waitress came to take our plates away. "So," Bennett said, steepling his fingers on the table. "I assume this won't be the last time I see you."

A giddiness filled me, like I'd breathed in something other than air. "Oh? You do?"

"I mean, you're going to Emerson Leigh's party, right?"

The giddiness leaked out of me. "Oh. Yes." Of course he'd be going, too. I cringed at the thought of him there in his nice suit, chatting with the guests while I walked around with trays of champagne and hors d'oeuvres. "She asked me to help out. Work it." I tossed my hair so that I didn't have to look right at him, already feeling self-conscious. Imagine how much worse it was going to be when I was wearing yellow, the world's least flattering color on me. "Hard to turn down the overtime pay, you know?"

Of course he wouldn't, but he nodded anyway. "It should still be fun," he said. "I'm looking forward to hearing about her business. I'm sure it's going to be a great success."

I couldn't hold back a snort. Or maybe it was that I could have, I just didn't want to. Because thinking about working that party while Bennett was there as a guest, and knowing that Emerson Leigh had put me in that position, made me both careless and mean. Not the best combination. "Emerson Leigh's pet yoga business is the most ridiculous thing I've ever heard of in my entire life. How do you even get a fish to do yoga?"

Once it came out of my mouth, I immediately felt bad. But Bennett's lips quirked up in a smile. "All right, it is a little far-fetched. Maybe even ridiculous. I think she's only booked her sister so far."

A switch flipped in me from careless and mean to protective. It was like how my brothers would make fun of me nonstop for being smelly and ugly and stupid, but when the kid next door mocked me for having a mustache, all three of them swarmed him and beat him up (even though kid me totally did have a mustache). "I don't know, I guess it could be worse. Like, she's trying to do good," I said. "And it might just be that I don't 'get' the concept of pet yoga. Like, I'm not a part of your world."

Bennett's eyebrows raised so high they lifted above the rim of his glasses. "My world?"

Curse the English language for no longer having a plural second person pronoun. "Like, yours and Emerson Leigh's and Maisie's and, you know, the rest of your circle's."

Bennett laughed softly, which sounded the way rubbing velvet between your fingers felt. "It's not like we live on another planet. We're still here on the same world as everyone else."

This time I could absolutely control my snort, and I made it as loud and obnoxious as I possibly could. "The wealthy might as well live in a different world. Like, I've been to your apartment. You're definitely not paying for that apartment on a food writer's salary."

"That's true," he acknowledged. "That apartment's one of my dad's holdings. Penny lives in another."

There it was. I couldn't stop the words from coming out along with a self-conscious laugh. "It's all just as well that you wanted to keep things professional after that kiss. That way you'll never have to come down and see where I live. It's nothing like your place, I can tell you that."

Before he could answer, but not before I could start to regret putting myself out there like that, the waitress popped back up with our entrées. Bennett and I didn't speak as we rearranged everything on the table so that it all fit, and then I had to take all my photos, which he no longer complained about, so by the time we were ready to eat, I thought he might have forgotten what we'd been talking about. I hoped, anyway.

Then he began, "Julie, listen—" and I knew he hadn't. I cut him off.

"We've got french fries on the table," I said. "In my experience, french fries need to be eaten immediately. Crispiness waits for no man."

And so we dug in. Maybe he'd forget for real by the time we were through with these dishes. For one, the lomo saltado was so delicious I thought I might forget my own name. It was beef tenderloin stir-fried so that the sugars in the marinade caramelized on the outside, making it crispy and chewy and as tender as the name in the middle, on a big blue platter piled high with roasted tomatoes, various salsas and chiles, and crispy fries. The idea was to wrap pieces of beef and the toppings in the scallion pancakes that came along with it. What resulted were flavor bombs, savory and spicy and fatty and crispy, all accentuated by the sweet, tangy pop of tomato. Flakes of scallion pancakes drifted from my lips down to my plate as my teeth crunched through each bite.

"I can't even handle how good this is," I said, then swallowed because I couldn't wait to say it.

The other two dishes we'd ordered were pretty great, too—a whole branzino marinated and charred so that we picked it clean off its spindly bones and ate it with greens and roasted peppers; a half chicken roasted with aji amarillo chile paste and served over shiitake mushrooms and a lime crema—but the lomo saltado was the true star of the table. I could already picture how it was going to look on my page. The golden-brown fries glistening with oil. The beef shaded from light pink in the center to deep brown on the edges. The ruby red tomatoes nestled among them. And the scallion pancakes serving as a lacy backdrop.

Maybe there'd been some nuggets of kryptonite cooked into the scallion pancakes, because my superpower was starting to fail me. My stomach was protruding from under my blouse, dangerously full. Eating another bite might make it explode.

"I think we'll need a few minutes before dessert," Bennett told the waitress. Then turned back to me. "Julie, what you were saying earlier about me wanting to keep things professional?"

I couldn't bear to look him in the eye. My cheeks might burst into flame. "It's okay, I shouldn't have said anything. We don't have to talk about—"

"I wasn't the one who wanted to keep things professional." I looked up then to find him appearing vaguely surprised at himself, maybe for interrupting. "I thought it was you. You were the one who ran out of the room after our . . . after we kissed, and who wouldn't look at me, so I thought I'd let you make the first move, if you wanted to, and you skipped the reservation, and then when I finally heard from you again afterward, you were saying you wanted to keep things professional. That wasn't me." He was out of breath by the time he finished, wicking away a drop of sweat from his forehead.

"No, it was totally you," I said, but I was less sure. In my mind, he'd been the one to . . . but no, maybe that *was* me, after I'd missed the reservation, and he hadn't wanted to scare me away. I cleared my throat, and because I had to be absolutely clear, I asked, "What does that mean? You don't want to keep things professional?"

He reached out and took my hands on the center of the table, pushing aside our mostly empty plates. His thumb brushed lightly over my knuckles, sending a shiver trembling from my wrists to my shoulders to my chest. "I want to keep things anything *but* professional," he said, voice low. It thrummed somewhere deep in my stomach. "I mean, unless you want to keep things professional."

I traced my own thumbs over his palms. They curled reflexively up into my hands. "I want you to stop saying the word *professional*. And thinking it." I swallowed hard. Once I said this, there was no going back.

But I didn't want to go back. "I don't want to keep things professional. At all."

"Then we're in agreement," he said gravely. "To be unprofessional. Together."

I nearly wrenched my shoulder from its socket waving to the waitress for the check. "No dessert tonight," I told her, trying not to look at Bennett's slow grin across from me. "I think we'll just have it at home."

17

NORMALLY, WHEN I LEFT A RESTAURANT, I WAS AL-
ready calculating in my head the precise combination of
subway lines and stops that would take me home in the
shortest amount of time.

Today? I stood on the sidewalk beside Bennett as he
waited for his Uber, pressed tight against his side. Cars
roared around us, exhaust filling the air. I was probably
breathing in all sorts of terrible things that would give me
cancer in twenty years.

And I didn't care.

Bennett was staring down at his phone to track how
far away the car was, his neck cricked at what had to be an
uncomfortable angle. He glanced up and caught me looking at him. His lips quirked in a smile, which made my
heart twist. I wished for teleportation. I wanted to be at
his apartment right this second.

"Julie?" Bennett said. I realized I was still looking at him.

"Bennett," I breathed. Screw waiting to get to his apartment, I couldn't wait. I reached up to kiss him, warm lips on warm lips, his hand pressing into my lower back, the sweet taste of the cherimoya dessert we'd skipped somehow on his tongue. Custard apple, people called it, rich and creamy and slippery, or maybe that was just him.

He pulled back, and my whole body seized in panic. He was going to tell me it was a mistake. That he'd forgotten that he didn't like kissing me, and we should keep things professional after all. That we should never have—

"The car's here," he said, breathless. "Come on."

We didn't kiss again in the back seat of the car. It was too weird, with the driver rattling on about the time he'd rear-ended a cop car over a soundtrack of jangling Bollywood hits. Instead, we sat side by side on the cracked leather back seat looking straight ahead, my right hand in his two.

Hand-holding, hot. It felt like I was in middle school again. But Bennett traced every inch of my skin, fingers skimming from my wrist up my palm, learning my life lines and my love lines, rubbing each finger from root to tip. My breath caught in my throat as his thumb rubbed an oval into my palm, sending tingles shooting up my arm. Muscles strained in my neck with the effort to keep looking forward as he raised my hand slowly, gently, to his lips and grazed the back of it with a kiss.

We tumbled out of the back seat when we reached his

building, and let me tell you, it was a good thing we had to pay ahead in the Uber app, because neither of us had money on the brain right then. We hurried past the doorman, who was perceptive enough not to try and make small talk, and then into the elevator. The doors whooshed closed behind us, and it was only then that I turned to Bennett and looked him in the eye.

The way he was looking back at me. How to describe it? Some delicate mix of awe and kindness and fear and hunger, the way you'd look at something you wanted so badly but were afraid of breaking. All of that blazed behind his glasses, those blue-gray eyes pinning me in place so that I went up in flames, too.

Into the hallway. We'd barely made it inside his apartment, the door closing with a click behind us, before we were together. My front pressed up against him, his front pressed up against me. His hot mouth moving on mine. His hands tangled in my hair, pulling it without hurting it, somehow. I couldn't think. I couldn't breathe. My only sense that worked was touch, as his fingertips blazed a trail over my body.

Damn clothes were in the way. I slipped my hands up under his shirt, exploring the divot running down his back, the way each muscle tensed and then relaxed at my touch. "Julie," he said roughly into my ear, and I guess my hearing worked, too, or maybe it was the way just one single word of his hot breath could make my insides melt into a warm, slick puddle.

My other hand fumbled with his buttons as he kissed

my ear, my chin, the hollow of my throat. I finally pulled that last button free, sending his shirt dropping to the floor, and turned my attention to his chest. I nuzzled the spattering of light brown hair that covered defined pecs, a soft belly, the hair growing coarser as it wound its way down under his dark jeans.

I panted as he pulled me back through the entryway, hands on my waist, kissing the whole way, and collapsed backward onto the gray leather couch, which felt softer than my skin. I fell on top of him, straddling his lap. He kissed his way down my neck and across the collar of my blouse, leaving a trail of fire behind.

"Enough of that," I panted, ripping my shirt over my head. Thank goodness I'd worn a decent bra today—blue satin with a bow in the middle, not frayed or torn anywhere. He eyed it with a growl of approval, but maybe it wasn't a growl for the bra at all, because a moment of fumbling over my back and—pop—I shook off my now unfastened bra.

"And to think you didn't like me at first." He drank me in unabashedly, his eyes roaming from belly to breasts to nose to eyes, and each inch his eyes traveled made me feel more and more powerful. Like I could go anywhere, do anything.

Except all I wanted to do was right here. I ground against him, feeling his cock already hard and strong under his zipper. "Who says I like you now?"

He gasped and pulled me tighter onto him. "If this is

what you do to people you don't like, what do you do to people you *do* like?"

I silenced him with another kiss as I rubbed up and down him again. Now my own sex was throbbing, and I sucked in a breath with every movement.

I kept moving up and down as he kissed my breasts, tongue tracing lightly over each nipple. When I couldn't take it anymore, I tumbled to the side, lying down on the couch and pulling him on top of me. Because his was an expensive couch and not the cheap one my old roommate had bought at Ikea, there was plenty of room for us to writhe without making me feel like I might topple off the edge.

He went down to kiss my breasts again . . . and kept going. His tongue slid down my stomach, did a lazy circle around my belly button. I clenched my teeth, holding back a beg for more as he slowly, slowly, way too slowly unzipped my skirt and tugged it down. I kicked it off, along with my underwear, when he reached my knees, nearly clipping him on the ear.

His soft laugh nearly undid me. What actually did undo me was when he kissed his way back up, shivering up the inside of my thigh, and landed between my legs. He swirled. He sucked. He kissed. I closed my eyes, my hips bucking involuntarily.

When I felt close to the edge, I reached down and pulled him up. My hand moved down and took over, zeroing in on just the right spot on my clit. It didn't take long.

I shuddered against his shoulder, biting back a cry, then wondered why I was biting it back and let it out.

Breathing hard, my head collapsed back into the cushion. I was a little worried that now post-orgasm clarity would descend upon me and be like, *What the hell are you doing, Julie?* but the post-orgasm clarity seemed to approve. With a wink and a nudge, it made me pull away, and the desire roared back inside me. "That's why it's great to have a clitoris," I told Bennett. "Multiple orgasms."

Before he could question the continuation of my inner monologue, I slid out to the side and moved atop him again, straddling his hips as he lay down where I'd been just before. I reached down and unzipped him. His cock sprang free, and as I wrapped my hand around it, it twitched hot under my fingers. Bennett moaned, the breathing already ragged in his throat, even more ragged when I lowered my mouth and teased the head with my tongue.

When I lifted my head, he pulled me up and toward the stairs to his loft. His pants and boxers got lost somewhere between the couch and his bed. My mind got a little lost, too, tangled up in the hitches in Bennett's throat and the hard length of his naked body up against mine and the few seconds we had to separate to go up the steep stairs to his loftlike bedroom, aka horrific torture. But then we tumbled into his bed together, rumpling the impeccably made navy blue bedspread, and he was all hot lips and moans and want.

I could only take it so long. "Do you have a condom?"

He responded by reaching into his nightstand drawer.

I hadn't even noticed the nightstand. My whole world was him right now, him and the desire coursing through me. He tore the foil packet and rolled on the condom. I pulled him on top of me, and he leaned down for a long kiss, a kiss that stole every thought other than *now, now, now.* He gasped as I guided him inside, then growled into my neck as he plunged into me. I ran my hands over his back as he moved inside me, tangled my fingers in his hair, tugged him as close as he could possibly be. He pulled his glasses off and set them on the nightstand at some point, and the way he looked into my eyes was so bare, so open, that I didn't know if I could take it anymore.

So I flipped him over. Together, we moved as if we'd trained at it for years, putting him on the bottom, me sitting up on top. He'd popped free, and Bennett groaned as I slid myself back onto his length slowly, exquisitely, holding his arms down so that he couldn't reach up and pull me faster. I leaned down and sucked on his bottom lip as we began rocking together, me moving up and down on top, him thrusting from the bottom. We moved faster and faster until he grabbed my hips and pulled them to him, letting out a guttural cry into my neck as he came.

He ran his hands up and down my back as I moved up and down a few more times, shuddering with each thrust. The look in his eyes could only be described as worshipful. Pleased, I slid off and nuzzled up to his side, tucking my head into his shoulder. A crinkle as he disposed of the condom somewhere I couldn't see, and then he was hugging me close, breathing hard into my hair. I splayed my arm over his chest, marking him as mine to anyone who happened to be watching. Which was (hopefully) no one.

"I've wanted to do this since you yelled at me at the Central Park Food Festival." Bennett's voice was thick, already sleepy. Men.

Then again, I was feeling a little sleepy, too. The room was dark and cozy, the bedspread even softer and plusher when Bennett and I wriggled beneath it. "You must be a masochist."

I could hear the smile in his voice now over the sleep. "Maybe."

We fell asleep in each other's arms.

I WOKE UP a few times during the night to use the bathroom (which, as it turned out, was inside the second door I tried, after having stumbled into his closet and gotten lost among the suits and ties) but didn't wake up for real until light was filtering in through the blackout curtains. I squinted at Bennett's analog clock, which was probably an antique worth thousands of dollars. Seven thirty in the morning. Far too early for a Saturday. I tried to fall back asleep, but as cozy as Bennett and his nest of blankets were, my body wasn't having it.

So I tried watching him sleep for a little bit, smiling to myself. He was a really cute sleeper, not drooly or snory, at least not much. I was happy to be here. Would this be a relationship? I didn't want to get ahead of myself.

But . . . I could see it.

It turns out you can only watch someone sleep for so long without feeling like a giant creeper. I rolled myself out of bed quietly so that I wouldn't wake him up and then rifled through his bureau, finding, to my absolute delight, the terrible dead squirrel T-shirt from that night at the bar. It was so big it went past my butt. I slipped it over my head, feeling like I was starring in a romantic movie.

His living room looked different in the warm light of day: the city waking up through his floor-to-ceiling windows, the bookshelves inviting and ready for reading. Maybe I'd make him some coffee. That would be considerate. Though maybe it wouldn't be considerate if his kitchen went up in flames again, as it had the last time I'd used it.

I'd look through the bookshelves, then, pick out something to read. He'd find me cozy on his couch in his T-shirt, nose in one of his favorite books, and his lips would curl in a smile like steam from a cup of coffee.

Resolved, I stepped from bookshelf to bookshelf, scanning what he had. I'd only seen the food writing shelves last time, but he had a plethora of other options. Ancient *Dungeons & Dragons* manuals from the 1970s. Comic books and graphic novels. Shelves of fat fantasy books with elves and goblins on them, including what appeared to be the full line of licensed *Dark Avengers* novels. I scanned for the first in the series—maybe it would give me the dirt on that coveted Blood Sword of Destiny and Fortitude.

I didn't see it . . . oh! There was what looked like a thick

fantasy novel on Bennett's desk. I headed over to the sleek
white piece of furniture stacked with neat piles of papers.
Grabbing the book, which was indeed the first in the series, I took a moment to admire his pen collection. Would
he notice if I borrowed the green tortoiseshell beauty?
Forever?

That could come later. If there was a later. I turned,
but before I stepped away, my eyes snagged on a printout
on his desk. It looked as if it were an email.

And my name was in it.

I didn't touch the paper, because that would be prying,
but I did tilt my head nearly forty-five degrees so that I
could read it. I mean, it was sitting right there, out in the
open. As my eyes traveled down the bullet points, they
blinked longer and longer in shock, as if they might be
mistaken about what they were seeing.

What I learned about restaurant-review influencers
during my time with Julie Z.

- Reviews on social media lack depth and nuance.
  Influencers don't have the breadth of knowledge or
  even the interest in food that a traditional reviewer has.

- Influencers spend more time trying to get a pretty
  photo than actually dissecting how the food tastes. The
  dishes Julie Z. spotlights are not the best ones, just the
  best-looking ones.

And so it went, a list of points all in the same vein. Things Bennett had learned from me.

I backed away, feeling sick. No, not just sick. Full of sick. I actually thought I might vomit all over Bennett's impeccably laid out desk.

Those were all things I'd secretly worried were true, but Bennett had helped me realize they weren't. Except he didn't think that at all, did he? Not if he was busy writing an article for the *Scroll* about how I was trash. About how what I did, what I was passionate about, what I lived for, was something to denigrate and mock in a major newspaper.

So much for keeping things professional. Or *un*professional.

I didn't realize I was crying until I reached up to investigate why my vision was suddenly so very blurry and found my fingertips wet.

Up in the loft, something rustled. "Julie?" Bennett called sleepily.

I wished I could turn back time. Not see that email draft to his editor. Settle for the second book in the *Dark Avengers* series.

But I couldn't. And I also couldn't just climb back up there and pretend nothing was wrong. And it was for the best, wasn't it? Better to find out now that Bennett was even more of a dick than I'd thought he was at first than later on when I would be even more attached.

Fortunately, all of my clothes and other things were

still down here from when we'd frantically shed them last night. Tears stinging my eyes, I shrugged off Bennett's cozy T-shirt and changed back into my own clothes from last night, which were now rumpled and chilly from their time on the floor. I gathered my stuff.

"Julie?" Bennett called again, sounding slightly more alert. Any moment now, he'd roll out of bed and come find me.

So I ran out of there before he could.

18

MY PHONE BUZZED THE ENTIRE SUBWAY RIDE HOME, even deep underground where I really shouldn't have had a signal. All texts from Bennett. They started out confused. **Where are you? Did you leave?** Then got concerned. **Is everything okay? What happened?** Then got upset. **Did I do something?** He tried calling multiple times, too, but I hung up on him each time. Didn't bother listening to the voice mails. Who still left voice mails, anyway?

Marcus wasn't home, which was good, because I didn't like bursting into tears in front of people. I collapsed onto the couch sobbing, shoving my face into my hands. Which still smelled like Bennett. Damn it.

I wanted to scream into the void, but I couldn't do that in my apartment. My walls were too thin, and the chances were too high that my landlord downstairs would think I was being murdered and barge inside to check on me. So I did the next best thing: I called Alice.

"Julie, what's up?"

Spilling the whole story felt like vomiting. Only unlike vomiting, my stomach didn't feel any better once it was all out. "I don't know what to do."

"Oh, fuck him," Alice said immediately. "How dare he? You're great. What you do is great. You're better off without any guy who would put you down."

Really? Because I'd felt better with him.

I said that to Alice, and she told me, "Everybody feels that way after a bad breakup. You'll cry for a while and then you'll get over it. And maybe you should start looking for a new job, get out of that circle. You're too good for the Deckers, too. Hey, we can job hunt together!"

I could look for a new job, though it would cut into my reviewing time, and I'd be risking finding something with worse hours that would cut into my reviewing time even more. But was she right that I always felt that way after a bad breakup?

I'd certainly mourned the breakup I'd had with my college ex, but I'd known the whole time that he'd made me into a worse person while I was with him: jealous, suspicious, possessive (and rightfully so, considering he spent months cheating on and off with his ex-girlfriend). I hadn't mourned the person I'd been with him. But I felt like that was what I was doing now. I really liked Bennett, but I also really liked the person I'd become with him. The person who wasn't afraid to be honest and authentic. The person who felt joy about being an influencer, something that used to make me insecure. The person who felt respected and encouraged.

That's not the real him, I told myself, which only made me feel worse. *That was all a facade.*

I faked a laugh for Alice. "Yeah, I hope you're right."

I didn't think she was.

"Let's go review somewhere new and fun," she said. "Get your mind off of it. Is there anywhere you've really been wanting to go?"

I honestly didn't know if I could handle a full-on real restaurant review right now. It wouldn't be fair to the restaurant that all their food might taste like bitter almonds on my tongue. "One sec. Let me get some advice."

I put Alice on hold and clicked over to my texts. Opened up a new one to Jada Knox. We'd traded thoughts on chefs and breaking restaurant news on several occasions in the time since our joint restaurant crawl, so I didn't feel like I was going in out of nowhere. **Random question: Where would you go to drown your sorrows after a bad breakup?**

The response came before I'd even clicked back over to Alice. **Don't drown them with alcohol; that's how you end up on the floor crying (personal experience). Soak them up with doughnuts. Let's go? Yes?**

I blinked. I was dazzled. **Sure.**

She texted me the address for Wendy's Doughnuts up in Prospect Heights, only a few subway stops away. Excellent. And I didn't waste any time wondering if Alice would be on board with an extra guest, because I knew she'd be just as dazzled.

The three of us met up at Wendy's Doughnuts a little over an hour later. The weather was one of the few pleasant days New York City gets in a year, dry and sunny and not painfully hot or cold. My olive green windbreaker was perfect, though being real, I didn't want any pictures taken of me today. I'd showcase some doughnuts for my followers as a fun in-between treat, but this wasn't going to be a full post.

The line for the doughnut place stretched out the door. I found Jada and Alice at the back; Jada was snapping a few selfies with other girls in the line, but she turned her glittering smile on me as soon as she saw me. "It was so great to meet you!" she gushed as the girls went back to their place in line. "Make sure to tag me so I can repost you!"

I hugged Alice, then Jada. Alice asked me, her mouth pinched with concern, "How are you?"

I didn't want to get into it in public here where people could take pictures of me crying. "You know," I said vaguely, then changed the subject. "How are *you* doing?"

Alice shrugged. "I've actually been hearing from a lot of recruiters, so clearly that letter didn't turn off *all* the tech companies out there?"

Jada's mouth fell open. "Oh! You're *that* Alice Wong!" Her hands clasped together over her phone, like she was presenting Alice with a sleek plastic and metal bouquet. "I was reading about you. You're amazing!"

Alice wasn't typically one for hyperbole, so I was surprised to hear her say back, "No, you're amazing!"

If there was ever a time for women supporting women, it was now. I let them do a little amazing-off for a while, their argument of who was more amazing and who was more impressive stoking a tiny warm fire in my cold, dead heart. I could at least be glad that some people were having a good day. And really, having the two maybe most amazing people in the world turn to me afterward and focus all their amazingness on me made me feel legit extremely special.

I'd already told Alice all the gory details, so I gave Jada, as somebody I didn't know as well, an abbreviated version. "So he's been trashing me behind my back the whole time and is planning on doing it to his readers, too," I said. A thousand tiny needles pricked the inside of my nose. *Do not cry, Julie. Do not. Do not.*

"What a fucking douchebag," Jada said. "You don't need that in your life. Trust me, being single is pretty fantastic. I'll take you out and you'll forget all about him."

I didn't want to forget all about him. That was the problem. "Thanks," I said miserably. My whole outlook had changed since I'd started going toe-to-toe with Bennett. I'd found value in myself. In what I did.

But it wasn't *because* of him. Jada had helped me there as well. And I still had my revelation at Sebastian. I still had the joy I'd found in what I did. It wouldn't go away just because Bennett did.

So I sucked the snot back into my head with a truly impressive and truly disgusting noise. I clutched my phone in my hand, felt the power in it. I looked between the two strong, brilliant, *kind* women, one old and one new, who were there for me. *Here* for me. When I'd needed them, they'd shown up.

Who needed a company like the *Scroll* when I had people like them?

The thought and the camaraderie kept me buoyed up a little bit as we hashed out what doughnuts to get, then purchased them and retreated to Prospect Park to eat them. We settled on a bench near the Arch, where we could people-watch to our hearts' content. The ratio of hipsters to normal people might not have been as high as in neighborhoods like Williamsburg, but there were still plenty of unicyclists and jugglers to keep us entertained. And the saxophonist playing somewhere behind us wasn't half bad.

Speaking of half bad, that was one thing that the doughnuts were not, either—they were all good. The dough itself was flaky, almost more croissant-like than doughnut-like, and glazed with a crystalline crackling of sugar. The lemon doughnut gushed with sweet and tart filling, the guava and cheese was gooey and creamy, and the plain glazed was still warm from the oven. I took a photo for Jada as she bit into the lemon cream, the bright yellow filling dripping onto her chin, and then she took a video of me pulling apart the guava and cheese so that the sunlight gleamed against the striped pink and white. I advised her on what angle made the yellow of the doughnut pop without washing her out; she helped me figure out what filter looked best so that the pink guava and white cream cheese were vibrant without overshadowing the shine of the dough.

It was really, really nice.

BEST SERVED HOT279

"These were so good." Alice popped the last bite of the plain glazed in her mouth, not asking if either of us wanted it. I didn't blame her.

"Do you live near here?" Jada asked her. Alice shook her head. "Too bad, because sometimes they give out the extras at the end of the night for free."

"I might just move here for that," Alice said. She sounded so serious I honestly wasn't sure whether she was kidding.

"I've considered it," said Jada. "It's a shame to think of all those doughnuts getting thrown out at the end of the night."

Alice's eyes nearly bugged out of her head. "What?"

"They give some out, but sometimes they just make way too many." Jada sounded kind of like her pet had died. "And they have to toss them."

"That's awful!" Alice cried. Had I ever heard her sound so passionate about anything? "There's got to be something they could do!"

At least that one night, they gave some to me. Because I went back right before closing, and Marcus and I feasted until dawn.

A DAWN THAT found me feeling terrible, and not just because my body was now at least sixty percent fried dough. No, because I woke up to my phone dinging with a calendar reminder. I blinked at it. Emerson Leigh's party. It was tonight.

Oh hell no.

I might have been feeling slightly better than before, thanks to Alice, Jada, and Marcus, but there was no way I could work this party tonight. I didn't think I could paste on my big fake smile tight enough to keep it from springing a leak in front of all the guests.

Much less Bennett. My face swelled up with tears and spilled over.

I wiped my nose, then wiped my eyes, then realized I probably should've done it the other way around. I'd call Mr. Decker and feign illness. I certainly sounded congested, from the crying now and, okay, the crying last night after I got home. Surely, he wouldn't want me giving his guests a cold or the flu or anything.

"Hello?" he said into my ear. Even though I knew his screen said Julie Zimmerman Cell, because I'd programmed my number into his phone myself. I suppressed a sigh.

"Good morning, Mr. Decker, it's Julie."

"Oh, good morning, Julie." He sounded distracted, like he was reading the paper while he spoke to me. He probably was. "I'll see you later tonight, right?"

"That's the thing, actually." I forced a cough. "I woke up not feeling so—"

"Because Emmy is so excited to have you there, helping out. You're the only person she asked. Will there be a problem? You've always been such a good, reliable assistant. I would hate for that to change."

My fist clenched around my phone. Something beeped in my ear. I eased up a little bit, but not because of the sentiment.

Mr. Decker had just as good as threatened me. Told me I'd fall in his eyes if I didn't show tonight. He probably wouldn't fire me, but what if he did? It could be hard to get another job as good as this one, with ample free time to do my own thing during the day, and dental insurance, especially knowing that I wouldn't get a good reference from him. I'd be stuck temping again, or else working as the assistant at some scrappy start-up where the head honchos paid partially in fun snacks and required you to work overtime every day. I couldn't do that if I wanted to keep reviewing.

I sighed heavily, then swallowed down an actual legitimate cough. Maybe I was getting sick for real. It would serve him right if I gave it to him later. "No, no problem," I said weakly. "Just . . . um, I'm supposed to be at the boutique at five thirty, right?"

"Make it five fifteen," he said. "Emmy might want to train you to recite a poem as you rotate through the room."

Horror shuddered through me. Fortunately, Mr. Decker wasn't so pedestrian as to say things like "goodbye," so he just hung up without expecting me to say more.

19

I SPENT MOST OF THE REST OF THE DAY DIRECT-
ing my ire at the terrible yellow dress I had to wear tonight.
I hadn't owned any yellow clothes since yellow looked terrible on me, which meant a trip to the thrift store. This
terrible dress had been the least terrible option out of all
the other even more terrible options. It was an almost
golden, kind of mustardy color with puffed sleeves and a
weirdly high neckline, but the silhouette was at least flattering, the fit tight over my boobs before it nipped in at my
waist and flared out into a full skirt. The effect of all that
ire direction meant that I was slightly less focused on Bennett and Emerson Leigh when it came time to leave, but
also that I felt extremely ugly when I looked in the mirror.

"What do you think?" I did a twirl for Marcus, who'd
returned by then, bearing tales of a hookup who looked
eerily and suspiciously like Santa Claus.

Marcus's nostrils flared. "It's . . . something."

I sighed. "I guess that's the best I can expect."

"That color just isn't the most flattering on you," he said. "The shape is nice, though. At least from the chest down."

I sighed harder. "Thanks?"

I couldn't focus on my book on the subway no matter how hard I tried even though I had a plum seat along the side of the car, so I stowed it away in my bag and turned to stare out the window as the Q train trundled over the bridge into Manhattan. I'd have signal here, but I didn't want to look at my phone, either. Anything I'd pull up would only make me feel worse.

Unless . . .

I'd gotten a lot of support the night I'd been honest with my followers after Bennett's and my cooking disaster. It had made me feel better. And Jada had talked about how she loved being honest and authentic with her followers. Obviously, I wouldn't spill everything—I didn't want to be that open online. But I could be vague.

I opened up my video and stared into my lens. Made a funny face to break the tension I was feeling. "So . . ." I began. "Do you ever have to go somewhere that you just know is going to be the worst? Like, when you're back in your hometown, and your friends want to take you to the local chain restaurant where all the food is microwaved to soggy death, and then you show up and your friends aren't actually there at all. It's your childhood bullies there to laugh at you all night as you choke down lukewarm, unsalted mozzarella sticks?" This metaphor was getting away from me a little. "Oh, wait, that was just a nightmare I had." I tilted my head back against the subway window, inviting millions of mutant bacteria to take up residence in my hair.

If one could make me sick enough where Mr. Decker couldn't in good conscience make me work, they were welcome. "Anyway, that's where I'm going. If you have any good thoughts for me, DM away."

I really hadn't done much. And yet as I tucked my phone back in my bag beside my unread book, I felt a little bit lighter.

And even lighter than that when I stomped up the stairs of the subway exit and tucked myself against the side of a nearby bodega to check my phone. The time was 5:05 on the same day, which meant that unfortunately my train hadn't entered a wormhole and come out into tomorrow. That would've been nice. But also waiting for me were a hundred DMs. I didn't have time to read them all in detail, but I skimmed through them, my heart growing warmer and warmer the more my finger flicked. A few trolls had slipped in, but probably ninety-seven of them were supportive and encouraging and kind.

> Girl, my partner and I broke up while we were at the resort for her sister's three-day destination wedding, and I had to go as her plus-one the next day and make nice with all her family knowing she didn't love me.

Hey Julie, no specific advice, but just wanted to say that
you're amazing and following your posts has made living
in NYC so much better!!

I had an army on my side. And knowing that so many
people were following me, so many good and kind people,
was enough to make me lift my chin high and square my
shoulders.

Emerson Leigh was holding her party at her sister's
boutique, both downstairs and upstairs in the private
event space. I wound my way through the tables of loofahs
and held my breath as I passed the perfumes. I took shaky
breath after shaky breath, trying to push down the wave of
nausea swelling up my throat. *You can do this, Julie. You can
do this.*

Eventually, I had to stop procrastinating. The second-
floor event space, where I assumed stock usually waited,
had been set up for a party, small round tables with cheerful pastel tablecloths littered throughout, a low platform
with a podium set up on one end. Otherwise, it was empty.
Of people. As in, I was the only person there. I took a few
steps in, looking around. Maybe everybody had forgotten
and I'd get to go home.

"There you are, finally!"

I jumped at the sound of a familiar voice. "Maisie?" I
said, turning. Mr. Decker's elder daughter looked a lot
like her younger sister, but the similarities ended there.
Maisie had never been all that nice to me. Once, when

she'd stopped in at the office unexpectedly and caught me walking around without my shoes, she'd gone and tattled to Daddy.

Maisie stalked toward me, her sleek black dress and red stilettos a far cry from what I was wearing. "I've been waiting."

I snuck a surreptitious glance at my phone. "I'm five minutes early."

She didn't seem to hear me. Maybe my voice couldn't penetrate that shiny helmet of blond hair. "Emmy asked me to help facilitate this little shindig. Though . . ." She scanned the room. "She seems to have it quite under control. For the most part."

"It does look good in here," I said, relaxing slightly. Maybe I'd only have to see Emerson Leigh from afar. Maybe Bennett wouldn't show up. Maybe this wouldn't be as terrible as I thought it would be.

Again, Maisie didn't acknowledge what I'd said. "Come, I'll show you what to do."

As I followed her to the side of the room where a table was piled high with assorted items, I braced myself for having to memorize Emerson Leigh's poetry or do flash cards on the guest list so that I'd be able to call everybody by name, but all Maisie did was reach down into a cooler beneath the table and pull out some bottles of what were probably very expensive champagne. "There are sparkly plastic goblets under here somewhere," she said, waving her arm vaguely at the table. "Just pour the champagne into the goblets and walk them around on one of the trays. Make sure everybody has one before the big toast."

"Okay," I said. That wasn't very hard.

Maisie sighed, like teaching me had indeed been very hard. "It's so lucky for Emmy that you volunteered to help. Otherwise, she would've had to hire strangers who didn't know anything about her or feel invested in her success."

I dropped the plastic goblets I'd uncovered. "I what?"

Maisie looked at me like I was an idiot, which really wasn't too many shades off from her usual look. "Emmy. Is. Lucky. You. Volunteered. To. Help," she said, slowly and loudly. "Otherwise. She—"

"I heard you," I said. My mind was racing. I definitely had *not* volunteered. "Did she tell you that?"

"Yes," said Maisie, still speaking slowly and loudly. "Excuse me. I have things to do." She removed herself and went to the other side of the room, where she stood and stared at her phone, occasionally laughing at the screen.

I didn't even care. As I sorted through the pile of things on the table, pulling out the trays and various packages of goblets, my mind continued to race. Emerson Leigh was so entitled. So entitled. She'd just assumed that I, as an employee of her father, was available to work for her off the clock. Like I was *made* to assist, not a full person of my own with a real life and real goals and real dreams. How many other things and people in her life did she not see, who she thought were just there? Her family fortune that she took for granted, her friendly condescension toward anyone who actually had to worry about money, that blithe feeling that she could literally do anything she wanted anytime she wanted?

She and Bennett were just alike. All the better that I no longer had to be a part of his world.

I wondered about it as I poured goblets of champagne and arranged them into concentric circles on the sparkly clear plastic trays she'd brought to match the goblets. The pair really made a cool-looking design: they made the champagne look glittery, too, fun and playful. Then people started filtering in, all people whose clothes fit perfectly in ways that meant they'd been tailored, and I pasted on my big fake smile, praying to every god that had ever been prayed to that Bennett wouldn't show or that, if he did, they'd take care of me. I wasn't picky who responded. If it was Zeus who struck me down with lightning, that was okay. Anubis pulling me down into the underworld was acceptable.

For a while, it seemed to be working. People kept on coming in, but the only ones I recognized were Mr. Decker and his wife—who gave me genuine smiles and thank-yous as they took their goblets—and a few of his business associates, who looked right through me. Maisie had eventually gotten off her phone and set up an hors d'oeuvres table on the other side of the room, where people gravitated for hummus and pita chips or vegetables and ranch dip. No matter how much money they had, people loved free food.

I actually started to relax a little bit. We were at six thirty, and even if the champagne was now warm waiting for Emerson Leigh's toast, Bennett was never late. He would've been here promptly at six if he were coming.

A hush settled over the room. I turned to see Emerson Leigh emerging onto the stage, a brilliant smile on her face. A pit soured in my stomach. She wore a sleeveless vintage yellow-and-green plaid dress, a tight sheath that had probably belonged to an especially fashionable 1960s secretary. "Welcome, all!" she trilled, smiling even harder into the microphone at the podium. "I'm so honored that you all came out tonight for the launch of my new business!"

I took deep breath after deep breath, but I couldn't stop my gaze from burning in her direction. Would she even thank me for being here, or was I just a piece of furniture or decoration to her? If my insides boiled any harder, they might spark one of the faux-fur scarves and cause the whole building to explode. Which would probably evaporate Maisie's perfumes into a poisonous gas and eradicate the entire block.

Emerson Leigh was going on about how she created her business. "I was, like, hard-core inspired by feminism," she said. "Because as a woman, why shouldn't I start a business? We all love our pets and want them to lead better lives. If my cat could say what yoga's done for her, she totally would. I actually brought a testimonial from her to recite on her behalf: 'meow, meow, purr.'"

The crowd laughed. Emerson Leigh's smile widened.
Deep breath.

"They're also inspired by feminism because *I'm* only here because of feminism. Because of the belief that I, as a woman, can do anything a man can," she said. "I'll be humble tomorrow, but tonight I want to thank myself for getting me to this point. My hard work and my talent and my drive." She paused for a moment, giving me a chance to subtly snort. "If I can do it, anyone can do it!"

This time I full-on rolled my eyes. Fortunately, I was still near the back of the room with my tray of champagne, and nobody would be able to see me.

She asked if anyone had any questions, and hands went up. She called on a girl who looked around her age, probably a friend or acquaintance. "Do you have any tips for someone else looking to become an entrepreneur like you?" she asked earnestly.

Emerson Leigh's face glowed as she answered just as earnestly. "I threw everything I had into this business, making it my full-time work from the beginning. You really have to be willing to commit yourself to your passion if you want to make it work." The people around me were nodding as if she weren't speaking an entire alien language. "Your time is precious. Keep it for yourself; don't give it to someone else. And work hard. That's what I did, and it's basically all you need."

I didn't just roll my eyes at that, I rolled my entire body, my right hand flying up to cradle my head.

Unfortunately, I forgot that I was holding a tray of champagne. All eyes turned toward me at the crash, at the waterfall of liquid turning my mustard dress to gold—just kidding, to darker mustard. The glasses were plastic, so they didn't break, but they did go everywhere, creating a circle of space around me that put me even more in the spotlight.

My face flamed. "Sorry," I whispered, patting down my front like that might dry it. Nobody stooped to pick up the cups, and I couldn't bring myself to crouch down and scoop all that wet plastic into my arms as the entire room watched me, a bug under a microscope.

Emerson Leigh let out a tinkling laugh a few notes higher than her usual one. "That's okay! Don't worry!" The room was still looking at me. My skin crawled. I wished she'd just look away and start talking about something else, taking the focus off me and this terrible wet dress, but she said kindly, as if she were doing me a favor, "Julie, do you want to ask me for any advice? I know you're trying hard to make your own little business work."

The flames spread from my face down my body, igniting in my chest and stomach.

I just want to make it clear: I knew as soon as the words started coming out of my mouth that what I was saying was rude and unnecessary. But I was on fire, furious at her and Bennett and her and mostly Bennett for making me feel small, for making me feel less than, for making me feel like they were better than I could ever be because of the sheer accident of birth. "Sure, I'll ask for some advice." My voice carried around the room, bouncing off the walls and ceiling. "Do you have any advice for someone who wasn't born with a massive family fortune? Who can't decide to quit their job and start a ridiculous business on a whim because they don't have parents who can pay their rent and invest in their ridiculous business?" I paused. "Did you even think about me working here tonight, or did you just assume? I don't work for you, but you assumed I'd be here working anyway. I have a life, too. Does that even matter to you?"

Emerson Leigh's face fell. Her lower lip trembled.

I was a terrible, *terrible* person.

"Sorry," I said, but somehow my apology seemed to come out quieter than my questions. "Sorry, sorry. I shouldn't have said any of that."

I suddenly caught sight of Mr. Decker in the crowd. I realized that, under his crystallized O of surprise, he'd taken my advice. Worn the charcoal gray jacket and pink tie with normal matching gray pants. When I looked back up, his face was darkening with fury.

Okay. Time to flee.

I spun toward the exit and stopped short. Because there was Bennett, his face red and sweaty, looking as shocked as everybody else. For a moment I wanted to run into his arms for a hug, and then my heart hardened. Screw him. I might be terrible, but he was more terrible. I bolted out of there, down the stairs, and out into the warm night.

I slowed when I made it around the block, because running in stiff ballet flats was not comfortable. I hobbled the last few steps then braced myself against the crumbling brick wall of a tenement building, turning my shoe sole up to check out the gum and rocks and other debris that had stuck themselves to it. In the cool night air my dress was cold and clammy, clinging to my body and making me shiver.

The reality of what I'd done was just beginning to sink in amid the laughs and cheers of NYU students striding out on their way to dinner like they owned the world. I sighed heavily, letting the back of my head rest against the building, too. My hair was going to be *so* gross later.

My phone dinged. I didn't even want to look at it. I didn't know whether I'd rather it be a text from someone like Bennett or Emerson Leigh who'd just witnessed what I'd done, or a blithely ignorant text from someone like my brother showing off how many tacos he was about to eat. But I couldn't resist. I raised it up to my face, letting it do the passive work on unlocking it.

Mr. Decker. **Julie, I'm shocked by your display. Needless to say, you're fired for gross insubordination. I'll have your things shipped to you.**

I lowered my phone, eyes shockingly dry. Well, that was both surprising and obvious at the same time.

"Unemployed." I tested out the word. It was almost sweet. "No more health insurance." Well, that one was decidedly more bitter.

"Julie?"

Bennett.

I didn't have the energy to yell or cry or run away. I was all yelled out and cried out and painful shoed out. I just sighed again. "What do you want?"

He shifted back on his heels. His arms hung loosely by his sides, his palms facing toward me as if in supplication. He cleared his throat but then didn't say anything.

I sighed once more. I was going to sigh out all the air in my body at this point, suffocate to death right here on the sidewalk across from a bong shop.

All I wanted was to nestle into his arms, for him to whisper into the top of my head that everything would be okay.

He didn't come near me. Probably wisely. "Julie," he said again, taking a deep breath. "Julie. I'm sorry."

If I had feathers, they'd be bristling right now. "Sorry for what? For writing an article for the *Scroll* about how frivolous and dumb and ridiculous influencers like me are? Or just for leaving your outline for the article sitting on your desk where I could see it?"

"It's not what it looks like," he said in a rush.

I rolled my eyes. "It's pretty hard to interpret it in a different way."

"I'm not writing that article. Or any article like it. My editor wanted me to write an article about my experience working with you and sent me those talking points for what he wanted the article to say. He really wanted me to push the point forth that we were the only outlet readers could trust for their reviews. I copied the points into a draft email to mull over and think if there was any way I could make his point work in an article without putting you down but dismissed it almost immediately. What he wanted me to say just wasn't true, and I felt embarrassed even considering it."

"I don't know," I said. I wanted to believe him, but my feelings were still hurt.

He took my hand, holding it between the two of his. I let it happen, softening at the feel of his skin on mine. His palm was dry. Maybe he'd been so upset when I stormed off that he'd forgotten to moisturize.

"I know how it looks. I should've discussed it with you." He took a deep breath. "I'm truly sorry, Julie. I just wish you'd given me a chance to explain instead of running off."

His voice sounded sincere. I softened, like butter left out on the counter. Any further and I'd melt. "Yeah. I probably should have. I'm sorry."

"I understand." He gave me a tiny smile. I tiny-smiled back.

But my tiny smile totally evaporated when I remembered where I'd just come from. "And oh my God, I'm so sorry for what you had to see in there. I don't know what came over me. I can't believe I ruined Emerson Leigh's party like that." My stomach was sinking, and not just because I'd lost my job. "She might be totally oblivious, but she means well."

Bennett shook his head. He moved his lips, but an ambulance sped by, siren wailing, followed by a couple of cop cars speeding through the intersection, making pedestrians with headphones on leap back onto the sidewalk.

I leaned after it, making sure it wasn't going to Maisie's boutique—what if the shock of the evening had given Mr. Decker a heart attack?—before turning back to Bennett.

He was saying, "You're right. But I can hardly blame you after listening to what she was saying. Even I, who grew up in a similar bubble, found it absurd." He shook his head. "She's trying her best. She really is. But she was born into a world where expectations are different."

I couldn't help but snort. "Yes, poor Emerson Leigh." I wasn't going to spend too much time feeling sorry for the beautiful girl who'd been born into one of the richest families on the planet, who'd had every need and every want accounted for her entire life, who got to do whatever she wanted whenever she wanted.

"I know. It's not the most sympathetic story," Bennett said. "But she's never worked for anything. Never gotten to fail at anything. Never had to stick her neck out or learn what she's good at. She doesn't know who she is or what she wants or what she's good at. She's so jealous of you, Julie, so jealous it hurts her, and I imagine it must have hurt her more to hear what you really think of her like that."

"Jealous of *me*?" I laughed harder, so hard I had to take one of my hands back to wipe the tears from my eyes. "Yes, if I were the daughter of a near-billionaire who has everything handed to her on a silver platter, I would also be jealous of her dad's assistant, who lives in a shitty apartment with a roommate and can barely pay her student loan debt. Do you think she even knows what student loan debt is?"

Bennett tucked a stray curl behind my ear. A pigeon cooed overhead. If some guy hadn't been yelling about how big his dick was somewhere down the block, it would've been a really beautiful moment. "She's jealous of Julie Zee Eats NYC. The Julie who's hungry, who built something amazing out of nothing with grit and will and perseverance. The Julie who's had to work hard because if she fails, the failure means something. That's not something Emerson Leigh's ever known."

He was just making me feel worse and worse. "I'll apologize and explain why I felt like she took advantage of me. But not right now. I can't go back in there."

"I'm sure you'll see her at the office," Bennett said, and I grimaced.

"Mr. Decker fired me."

Bennett didn't look all that surprised. "Maybe that's a good thing." Bennett squeezed my hand. "It's a push to do something new."

I snorted and pulled my hand away. "Easy to say that when you've always had a safety net." Though I did, too, really. If I couldn't find a new job, I wouldn't be on the street. My parents might not have much, but there would always be a room in their house for me. They'd feed me and help me figure out how to defer my student loans until I could pay them again. It was important to remember that I was privileged as well, even if nowhere to the extent of Emerson Leigh.

"I'm sorry," Bennett said. "What I was attempting to say, insensitively, is that maybe now you'll get to try something else out. My safety net is held together with all sorts of connections. I'll put the word out that I have a brilliant friend seeking a new job. I'm sure something will turn up. Maybe even something at the *Scroll*."

I waited for my insides to jump in excitement at the mere possibility, but they were still and cold.

"In the meantime," Bennett said, "perhaps you'd like to come over for a snack? I have some new potato chip flavors I thought you might want to try."

"I don't know," I said. While I loved potatoes and he may have explained that article, tonight had reminded me that he was part of a world I'd never really belong to. I might care about him, but we came from such different places. I'd always have to be watching my mouth, worrying about what I'd say, worrying everybody around him would always see me as less than. "I need time to think."

He reached out and touched my shoulder. "I understand." Did he, though? "I'm only a phone call away if you need me. Or a text. Or an email. Or—"

"I got it," I said. I covered his hand with mine for a moment, only for a moment, so that I wouldn't get sucked right back into the warmth of his skin, the heat of his kiss.

And then I pulled away.

20

I CALLED ALICE A FEW TIMES ON MY WAY HOME, but she didn't pick up. I texted her the highlights anyway and expected at least a few shocked emojis, but still nothing. Over the next few days, it was nearly impossible to get her on the phone. I only got a few vague texts expressing her sympathies and telling me that she'd have huge news for me soon that might help. Somehow. I had no idea how huge news on her part would help me with my lack of a job and my social obliteration, but I had faith in her.

I texted with Bennett a few times, too. Nothing conclusive. I just couldn't see how we'd be able to make it work.

Marcus was the absolute best, stepping up to fill Alice's small, expensive shoes. To his credit, he didn't immediately ask if I'd be able to keep paying rent (he waited until the next day). We spent three nights in a row eating his homemade pecan pie ice cream from the freezer, making our way through the cardboard container. I cried snottily into his shoulder two of those nights, which, really, was a terrible thank-you for the ice cream. Though he did take the opportunity to take his snotty shirt off, which he loved, so maybe I'd done him a favor.

"Have you ever thought about opening an ice cream shop?" I asked him from where we sat side by side on the couch on the third night, some reality dating show playing mindlessly on the TV.

"I've considered opening a combination ice cream shop / arcade," said Marcus. "Does that count?"

"Whatever it is, you should perfect this and make a buttload of money." The ice cream's texture wasn't perfect, a little grainy, but the taste was on point. Buttery vanilla studded with chunks of crunchy candied pecans and a graham cracker swirl, sweet but not sugary sweet, a little salty and spicy for variety.

"Tell me more."

Before I could flatter him further, our buzzer rang. I leaped up. Hopefully it was my Thai food. I couldn't wait to shovel an entire plastic container of sugary takeout tofu pad thai into my face. A-plus coping strategy. I hit the button to open the downstairs door, then opened my own apartment door, so ready to take that warm plastic bag in my hand, and—

"Julie?" Emerson Leigh peered up at me from the bottom of the staircase. "Can I come in?"

I blinked down at her. She was hunched in on herself,

her tailored tan trench coat clutched tight around her body, her arms wrapped around her designer purse. Seeing her here, at my apartment, just did not compute. It was like ordering a strawberry cupcake at a bakery and having them hand you a sparkling Christmas ornament. Not entirely unwelcome, but like . . . what?

She cleared her throat, and I realized she was waiting for my response. Might as well get it out of the way early. "Emerson Leigh, I'm sorry," I began. "I shouldn't have—"

"Can you apologize to me inside, where it's safe?" she asked through clenched teeth, glancing over her shoulder like there were muggers lurking in the shadows behind her. I backed up, letting her scurry up the stairs. She poked her head in first before entering, still wrapped up tight around herself. She shut the door hard behind her and flipped both locks, even the second dead bolt that had the tendency to stick. "Okay. That's much better."

I bit my tongue, not wanting to get into how I did not actually live in a dangerous neighborhood. "Come in, sit down."

She kicked off her stiletto heels in the entry, which was good, because they probably would have marked up our wooden floors. For a moment, I wondered how she'd navigated the subway stairs and the walk here over the cracked sidewalks in stilettos, until I realized that of course she'd just hired a car to get here. I glanced out the window before sitting back on the couch beside Marcus. Sure enough, a shiny black SUV idled on our curb.

Emerson Leigh raised her eyebrows in surprise as she

entered the room. "Julie, who is this? I didn't realize you
lived with someone."

"He's my roommate, Emerson Leigh," I said wearily.
"I found him online."

"Ooooh." She sat gingerly on the opposite end of the
couch, avoiding the dried wine stain from two roommates
ago that had never come out (pro tip: only drink white
wine on a white couch). "I don't think I could ever have
roommates. I just like living on my own." Before I could
even think of rolling my eyes, she held up a finger as if she
were correcting herself. "That was my privilege speaking.
Wasn't it? Because most people don't have roommates for
fun; they do it because they need to do it. For financial
reasons. So I shouldn't say things like that."

My jaw dropped open at her self-awareness. That was
certainly new. Marcus said, very seriously, "Yes, I actually
hate Julie. I'm only here because I need to be. For financial
reasons."

I swatted him as he jumped up, chortling. "I'll go finish my ice cream in my room and leave you guys to it," he
said, and indeed went into his room. I was impressed he
could resist the sure drama to happen. At least until I realized he'd left his door open.

Whatever. I didn't care if he listened in. He'd heard me
cry from breakups and have diarrhea not just once but
twice, even if he didn't know my middle name. It was the
strange intimacy of a New York roommate.

I took a deep breath. "Look, Emerson Leigh, I'm surprised to see you out here, but I'm happy, too," I said. "I owe you an apology. I shouldn't have said those things to you at your party. It was rude and mean and I regret it."

She cocked her head, peering keenly at me with those green eyes. "But you meant everything you said, didn't you?"

"I—" Couldn't deny it. "Yes, I did, but still, I shouldn't have said them there, or said them the way I did, and especially not in front of all those people like that. I'm really sorry."

"I appreciate the apology," Emerson Leigh said. She took her purse from where she'd been hunched over it on her lap and placed it on the floor between her feet. She must have felt safe enough from any living room muggers crouched behind the bookshelf. "But I should apologize, too. I feel terrible how I didn't see so much of the privilege I had." She blinked. "Still have."

My first instinct was to comfort her and tell her that wasn't true, but that was a leftover from working for Mr. Decker. I didn't work for Mr. Decker anymore. "You are a little oblivious," I said. "But it doesn't make you a bad person."

"Just a kind of ignorant one." Emerson Leigh let out an airy laugh, but this time there was an edge beneath it I hadn't heard before. "I feel silly that I've never really thought about the role my family's money plays in my life. And I can't believe how I just assumed you would work my party. It was wrong. It was all wrong."

It might seem like a ridiculous revelation to have, but these were huge steps for her. "How did you . . . come to these conclusions?"

Something creaked inside Marcus's room. Probably him leaning over to hear better.

"Well, after you had your little outburst, the party went on and I put on a brave face," Emerson Leigh said, lifting her chin and perhaps mimicking her brave face, which looked a little bit like she was leading an army into battle. "After the party ended, I went home with Mom and Dad since I really needed some comfort in my old childhood bed. And my dad was telling me in the car that he fired you, that you didn't know what you were talking about, that you were just bitter and jealous and hating on me because my business was doing so great.

"And I just looked at him and knew he was wrong. I don't know how, maybe it was spending so much time with you and knowing that you weren't that kind of person. And maybe part of me knew that my business *was* a little ridiculous. And that it's not doing great. And that I've only been working on it because I don't know what else to do with myself." She bit her lip. "But I asked the driver to drop me off at Bennett's so I could hear what he thought. And he really . . . he really helped me realize how much privilege I have." She looked at me earnestly. "You know, he's a really good person."

Bennett. Bennett had helped her realize all this. Maybe . . . maybe that meant something.

But I had something to address before thinking about

that. "Your dad wasn't entirely wrong." I swallowed hard. "I was really jealous of you. Am still really jealous of you, maybe even a little bitter. I think that's one of the reasons I was so hard on you at your party."

Emerson Leigh's eyes went wide and round as I continued. "I'm so jealous that you get to do whatever you want, whenever you want, and you don't have to worry about rent or student loans or anything like that. You can quit your job to pursue any passions that cross your mind without any kind of business plan or plan B because you've never had to worry if they'll make you money or not. I'm so, so jealous of you that it burns sometimes."

Though funnily enough, admitting it did make me feel the tiniest bit better.

Emerson Leigh crossed her legs at the ankle, pushing her purse farther to the side. She wasn't even touching it anymore. "I understand. But I'm jealous of you, too." That was what Bennett had said. *No, Julie, stop thinking about Bennett right now.* "Like, you know exactly what you want, and you go after it." She looked down, folding her hands in her lap. "I have no idea what I want. I feel lost." I remembered back to a few times before when she'd let it slip how she felt lost or anxious. "My dad was a big businessman, and I grew up feeling like he wanted me to do something like that, too, but I've never known what I want to do, and that makes me anxious. Maybe it's because I have too many choices." She looked back up, eyes widening in panic. "Oh no, I know I'm lucky! Except maybe by having to work, you had no choice but to figure yourself out."

I couldn't help but laugh. "It's okay." And sobered. She was probably right, at least partially. My series of jobs and internships had taught me the things I liked doing with my time and the things I really didn't like. "I don't know, you're in a fortunate position where you don't have to work, and there are plenty of people who don't find fulfillment through work. Maybe you're one of them. Or maybe you're not, you just haven't been forced to figure it out yet."

She just furrowed her brow.

I said, "I have to tell you, the party the other night was really good. Everything was put together well and it seemed fun. And I know your dad was looking for someone to plan events for his charity, and other people out there are always looking for event planners for all sorts of interesting parties and galas. I imagine that would be pretty fulfilling and would make you feel like you're doing something good. And even if it's not your thing, who knows? Maybe going outside of your comfort zone will help you figure out who you want to be."

"Maybe," she said slowly, then clapped her hands together. "Speaking of going outside of your comfort zone. I'm not the only one who needs to do that." She closed one eye and looked intently at me through the other. Was she trying to wink? "Have you forgiven Bennett yet?"

I choked on nothing. I hadn't even been taking a breath. There was really no excuse. "What?"

She repeated it, slowly and loudly, as if the problem had been that I hadn't heard her. I shook my head. "Yes, I heard you. I just . . . I don't know."

Except . . . didn't I? Maybe I was just hiding from this relationship because I was scared of going outside of my comfort zone, into this world of Bennett and Emerson Leigh and the Deckers.

Maybe I should give my own advice a try.

I put on my own battle face. "You know," I said, "I think I have." I jumped to my feet. "I should call him."

Emerson Leigh stood, too, though she was much more graceful about it. Somehow she even managed to scoop her purse up at the same time. "No need." A mischievous smile crept over her glossy lips. "I'm here to take you to him." She paused and considered. "That, and to tell you you've got your job back."

"Wait, what?" I blurted. I wasn't even sure which of those sentences I was responding to. I put my palm up in the air to stop her before she could slowly, painfully repeat what she'd said. "You're taking me to Bennett? And what do you mean about my job?"

"I mean that I told Dad to rehire you, and of course he listened to me. You should be hearing from him soon." She spoke over her shoulder as she strode confidently down the hall toward her shoes. "And also that it's good you forgave Bennett, because I don't know what I would have done if you hadn't. Or what he would've done, honestly." She bent over to wiggle her shoes on. "I guess he would've just sat there alone all night, all sad."

"Sat *where*?"

"You'll see." She snapped her fingers. "Now go put on something presentable." She cast a critical eye over me, which was fair, considering these sweatpants were on their third day. And on the second day, I'd dropped ice cream on them. "And maybe brush your hair."

FIFTEEN MINUTES LATER, my hair was brushed, and I'd put on a mostly clean pair of jeans. No matter how many times I asked Emerson Leigh where her shiny black car was taking us, she wouldn't say a word, only smiled at me like the Cheshire cat. So I sat back on the supple leather seat that was somehow my exact body temperature and hoped that she wasn't taking me somewhere to kill me.

If she was, it was the worst possible place for it, because any decent investigator would trace the murder right back to her. Her car glided to a stop back outside Maisie's boutique. Emerson Leigh gestured for me to get out. On the sidewalk, I turned, waiting for her to follow me, but she just slammed the door shut and waved out the window as the car drove away.

The front door would usually have been locked at this time of night—opening hours for the boutique were generally whenever Maisie felt like getting up to whenever she got bored of being there—but it swung open easily when I pushed it.

I gasped at the inside. The tables of artisan faux-fur scarves and self-published poetry books by Maisie's friends were back in their places, but an aisle of lit candles wove its way among them, tracing a path deeper into the store. Banishing thoughts of how wise it was to have lit candles flickering a little too close to what appeared to be very flammable polyester, I followed the path back to the stair-way, where candles framed every step. They danced and glowed beside me as I climbed, making me feel a little like I was tracing a fairy path in the forest.

"Julie." My heart leaped at the sound of Bennett saying my name. There were more candles upstairs, some lit, some not. In the middle of the open space, topped by can-dles and a bouquet of peonies so fresh I could smell them from where I stood, sat a white-clothed table for two.

And of course there was Bennett standing beside one of the chairs, the flames reflecting against his glasses, giving him fire in his eyes. His button-down was red-and-purple checked today, his hair in that characteristic swoosh, and my heart squeezed hard at the sight of him.

"I hope we're not summoning demons tonight," I said, sweeping my arm out at the candles. Bennett's lips quirked. "Though if we are, I call dibs on not being the blood sac-rifice."

A buzzer sounded downstairs. Bennett stepped around me. "That's the blood sacrifice now," he said.

"You really can get anything delivered in New York."

Of course, when he came upstairs, he was carrying two slightly greasy paper bags. "Our first course," he said, set-ting them on the table and opening them up. "Emerson Leigh arranged for us to get takeout from West. They don't usually do takeout, but somehow she worked a miracle."

Two missed reservations and finally we'd get to try it. "That's amazing." I waited for him to carefully divide the food up onto our plates—he seemed to be using the fancy gold plastic leftovers from Emerson Leigh's party—then gallantly pull out my chair. I sat down and let him push me in, then he took his seat.

I knew there would be a talk coming, but obviously we couldn't let the food get cold. Or warm, in the case of the tuna tartare with benne seeds I finally got to compare to Jada Knox's review. It really did taste a little bit like coffee, which, contrasted with the cold, clean chunks of tuna and hits of acid, was the perfect mellowing factor. The red stew, with a tender chicken thigh nearly falling apart in the spicy, sharp broth, was both hearty and exciting, the bland, fluffy fufu it was served over the perfect contrast. And the curried goat with roti and crispy potatoes? The whole fried red snapper with jerk seasoning? All the contrasts of flavor and texture made me want to eat and eat and eat until I burst.

We kept our conversation strictly food-related until we were both picking bits of flesh off snapper bones at the end of the meal. "This was amazing," I said. "Both the food and the ambience. How'd you light all those candles?"

He ducked his head modestly. "Emerson Leigh let me know when you were on your way. She helped me set this all up. You remember when we got stuck in the copy room together?"

"I could never forget that."

He looked up and met my eyes. "That was her, too. She was trying to set us up."

I snorted. "Well, it worked." I reached for his hands, which were lying on the table tantalizingly close to mine, but he pulled them away. "Did she also tell you that I forgave you for lying to me?"

"She didn't. But I'm happy to hear it." He reached under his chair, coming up with another paper bag. "This is for you, too."

Pastries? I crossed my fingers for Dominique Ansel, my favorite bakery. But as I took the bag and unwrapped the box inside, I pulled out the most perfect thing I'd ever seen. "The beagle teapot!" I cried. I'd nearly forgotten about the adorable porcelain appliance—its ears the handle, its snout the spout—that I'd admired in the window of the teapot store on our way to Wander. "You remembered!"

"I remembered." This time, he took my hands. I set the teapot down gently in the middle of the table, and while it was hard to stop gazing at such a thing of beauty, I looked over at him. His eyes were soft, watching me admire the teapot like he was admiring something even more exquisite and beautiful. "Julie."

Hearing the sound of my name coming out of his mouth, spoken like he'd just eaten the most delectable chocolate croissant, set my whole body aglow. "Bennett."

From the way his face lit up at the sound, it was safe to assume the same was true for him. "Let's do this," he said, squeezing my hands. His thumbs rested in the cups of my palms. "For real. I want to be with you."

I squeezed back. However cheesy it sounded, it was like my heart was literally singing in my chest. I felt I might burst out into song myself. "I want to be with you, too."

And suddenly he was by my side and I was standing and he was ducking down to kiss me. Our lips met with a gentle thrill down the back of my neck. This wasn't a fiery kiss, one that foretold clothes tearing and *fuck me*s. It was a soft kiss, a sweet kiss, one that brought with it promises of waking up next to each other every morning and him bringing me chicken soup when I was sick and me slowly stealing all of his hoodies because they smelled like him.

I pulled away and nestled my cheek into his shoulder. He leaned his head down and pressed a kiss to my forehead. "Does this mean you're my boyfriend now? However high school that sounds."

"It means I'm your boyfriend," he said. "Does it mean you're my girlfriend? Do you want me to write a note where you can check off the yes or no box?"

This next kiss melted me. Now came the clothes tearing, the sweeping of plastic plates off the table, the gasping as he bent over me and I bit his earlobe and he groaned into the curve of my neck.

Who needed pastries? This was better than any dessert.

21

TRUE TO EMERSON LEIGH'S WORD, MR. DECKER called me the next day as I woke up curled into Bennett's side in his bed (we'd cleaned up Maisie's boutique very well before relocating to his apartment). Every word grudging, my former boss told me, "Julie, I shouldn't have let you go so quickly. I hope you'll come back." He paused afterward. Maybe he was waiting for my answer, or maybe he'd choked on his first ever apology and was writhing around on the floor clawing at his throat.

I told him I'd need a week to think it over. Because, as it turned out, there was a reason Alice had gone radio silent for so long. She called me a couple days into what I told Marcus would be a vacation and time to catch up on JulieZeeEatsNYC but that in reality turned into me lying on the floor obsessing over every possible path forward, my stomach churning with stress.

"Julie, I have news," she said into my ear. Then she stopped, which I assumed meant she was giving me time to guess what the news was.

Obviously, my first thought was something job related, but I didn't want to say that, just in case. I knew firsthand how everybody constantly bringing up job stuff could really hurt when you were unhappily unemployed. "You're pregnant?"

"No, considering I haven't had sex in a year, and I have not yet mastered cloning," she said. "Which is unfortunate, because I think it might be fun to raise a small version of myself."

"Will you give her the same bowl cut you had as a kid?"

I could hear the shudder through the wireless connection. "Don't remind me." Another pause. I hoped she didn't want me to guess again. But then she said, "You know, I want to tell you in person. Dinner?"

And just like that, some of the day's tension melted away into the floor, hopefully not leaking into the downstairs neighbor's bathroom the way our shower had a few months ago. "I know just the place."

We met a few hours later at Taiwan Garage, a Taiwanese place in Brooklyn I hadn't realized I'd need to take the bus to get to. Because of the unexpected traveling conditions, I ran into the restaurant a few minutes late. Then ran back out, because Alice was waiting outside. She said, "They only seat you if the full party is here."

"Sorry sorry sorry," I said breathlessly. "The bus stopped for ten minutes because a woman with a stroller wouldn't close it, and the driver refused to move until she did . . ." I trailed to a stop when I realized Alice wasn't scowling at me. She was smiling. "You look . . . pleased with me? Even though I'm late?"

"Oh, I'm not pleased with you at all," Alice said, but she was still smiling as we walked inside. The restaurant was expansive, the space formerly a garage; tribute was paid in the form of a few rusted mechanic's tools hanging on the walls between what seemed to be black-and-white photos of the chef's family or landmarks in Taiwan. The effect was fun and funky, though I had to admit I was relieved to be seated at one of the tables beneath a photo and not a tool. I didn't particularly want to have to stress about that rusty wrench falling on me.

I glanced quickly through the menu for any changes from the menu on which I'd taken careful notes on my phone. A few little alterations, but nothing big. Then looked back up at Alice, who was *still* smiling. "Okay, you *have* to tell me what's going on now," I said.

"Let's order first."

"Then I'm just going to pretend you're smiling at me for being late." I tilted my head, tapping my temple. "I want you to keep smiling, so I guess I'll just have to be late more often."

She scrunched her face up into a mock frown, but even that looked like a grin.

Thank God the waitress came quickly, or I might have bargained away my firstborn to Alice (which she would not have taken, so it would have been a terrible bargain). I ran down my order, nearly vibrating with impatience as the waitress warned me about various spice levels. As she walked away, I turned to Alice and slapped my palms on the table. "Tell me what's going on, or I'm going to flip this whole thing over."

Alice folded her own hands neatly before her. "I'm desperate to see that."

"You know I'm not actually going to flip the table."

"Damn. Fine. Okay." She positively beamed at me. "Kelsey and I are sick of working for the man—we're founding our own start-up!"

I began to applaud. A few of the other diners gave me a look, but I didn't care. "That's amazing! Congratulations!"

"Thank you!" Her smile faltered a tiny bit. "It's actually terrifying. It might be the worst idea ever."

"No way. It's the best idea ever."

"You don't even know what the idea is."

"I know you had it," I said. "And you only have good ideas."

"Even when I advised you to give the taxidermist one more chance?"

"You have *mostly* good ideas," I relented. "So what's this one?"

I could barely keep my excitement contained as she told me. It wanted to come up in a squeal, and I was not a squealer. "It's an app that helps reduce food waste," she told me. "Jada actually inspired it from what she was telling me when we went out for doughnuts, so maybe she'd be willing to become a partner or something." Basically, restaurants or grocery stores or other food establishments could sign up and pay a small commission to sell discounted packages of food or meals that would otherwise get thrown away at the end of the night. "And for users, it's almost like a game. Maybe one or two items from each place will pop up at a time, and they earn points with each one they nab. Always wanted to eat at Sebastian but couldn't afford it? Now here's your chance." And you could purchase or put points toward donating some of the food, too. "So what do you think?"

"I love it," I said immediately.

"Good," she said. "You know who else loved it?"

"Who?"

"Venture capitalists!"

I couldn't hold back my squeal this time. It earned me another few side glances, but I could not possibly have cared any less. I didn't know a ton about venture capitalists, but I did know that they were people with a lot of money who chose certain projects to give that money to in exchange for a certain percentage of the project, which ideally would grow and earn them back their investment plus a profit. Like on *Shark Tank*. "That's *amazing*!"

"Yeah." She let out a long, deep breath. "It's all happened so fast."

You know what else was fast? The food. The waitress showed up then with our order, and we had to set to arranging our table so that none of the appetizers fell off. I wouldn't want to have lost any of the crunchy cucumbers

marinated in a sweet, tangy vinegar, not quite long enough
to become pickles but long enough where they weren't cucumbers anymore, or a single bite of the candied pork
belly, rich and marinated in sticky sweet soy sauce, tucked
in between pillowy buns and scattered with the crunch of
peanuts.

Alice pushed the third appetizer, which had only been
called *Fried Eggplant* on the menu, toward me. "Eat this."

I obeyed, closing my eyes to focus. The thin sticks of
Chinese eggplant crunched with breading on the outside
and melted creamy smooth in my mouth on the inside,
made even better with a swipe of the silky, mild tofu sauce
coating the bottom of the plate. Every time when I was
starting to feel like it was too rich and I might need a
break, my tongue would hit a sprinkle of tart black vinegar
and reset the richness levels. "Heaven."

"Jada might have been the inspiration for the final
idea, but you inspired me, too, you know," she said in the
same matter-of-fact tone as she'd told me to eat the eggplant. For a moment I kept chewing, and then my eyes
popped open.

"What?"

"To work in a food-related business," she said. "I always loved food, but it was never something I thought of
in a businessy way. Until you and your business. A business you're so good at. I really learned how to love food
and admire food and think about food as more than, you
know, something that tastes good, through you."

If this were six months ago, I would've told her I didn't

have a business, that I just reviewed restaurants for fun. Now, I just let her go on. "You honor me."

"That's why Kelsey and I want you to come aboard as our social media manager."

I choked on a piece of eggplant. "What?"

She seemed to take that as me questioning their business. "We're for real, you know. We can pay you a salary and everything. It's a start-up, so who knows if we'll survive for the long term, and we probably can't afford to pay you as much as Mr. Decker does, but we can give you health insurance and everything, too." She took a deep breath. "But probably not dental."

"I've always had good teeth," I thought aloud.

"Great teeth," Alice said. She was tapping one of her chopsticks on the edge of her plate. "So what do you think?"

The waitress came to clear our appetizer plates, giving me a few moments before I had to respond. It seemed like it always worked out that way. Maybe they'd all taken a course or something in how to defuse awkward moments.

And then she was gone. "I think it sounds awesome." I was totally sincere, and I hoped Alice could see it. She set the chopstick down, which I hoped was a good sign. "I love the idea. I think it would be so much fun to work for you. And not just for you, but *not* for some old stuffy rich dude. And how many people actually have dental insurance?"

"Probably not many."

"Exactly." I took a deep breath. "But could I have all

the details of the offer? I love you, and I trust you, but I have to think it over against my other offer."

"Of course. I'd be insulted if you didn't."

The strong urge to give her the biggest hug I possibly could swamped me. But then our entrées came, and sorry, Alice, but they smelled so good I only wanted to hug them. Which I did not do, because then they'd be all over my shirt and not in my mouth. Which was the only place I wanted the beef roll, tender shreds of beef braised in garlic and ginger and soy sauce all chopped up and snuggled tightly inside a flaky, oniony, tender scallion pancake. The effect was something like beef Wellington, but better. Alice and I gobbled it down, using our fingertips to scrape up the last few flakes of pancake in the hot, peppery sauce.

Then we turned to the other dish. "Is this . . . a doughnut sandwich?" Alice asked, cocking her head and blinking.

"Yes," I said with relish.

Alice's entire face lit up. "*Excellent.*"

And it was. From the outside, it looked like any normal glazed doughnut, shiny with hardened sugar and puffy from the heat. But the chef had sliced it down the middle and filled it with the most delightful combination of ingredients: a salty, savory aged prosciutto-like ham that melted in my mouth; little bits of tart, sweet pickled pineapple; leaves of grassy cilantro. Together, when they came into contact with the sweet, fluffy doughnut, everything crashed into a bite that was sugary and crunchy and tart and spicy and bright, so bright.

22

TWO DAYS LATER, THE PRESSURE WAS MOUNTING on me to make a decision. Or at least it was in my head. I still had one more day before my deadline. I just wanted to have everything squared away, to be able to look forward, excited, to my future.

Right now I was looking forward, excited, at Bennett over a table of food. Not at a restaurant. At his home. And it was a meal he'd cooked himself. When I'd arrived, the doorman had buzzed me up, and I'd entered to capital-S Smells drifting out of the kitchen. Some good, some that made me a little nervous. "Don't come in," he called, and I was all too happy to oblige, drifting into his living space to watch the sun set through his giant windows.

But now that he was looking at me nervously over plates of linguine and clams and bowls of salad, I didn't want to look at anything except him. "Smells good," I said. "Do you think you've proven yourself?"

"I just hope I don't give us food poisoning," he said, picking at his pointer finger and grimacing.

I glanced down at the plate. The pasta was glossy with butter and scattered with bits of something fresh and green, the clamshells open and pointing photogenically toward the ceiling. "I mean, I'm not totally sure, but I think that if the clamshells are open, they're safe to eat." I *was* totally sure; I'd googled it on the way over when he told me he was making clams. Just in case. "Let's dig in?"

He took a deep breath. "Good luck." I hoped he wasn't talking to me.

As it turned out, I didn't need it. The pasta was maybe a little bit overcooked, but not mushy, and the plate was bright with lemon and rich with butter. The garlic could have been chopped more finely, and—

No. Turn off JulieZeeEatsNYC. Tonight, you're just Julie eating a meal your boyfriend cooked for you. Boyfriend. He's your boyfriend.

"You're smiling," Bennett said. "That's a good sign."

I swallowed. "It is. Really. Good." I mock-frowned. "I guess this means I'll have to cook something for you next."

He cocked an eyebrow. "If you think you're up for it."

"Well, *now* I definitely have to."

The conversation turned from the food to the Decker office. "I hear he's lost without you," Bennett said. "Keeps ghosting on lunches and not responding to emails. The temp they sent over can barely answer the phone."

I wasn't going to lie: hearing that felt good. Maybe if I went back, he'd appreciate me and what I did. Perhaps with a healthy raise. "I know. I've been hearing the same thing from Emerson Leigh. She thinks it's hilarious."

He snorted. "I kind of do, too. Did you hear what she's doing now? She just told me before you got here."

I hadn't checked my texts since I got on the subway. "Hopefully not painting me another nude portrait?"

"Oh God, you got one, too?" Bennett asked. At my grimace, he laughed. "It's somewhere in the back of my closet. Anyway, she signed up to volunteer with Ellen's Promise."

"Her dad's charity?" I said, surprised. "Since when did she develop a passion for curing ovarian cancer?"

"She's developed a passion for helping out with the skills she has. Meaning, throwing parties and events," Bennett said. "I think it'll be good for her."

I smiled to myself. I thought so, too.

"Anyway," I said, "I'm still totally torn about what to do next."

"I know exactly what you should do," he said. "Help me win the Halo of Absolution."

I rolled my eyes. "Come on, I can't do that," I said. He looked disappointed until I said, "I'd have to win the Wings of Destiny and the Staff of Fortitude first, and that'll take forever."

Now his face lit up. "You read the first *Dark Avengers* book!"

"It was surprisingly fun. And dark. Who knew you

could cut heads off in so many different ways?" I shook my head in bemusement. "But anyway, no, I am torn of heart, but not literally. What do I do? Go back to the stability of Mr. Decker's office, where I know exactly what I'm getting—including good benefits, by the way—or take a risk with Alice and Kelsey, which would definitely be fun, but also might lead to me having no time for my own stuff and also having no job in a year if they flame out? Because being real, most start-ups flame out. I don't know if—"

He silenced me with a kiss on my hand, which let the panicked racing of my heart slow down just a little bit. "Whatever you choose, you'll be fine."

"Easy for you to say," I muttered.

"It's true, it is a lot easier for me to say that," he acknowledged. "But either option is a good one. Worst-case scenario if you're unhappy at Mr. Decker's, you can still help out Alice and Kelsey. Worst-case scenario if you go with Alice and her company flames out, you have lots of admin experience and a good recommendation. And there's always temp work."

My breathing eased up. Deep breath in, deep breath out. "That's true. But that makes it almost harder, because there's no wrong choice! It would be so much easier to choose if one was obviously wrong, the way *Dark Avengers* villains are always obvious from their first introductions, because they have names like Malva the Venomous or Lucifer the Suspicious."

"I always did think that was unrealistic," said Bennett.

I bit my lip. "And I promised I would decide by tomorrow end of day. Can't you just tell me what to do?"

"No," he said kindly. "But I have faith that you'll make the right decision, whatever it is."

I wished I shared that same faith. "Well. I have until tomorrow, at least."

"Oh yeah? What are you going to do until tomorrow?"

The plates and bowls were empty. I stood to bring them to the kitchen. Bennett followed me with his own. "Oh, I have some things in mind," I said over my shoulder as I set the plates in the sink. Bennett put his down, too, then stood behind me, wrapping his arms around me and pulling me back into his chest.

"Like what?" His voice hummed against me, and I could feel it vibrate all the way down into my bones.

"I was thinking . . . dessert." It didn't come out as sexy as I wanted, so I grimaced. It was a good thing Bennett couldn't see me, though, because I felt his reaction poking me in the ass. I ground against it, making him groan deep in his throat.

He flipped me around and bent to kiss me deeply. "I might be ruined for other desserts."

I didn't give my decision a single thought for the rest of the night.

I WOKE UP curled against Bennett, him snoring lightly into my hair. I breathed in deeply as I delicately extricated myself without waking him up. One of my favorite things about sleeping here was how his smell surrounded me totally, scented me like I was his. Weird, maybe, but yeah.

Having successfully made it out, I padded downstairs, phone in hand. Part of me wanted to read the second *Dark Avengers* book and find out what happened after the radiation that destroyed what was once Chicago mutated the survivors nearby into elves—it seemed unscientific to me, though Bennett assured me they dealt with the science in later installments—but I knew I had to think about job stuff. And my future.

Elves sounded more fun.

I sighed, sinking into the couch. Googled success rates for new start-ups, example résumés for influencers, how much emergency dental surgery costs without insurance.

It took a while. But by the time Bennett shuffled downstairs in his fleecy moccasins, I'd made up my mind. Without even going for his coffee, he sat beside me and took my hands in his. "So? What's the verdict?"

I took a deep breath. "It might affect what we want to do next year, but—" I stopped short. *We.* My cheeks heated, my tongue feeling thick in my mouth. "I mean, it might affect what *I* want to do next—"

"I like 'we.'" Bennett squeezed my hands and smiled at me. "'We' sounds good."

He liked my decision, too. "We're a 'we' now, so it's important I approve of your decisions," he said seriously, but he ruined the effect with the smile playing on his lips. I whacked him playfully on the chest. "But for real, I'm glad you're doing this. I think it's going to be great."

I let out that deep breath from before. "You really think so?"

"Yes," he said. "Now let's go. Make that call!"

"It's so early."

"It's not that early."

I took another deep breath. "Okay. Here goes."

Hopefully, this was the right decision. But I guess I wouldn't know how it all worked out for another year or so.

Epilogue

ONE YEAR LATER

THE SOUNDS OF BATTLE, CLASHING MACHETES, and screams of pain rang out from the other room. Meanwhile, up in Bennett's loft bedroom, I'd already admitted defeat. In a manner of speaking. After much straining, squeezing, and a pep talk to my boobs about how maybe they should just shrink for a minute, I'd realized I was not going to be able to zip this dress up myself.

"Bennett!" I called again. "ASAP! Please!"

The sounds of battle paused, a moment of truce, and Bennett trotted in. Even a year after we'd first become an item, my heart still did a little flutter when he entered a room. Especially in the outfit he wore right now. The usual pressed black jeans, but the button-down he'd paired it with was a soft blue-gray, just the shade of his eyes. "Sorry," he said breathlessly, like he'd actually been swinging a machete and not clicking buttons. "But good news—I got us the Key of Dominion!"

"Nice!" I high-fived him with a resounding slap. I'd joined his guild in *Dark Avengers* a few months ago after I'd completed all of the introductory quests and raised my new character to a respectable level. With the Key of Dominion, we could progress to the next dungeon. "Now help me zip this up."

He complied. I sucked in as tight as I could, and after just a little bit of tugging, the zipper ran all the way to the top. I sighed, letting myself loosen up. "Thanks."

"Anytime." He grinned. "Though I'm glad your boobs didn't listen to you. I quite like them how they are."

As Bennett called an Uber, I paused in front of the full-length mirror I'd insisted he install on his closet door when I moved in a couple months ago. Not to brag—no, I was in my own head; if I couldn't brag here, where could I brag?

I looked *amazing*. I'd found this Sachin & Babi dress for super cheap online, and the silky dark blue fabric hugged the curves I wanted accentuated and flared out to cloak the curves I didn't. Plus, it had pockets! I'd left my hair natural, letting the waves flow over my shoulders, and touched up my eyes with a little liner and mascara. Smiling, I pulled out my phone for an old-fashioned mirror selfie and posted it. On my way to the gala! Hope to see you there!

The Uber deposited us smoothly outside Calabaza. I took a moment just to soak in how funny it felt to be there with Bennett standing arm in arm, neither of us in disguise.

"Don't throw any wine on me this time," Bennett said, as if he were reading my mind.

I smiled up at him. "Then don't do anything that would make me want to throw wine on you."

Inside, the party was not quite in full swing. Which was expected, considering we were an hour early. Only a few people moved about, setting up tables and center-pieces, going in and out of the kitchen to make sure the food was on track.

I blinked, and suddenly Emerson Leigh was there in front of me, clipboard and pen in hand. The pen was a standard black Bic, cheap and translucent. Bennett and I had gotten her a fancy pen like his own green-and-gold one after she successfully completed her first six months at A Real Job, but she didn't like using it. She'd discovered she was a habitual pen chewer.

"How does it look?" she asked, her eyes bright and fo-cused. Her highlighted hair was up in a high, tight pony-tail, and she was dressed in a chic heather-colored suit. "One of the chefs called out, so I had to scramble for someone at the last minute. I hope he's up to the task."

"I'm sure he is, Emerson Leigh," I said sincerely. "And really, it was a stroke of genius to rent out a place like Ca-labaza for this. It looks great."

It really did. She'd kept a lot of the restaurant's gold decorations, including many of its little namesake pump-kins, but added so many personal touches to showcase the purpose of the gala: the anniversary of Alice and Kelsey's start-up. Framed photographs of all the articles showcasing the company, including the one from the *Scroll* that Bennett had pitched, and gauzy gold netting that swooped over the tables. Attending tonight would be some of the app's top point holders, people from the restaurants and stores that used the app, and representatives of the shelters and organizations who benefited from the app's philanthropy.

"I know," Emerson Leigh said modestly, and, with a tap of her pen cap against her shiny white teeth, she swept off to address some other crisis. I watched after her for a moment, feeling oddly proud.

Alice swept in to replace her. She looked incredible as well, garbed in a knee-length white shift dress that shimmered with silver threads. A shiny barrette tucked her hair away from her face. "How's my favorite person doing tonight?"

I leaned in for a squeeze. "So proud and impressed by *her* favorite person."

"Don't lie, I know Bennett's your favorite person now." Still, her face glowed.

"Not tonight. Tonight it's all you, baby."

I wasn't kidding. When I'd turned down Mr. Decker's job offer a year ago, I'd been tired of working for the man and wanted to do more to build my own brand. Working for Alice and Kelsey hadn't just been the best way to do that; it had been a way to do good. I'd been able to harness my knowledge of social media and my connections to help their app blow up in the food world. Jada did a few free promos, too. Places I reviewed got incentives to sign up with the app, and some restaurants would sign up in hopes of getting noticed by people like me or Jada. And now they were super successful. Which was obvious from the mere existence of a gala. Even if it was only "a small gala," as Alice had directed Emerson Leigh when she hired her to do the planning.

What Alice (and Kelsey) had built was incredible. Every day I felt lucky I got to be a part of it. JulieZeeEats-NYC had actually grown over the past year to the point where I could probably do it full-time if I wanted to, but I didn't feel ready yet. Not when we were doing such amazing stuff together.

Plus, Alice was the best boss ever. My hours were flexible around my reviewing, and if I were visiting a new place I thought might be a good fit for the app, I got to expense my meal.

"I love you," said Alice. She may have had a few glasses of champagne already.

"I love you, too, boss," I said. "Now we'd better go mingle!"

Over the next couple hours, as the party swelled into something that didn't look all that small to me, Bennett and I circulated around the room. We talked about his latest review with Jada Knox, who was resplendent in a sparkly blue Cinderella-like gown—he'd given the restaurant a high rating while she hadn't been impressed. We congratulated Kelsey as we snacked on the circulating hors d'oeuvres, which had been created by several of their partner restaurants. I was thrilled to see Marcus, who'd found another roommate who, he assured me, was nowhere near as good as me (even if she did alternate cooking with him some-times). Bennett's sister, Penny, gave me a big hug, and I only thought for a moment that she was trying to strangle me. Nobody spilled wine on anybody. It was great.

As if tempting me, a waiter circled by with glasses of wine on a tray. "Would you like one, ma'am?"

I smiled. "No, thanks. I'm not the biggest fan of wine."

Eventually, Alice stepped up to the front of the room and clinked a spoon against her champagne glass. "I wanted to quickly thank everybody here who's supported our epic growth over the past year," she proclaimed, and then proceeded to not quickly at all thank pretty much every single person in attendance.

Bennett leaned down to whisper in my ear, "I have something important to tell you."

I turned to look him in the eye. I'd never get sick of seeing how his eyes crinkled in the corners when he smiled. "What?"

"I love you." And he pressed a gentle kiss against my lips. The smile must have been contagious, because when he backed away, I was smiling, too.

"I love you, too."

"And Julie!" Alice cried from the front of the room. I jumped back to attention, but she was only up to my name in her list. "We wouldn't be here without her. Let's toast to a hundred and fifty thousand followers for JulieZeeEatsNYC!"

Before I could raise my glass, Bennett whispered again, "My favorite person."

The champagne was the sweetest I'd ever tasted.

Acknowledgments

I wrote this book in 2020 and early 2021, when most restaurants in the New York City area, where I live, were closed for dining in. It was totally wild to write a book set mostly in restaurants when I couldn't go to any in real life! I relied largely on the experiences I'd had at restaurants before the pandemic, the photos I took of all my food there (because I, like Julie, photograph all my food, which ended up working out well in this case), and some amazing-looking menus. I've written more about the inspirations behind Julie's meals and the restaurants she and Bennett go to in the book club supplementary materials, which you can find online, but just briefly, I want to thank the people behind Saltie Girl in Boston; Mercado Little Spain, Daniel, and the sadly closed Henry at Life Hotel in Manhattan; Hug Esan in Queens; Llama Inn and Win Son in Brooklyn; and Maido in Lima, Peru, for directly or indirectly inspiring some of the meals in this book.

Unlike Julie's side gig, publishing a book is truly a team effort. Thank you so much to the amazing team behind this book: Merrilee Heifetz, Rebecca Eskildsen, and the rest of the team at Writers House; Kristine Swartz, Mary Baker, Colleen Reinhart, Liz Gluck, Marianne Aguiar, Will Tyler, Rakhee Bhatt, Jessica Plummer, Elisha Katz, Yazmine Hassan, Christine Legon, and everybody else at Berkley; and artist Debs Lim for illustrating Julie, Bennett, and their dynamic so perfectly on the cover.

Many thanks to the YA Underground critique group for helping me workshop this tricky first chapter. Special thanks to Will Roth for coming up with the running gag of Julie and Alice replacing Bennett's middle names with food words.

I would've had a much harder time writing this book without such wonderful and supportive family and friends. Shout out to the Berkletes! And special thanks as always to my husband, Jeremy Bohrer, for being the absolute best.

And finally, thank you, the reader, for reading my book. I wouldn't be able to do this without you.

Best Served Hot

AMANDA ELLIOT

Discussion Questions

1. What's your favorite restaurant? What specifically makes it your favorite? Pretend you're giving it a glowing review on your social media or in your paper of choice.

2. Julie and Bennett spar over the course of the book about the superior method of restaurant reviewing—traditional media versus social media—and come to the conclusion that both methods have their strengths. Do you agree? Why or why not? If you are looking for a new restaurant, where do you prefer to look?

3. Julie spends most of the book hiding her dislike of wine so that her followers won't judge her for it. Do you agree with her decision, and with her ultimate choice to stop hiding it at the end? Why or why not? Have you ever hidden an aspect of yourself to keep from being judged?

4. Early on in the book, Julie says, "Sometimes being loved on social media meant being loved as someone who wasn't really you." Do you agree? Why or why not? What does social media mean to you?

5. Class, classism, and money are major themes and topics of discussion in the book. How do you feel about the way the story depicted them and the various characters in different classes?

6. Emerson Leigh's search for fulfillment and meaning in her life ends (at least for now) with her finding work as an event planner, which was encouraged by Julie. Do you agree with Julie that this was a good move for Emerson Leigh? What do you think it means to find fulfillment in a job or in life?

7. If you could choose one character from this book to share a meal with at your favorite restaurant, who would it be and why?

8. Imagine a bonus chapter that takes place five years after the epilogue and features all of the main characters. Where do you picture the characters' lives at this future point?

Keep reading for an excerpt from

Sadie on
a Plate

MY LIFE HAS THIS IRRITATING HABIT OF THROW-
ing its biggest changes at me while I'm completely in the
nude.

Exhibit one, ten years ago: I was seventeen and enam-
ored with a boy my parents hated, all for the completely
unfair reason that he skipped school most days to smoke
pot behind the local 7-Eleven. I'd snuck him up to my
room, deciding against the back door in favor of the tree
outside my window because it seemed so much more romantic. We were in the throes of quiet passion when my
door flew open.

"Sadie?" my sister said, and her mouth dropped open.
She was four years younger than me, so I would've felt bad
for traumatizing her if I wasn't so busy screeching and
scrambling for my clothes or a sheet or anything to cover
up our naughty bits.

"Get out of here!" I grabbed the closest thing within reach—an old soccer trophy—and hurled it in her general direction for emphasis. It landed with a thunk on the rug, which made her jump and blink her eyes. "Get ouuuuuuuut!"

"Okay. Fine." She blinked again and adjusted her glasses. As she turned to go, she said over her shoulder, "By the way, Grandma died."

Exhibit two, six weeks ago: I was getting out of the shower when I heard my phone ding with a text. It was charging on the nightstand, so I picked it up on my way to the dresser. All I saw on the lock screen was that it was from Chef Derek Anders, my boss, and it started with, **Hey Sadie** . . . I sighed, figuring he was probably asking me to come in for a last-minute shift on the line. I entered my PIN and read the whole text.

Hey Sadie, I'm sorry, but we're going to have to let you go.

Exhibit three, five weeks ago: I was walking around my apartment eating Nutella out of the jar with my fingers for breakfast, psyching myself up to put on fancy professional clothes and head out for my nine a.m. interview at the temp agency. My phone rang with a 212 number, which I knew was New York City, and the only reason I picked up was because I thought that the temp agency had its headquarters in New York and maybe they were calling to cancel the interview because *what are you thinking, Sadie? All you've ever done is work in restaurants, and all you've ever wanted to*

*do is have your own, so why are you trying to get an admin job at some
obnoxiously hipstery tech company?*

It's not like I want *to work at a tech company*, I argued silently with the temp agency. *It's that I've been blacklisted for
the near future from the entire Seattle restaurant scene and need some
way to earn money until all this fuss dies down.*

The temp agency scoffed in my head. *Yeah, okay. Like
you could do a fancy office job. All you can do is work the line, and
now you can't even do that anymore. You're worthless.*

I picked up the phone, my shoulders already drooping.
"Hello, this is Sadie Rosen."

"Hi, Sadie!" It was a woman on the other end, her tone
far too chipper for this hour of the morning. "My name is
Adrianna Rogalsky, and I'm calling from *Chef Supreme*. Is
this a good time?"

I almost dropped my phone. "Yes!" I cleared my
throat, trying to keep from squeaking the way I did when
I got too excited. "I mean yes, this is a good time."

"Great!" Adrianna chirped. "I'm calling to tell you
that the committee really liked your application and your
cooking video. Would you mind answering a few more
questions for me?"

My eyes involuntarily darted to my bookshelf, which
consisted mainly of cookbooks. I spent too much time in
restaurant kitchens to cook much from them—or at least,
up until a week ago I had—but I liked flipping through
them to gather ideas and marvel at the food photography.
Five were written by winners of *Chef Supreme*, and four by
runners-up and semifinalists. I'd watched every episode of

all six seasons, seated on the edge of my couch to goggle at every cooking challenge and winning dish and contestant who cried when eliminated.

Season three's winner, Seattle's Julie Chee, was my culinary idol. Derek, my boss, had taken me by her restaurant after-hours one day. She'd laughed when I told her how I'd been rooting for her all season, patted my head like I was a little kid, and then cooked me a grilled cheese with bacon and kimchi. It was the best night of my life. Right after that, I'd started dreaming about competing on the show myself.

"Hello? Sadie?"

And if I didn't get on my game, that dream was going to evaporate like a pot of boiling water forgotten on the stove. I mean, I didn't really think I was actually going to make it on the show, but it wasn't like I was going to hang up on someone from *Chef Supreme*. "Sorry!" I said. "Bad connection for a minute there. Yes, I'd love to answer some questions." I shook my head and grimaced. Love? *Love* was a strong word. I should've said I'd *be happy* to answer some questions. Now Adrianna was probably—

Talking! Already! "Your application from six months ago says that you're a sous-chef at the Green Onion in Seattle?"

I cleared my throat. "Well, um." This was not off to a great start. "I was a sous-chef there until last week. I decided to leave to . . . um, pursue personal business opportunities." Another grimace. Personal business opportunities? What did that even mean?

I really wished I wasn't naked right now. I knew Adrianna from *Chef Supreme* couldn't see me through the phone, but I still felt way too exposed.

Fortunately, job-hopping is fairly common in the food world. So Adrianna just said, "Great. And how would you describe your personal style?"

I hoped she meant food-wise and not looks-wise, because my personal fashion style consisted mainly of beat-up Converses, thrift store T-shirts, and constant calculations on how far I could go between haircuts before crossing the line from fashionably mussed to overgrown sheepdog. "At the Green Onion, I was cooking mostly New American food with some French influences and a bit of molecular gastronomy," I told her. "But my own style, I'd say, is more homestyle, with Jewish influences? Not kosher cooking; that's a different thing. I'm inspired by traditional Jewish cuisine."

Paper rustled on the other end. "Right, the matzah ball ramen you cooked in your video looked fantastic. We were all drooling in the room!"

I perked up. Forgot that I was naked. Forgot that lately I was a walking disaster. "That's one of my go-tos and will definitely be on my future menu. I've been experimenting lately with putting a spin on kugels . . ."

As I chattered on, I could practically see my grandma shaking her head at me. Grandma Ruth had cooked up a storm for every Passover, Yom Kippur, and Chanukah, piling her table till it groaned with challah rolls, beef brisket in a ketchup-based sauce, and tomato and cucumber salad so fresh and herby and acidic it could make you feel like summer in the middle of winter. *Pastrami-spiced* pork *shoulder? Really, dear?*

I shook my own head back at her, making her poof away in a cloud of metaphorical smoke. I had that power now that she was dead and buried and existing primarily as a manifestation of my own anxiety.

". . . so in that way it's really more of a cheesecake with noodles in it," I finished up. My blood was sparking just talking about my food; I had to do a few quick hops just to burn off some of that excess energy.

"I love your passion," Adrianna said on the other end of the phone. "So, I take it that opening your own restaurant is hashtag goals for you?"

"Hashtag goals," I agreed. And my shoulders drooped again, because that was a dream that was never going to happen now. After I got fired by the Green Onion and the chefs at all the other restaurants worth working at learned why, I became the joke of Seattle's restaurant industry. Who wanted to invest in the local joke?

She asked me a few other questions, pertaining mostly to my schedule and availability. (There were only so many ways to say, "I'm free whenever you want me, considering I no longer have a job.") I continued to pace around my apartment, circling the coffee table, bare feet padding over the rug. And then, "It's been lovely to speak with you, Sadie."

I stopped short, my shin slamming into the table leg. I swallowed back a curse. "It's been lovely to speak with you . . . too?" I finished with a question, because I couldn't ask what I really wanted to ask. *Is this it? Did I not meet whatever criteria you have? What's wrong with me?*

"We'll be in touch soon," Adrianna said. "Have a great day!"

I did not have a great day. Because of Adrianna's call, I was fifteen minutes late to my interview at the temp agency and arrived all sweaty and panting from the rush to get there on time. The interviewer's lip had actually curled in distaste as she touched my damp, clammy hand. The sugar rush from the Nutella had worn off by the time I hurried back out onto the street, and I was starting to feel a little shaky, but the only place to buy food in the vicinity was a coffee shop where I was forced to choose between a stale bagel and some slimy fruit salad.

And that wasn't all. As I chewed (and chewed and chewed and chewed) on my stale bagel with too much cream cheese caked on, I ran into an old friend. Like, literally ran into an old friend, as in our bodies collided as I was trying to catch the bus.

"Oh!" I knew it was her as soon as I heard that raspy voice, earned from years of smoking in alleyways behind restaurants. Her eyes widened as she took me in: the sweaty strands of hair sticking to the sides of my face, the thrift-store blazer that still smelled like the eighties, even though I'd washed it twice and taken the shoulder pads out. "Sadie! How are you . . . doing?"

I gritted my teeth at the false sympathy in those big blue eyes. "Hi, Kaitlyn. So you heard?"

Kaitlyn leaned in, bringing the smell of smoke with her. I fought the urge to step back. Even after years working in restaurant kitchens, where most everybody was a smoker at least when drunk, I hated the smell. "Of *course* I heard. I'm surprised you're still here. Not here in SoDo, like, in Seattle."

"I'm still here," I said through a clenched jaw. Kaitlyn Avilleira and I had quasi-bonded in our early twenties, a little over five years ago. We were the only two women on the line at Atelier Laurent, and we had to have each other's backs if we didn't want to get banished to the pastry kitchen.

Having her back didn't mean I liked her.

"That's really strong of you." Kaitlyn pulled me in for a one-armed hug that might actually have been an attempt to strangle me. "I'm rooting for you, girl!"

I gritted my teeth in a smile. This was the song and dance of our relationship: seeing who could pretend harder that we *did* like each other, because we were busy fighting so many stereotypes about women on the line that there was no way we could fulfill the one where the only two women were enemies. "Thanks, Kait!"

An uncomfortable silence settled over us. I looked in the direction of the bus. No, I *stared* in the direction of the bus, willing it with my eyes to appear.

Alas, I had not developed any magical powers in the past few minutes.

"We have to get drinks sometime," I said. "And catch up. It's been way too long."

"*Way* too long," Kaitlyn said. She tossed her long, shiny brown hair. Her eyes sparkled, and her cheeks were naturally rosy. *She* never had to wear blush or undereye concealer to keep coworkers from asking her if she was sick. "Wait till I tell you about working for Chef Marcus. He works me like a dog." She trilled a laugh. "I almost wish I could take a break, like you."

I clenched my jaw and told myself that I couldn't hit her or I'd get arrested, and going to jail was really the only way I could make my situation worse. Well, that or moving back in with my parents in the suburbs, into my childhood bedroom with the shag carpet and no lock on the door.

"Well, I'd better be going," Kaitlyn said just as I was saying, "Well, I'll let you go." Our words clashed, and we both laughed nervously before hugging yet again.

"You should finally open that restaurant now that you're free and have all this time," Kaitlyn said as she backed away. "I'll be there opening night!"

Thankfully, she was off before I had to respond. I made a face at her back. Of course I wanted to open my restaurant now that I was *free* and had *all* this *time*. But opening a restaurant either took lots of money, which I didn't have even before the whole unemployment situation, or a bunch of rich investors willing to throw their money away on my behalf, which, again, I *wished*.

The bus was delayed, obviously, and it took me twice as long as it should have to get home, the whole time crammed in next to a manspreader who kept giving me dirty looks for trying to sit in three-quarters of my own seat. I stared hard out the window, watching the warehouses and industrial lofts turn into the residential buildings and parks of Crown Hill. By the time I stumbled through the door of my apartment, I was done with today. I pulled off my clothes, dropping them in puddles on the floor, so that I could shower the stink of failure away and then eat something for my soul. Like more Nutella out of the jar.

My phone chimed. *It's probably the temp agency already rejecting me*, I thought glumly, digging it out of my bag. Sure enough, it was an email.

But it was from Adrianna Rogalsky of *Chef Supreme*. And it started with, Hey Sadie, just like my firing-by-text. *Fantastic.* I took a deep breath as I clicked it open, readying myself for yet another important food world person to tell me how inadequate I was.

Hey Sadie, I enjoyed our conversation earlier. Upon further discussion with the *Chef Supreme* team, we'd like to fly you out to New York for some more interviews and cooking tests to determine whether you'd be a good fit to compete on *Chef Supreme* season 7. Would next Wednesday work for you?

I dropped my phone. *OhmyGodohmyGodohmyGod.* What if I'd just shattered my phone and I couldn't afford a new one and I couldn't get back to Adrianna and . . . and . . .

I picked it up. It wasn't even cracked. I opened up an email and wrote Adrianna back about how, yes, I'd love to come in whenever they needed me because it was my dream to be on *Chef Supreme*, and I couldn't wait to meet—

Backspace. I cleared my throat. Okay, take two, and be more professional this time. Hi, Adrianna, thanks for reaching out! Yes, next Wednesday still works for me. I look forward to receiving the flight information.

I sent it off, chewing nervously on my lip even as I tried to talk myself down. *They probably have a hundred people come in to audition further for each season's twelve slots. And seriously, if they have a hundred people to choose from, why the hell would they choose* you? *Maybe you shouldn't even waste your time. Is it too late to email Adrianna back and cancel?*

I spilled this all on my parents the next night at dinner. I kept my eyes on my plate of eggplant Parm, and not just because my sister, Rachel, who sat across from me at our kitchen table, tended to chew with her mouth open. "So it probably won't actually turn into anything if I decide to go," I said. "But on the off chance it does, it could mean a new start for me. The goal is really not even to win but to get noticed."

"Get noticed by who?" asked my mom. She set her utensils onto her plate with a clink. My dad followed suit. Only Rachel was left chewing. Loudly.

I let myself look up and look left, at my mom, then right, at my dad. I was an uncanny mix of the two of them: deep-set dark eyes and big boobs like my mom; a round face and thick, wiry brown hair like my dad. Unlike Rachel, who was a blond, blue-eyed giraffe. Even sitting, the top of her head nearly brushed the brass light fixture hanging over the table.

I cleared my throat. "Get noticed by anyone, really. The top four is the sweet spot. They get noticed by the public and by investors. Are offered their own restaurants and fancy executive chef gigs."

My dad shook his head. "Do you really think you're ready for that?" His eyebrows were furrowed with both love and concern, but his words hit me like a kick to the stomach. I pursed my lips and stared over his head at the row of porcelain chickens in a perpetual march across the counter. "You've been through a lot lately. And you're still so young. I'm just worried about you, honey. Maybe going on TV in front of the whole country isn't the best idea right now."

"I'm not that young. I'm twenty-seven." I blinked hard, trying not to cry. "You don't believe in me?"

"Of course I believe in you," my dad said. He sounded wounded by my very suggestion. "I think you could win. I *know* you could win. But you've spent the past few weeks huddled up crying. Maybe next—"

"I think that's exactly why you *should* do it, Sadie." My mom's eyes were fiery as she reached out to grab my hand. Her squeeze made me sit up straight. "Follow your dreams. Why the hell not, right? Make it to the top four. Get noticed. Never work for a shithead man again."

Relief swept through me, lightening the weight on my shoulders, and that was just about enough to convince me that she was right. That I *should* do this. "I haven't even made it on the show yet," I cautioned.

"But if you do . . . This is what you've always wanted. Don't let it go."

I was pretty sure what I wanted to do, but I looked at Rachel anyway. Grimaced at the chewed-up mass of eggplant Parm that greeted me from her tongue, then the raised eyebrows of a question. She grinned without swallowing. "Do it."

So I got on that plane Wednesday with my heart hammering and my head held high. Jet-lagged and sleepless, I talked to producer after producer, random person after random person. I cooked more of my food for other random people, and sometimes they liked it and sometimes they chewed slowly and expressionlessly and nearly made me scream with anxiety. I sat down with a psychologist or a psychiatrist, I wasn't sure exactly, and he introduced himself too quickly, and I thought that maybe asking him to repeat himself would get me a black mark, and I tried to seem a lot less crazy than I actually was, which in turn made me paranoid that he'd see right through me, so I tried to seem a little crazy but not *too* crazy, and—

Well, anyway, they flew me back to Seattle and didn't even make me wait impatiently for weeks and weeks before they told me I got in. While I was changing into my running clothes, naturally.

Was it that I spent far more time naked than the average person? Either way, nudity never failed.

Author photo by Cassie Gonzales

Amanda Elliot lives with her husband in New York City, where she collects way too many cookbooks for her tiny kitchen, runs in Central Park, and writes for teens and kids under the name Amanda Panitch.

CONNECT ONLINE

AmandaPanitch.com

AmandaPanitch

AmandaPanitch

Ready to find
your next great read?

Let us help.

Visit prh.com/nextread

Penguin
Random
House